Link to Friendship

Part I of The Claddagh Trilogy

by Kelly Richelle

PublishAmerica

Baltimore

First printing

ISBN: 1-4137-6785-0
PUBLISHED BY PUBLISHAMERICA, LLLP
www.publishamerica.com
Baltimore

Printed in the United States of America

Dedicated to:

Michael~
you gave me all three pieces
to the ring and lent me the voice to share
the story with others

$\mathcal{P}$rologue

The letter was finished.

Patrick O'Connor knew it was his best work yet. Of course, his daughter would not think so. She would be very disappointed, he imagined, if not totally steamed, an expression he had heard his granddaughter use, and he rather liked it under the circumstances. He smiled because he was not used to thinking in this new person vernacular. Patrick had been old longer than he could remember, and even longer than that, he had loved his wife, Olivia.

Olivia was not going to understand this latest ridiculous adventure, but he really needed it before he accepted his calling. He had never been one to shy away from adventure, from the possibility of "what ifs." Unfortunately, Rose, the only offspring of their union, would not be in agreement. He wondered where they may have gone wrong but knew that kind of thinking would only get in the way of what he needed to accomplish, and at that moment, Patrick O'Connor needed to brace himself for leaving this world and moving into the next, whatever that may be. He gave some serious thought to the tale—as he liked to call it—that had gotten him this far. A part of him already ached at the idea of the task not getting accomplished. But he pushed that fear aside because if anyone could settle an historical vendetta, it would be his family—in particular, his grandchildren. They would settle the problem his own father-in-law had set into motion once and for all, and each would, at last, live with the gifts they deserved.

He carefully placed the letter into the envelope, his wrinkled old hands crippled with arthritis and moving slower than he could ever recall. He held the letter tight against his chest so that Olivia would find it in just a while when she came in to give him his mid-morning medicine and tea. Thoughts of his strong yet elegant wife floated in and out of focus, making him sleepy and content. Then he closed his eyes for a quick little cat-nap…

Chapter I

Kaleb McMurran loved this time of day. As he climbed to the top of the lighthouse in Grosse Ile, Michigan, his tool belt snug at his side, he breathed deeply. The water's clean scent drifted toward him and made him feel like he was—finally—home.

Upon reaching the top, he set his tool box aside and went to the balcony that overlooked the Detroit River. Not so long ago he would have imagined that he would not be feeling very comfortable here in this spot. Only a year before this moment had he returned from the western part of the country where he had thought he was going to make his life. Now that he was back in the community where he had been raised with his brother, he felt more settled and relaxed. And that had been a long time coming.

As he watched the early morning sailors take to their boats, calm settled over him. He went inside to his coffee maker and waited for it to finish brewing the pot he had programmed the night before when he had worked into the dark hours. Or, at least, he had tried to work. After Melanie Wilson had shown up with an honest-to-goodness basket of fried chicken and fresh lemonade, he had allowed himself to get sidetracked by the pretty blonde. Making her leave his side without having stayed the night had been difficult, but he had never allowed a woman to stay the night with him. This often created tension in his own shoulders, and the fact that he had yet to marry a woman and produce another McMurran like his brother was about to do created annoyance in his own family, but he had promised himself that he would never want for the company of a woman throughout the night.

Unless it was Anna Keller.

Just the thought of her had the coffee growing cold on his tongue as he took his first sip. Rumor had it that she was back from her high times in New York and would be sticking around for a while, which he knew would please her family, particularly her mother, Rose O'Connor Keller. That woman was entirely took uppity for her own good, and if there was one thing he could not tolerate, it was the kind of person that looked down on you because you believed in hard work, especially when you worked with your hands. He had always imagined Anna had not taken that kind of attitude, but after she took off for New York, he supposed he had been proven wrong.

That did not settle well within him, and anyone approaching him now would see it in his smoky grey eyes, in the way he hunched his shoulders as he stood looking out the little side window, as though he were braced for something but did not know what that something was. Almost too tall for his own good, the snug blue jeans that somehow fitted him better than a three-piece suit hugged a trim waist and narrow hips while his dusky golden hair curled around the edges of his flannel work shirt in a way that suggested he had forgotten to get a haircut about two weeks ago and did not care. It was the kind of look that had caused Melanie Wilson—and several other young women in Grosse Ile—to cook for him.

His brother, Evan, stood just an inch shorter as he watched him down the last of his coffee, and in the way of brothers, decided to wake him up out of his daydreams quickly. He dropped a 2x4 to the ground near him.

Kaleb almost dropped his cup on the floor and swore good-naturedly as he turned to him in the narrow doorway. "You have nothing better to do than come crawling up here at dusk on a Saturday morning and scare the bejeezus out of me? What's that matter? Michelle kick you out of bed?"

Evan took the reference to his wife in stride. "She needed some space." He stepped up to the cupboard and got out a mug. Kaleb, without missing a beat, poured him a cup. "She went to the doc's yesterday. Gained a bit more weight and is feeling none-too-happy about it."

Kaleb smiled wickedly over the rim of his cup. "Better you than me, bro. No way you see me tied down with a wife and kid. That's too much baggage right there."

"Yeah, well." Evan paced around the space, fidgeted. Kaleb looked at him, concerned.

"Everything okay?"

Evan tried to stall but knew it would be no good with Kaleb; he was the one person who could always sense his mood. "Just nervous. She's due in about six weeks. I—I feel like I may not be ready—to be a dad."

Kaleb wanted to point out the fact that it was already a bit too late for that, but since Evan looked so serious, he tried for another tactic. "You know you're going to do a better job of it than I could ever dream of doing. Besides, if you get lost along the way, you've got Michelle. I really don't know another human being more cut out for parenthood than her. And she married you. Why she did will always be a mystery, but nonetheless…"

"I know I ain't no prize, but hell, I guess we're both lucky." He emptied his cup into the small sink and walked the space again. Kaleb could sense there was more to his visit than he let on, but he allowed it to come from Evan in his own time.

"I thought I'd get started on the underside of the lighthouse today. Restoring this baby for the museum has been more a pleasure than I would have thought."

"So, you're glad you came back?"

The question was asked with such hesitancy that Kaleb almost called him on it. "Of course, I am. I get to be near my little niece or nephew soon, don't I?"

"Yeah." Evan watched Kaleb fiddle with his tool belt. "Did you hear who's also back?"

Kaleb did not need to look at his brother to know of whom he spoke. And the full purpose of his visit became abundantly clear.

"Yeah. I heard."

They moved around in silence for a few minutes. Then Evan spoke again. "She arrived two days ago and is staying with her family."

"Good for her."

"I heard she asked about you."

"Why would I care?"

And there was the temper snap Evan had feared was boiling under the surface. Kaleb caught it just a minute too late and tried to rein it in.

"I just thought you should be prepared."

Kaleb set his tools down and pressed his fingers to his eyes. He wanted to gather the right words. "Thanks," was all he managed to say.

Evan offered his help on the house for the day, and the two of them went to work.

* * * * *

Nine hours of good solid work in the early spring will get any man dirty, but for Kaleb, the look only assisted his already outrageous sex appeal as he sauntered into the corner diner. He went straight to the bathroom to wash himself before he came out to order his usual Reuben special. Sitting at the counter on a red leather-covered stool as old as his father, he waved to the owner.

"Hello, Frannie. What's cookin' today?"

She sauntered over in the same teal colored uniform he remembered her wearing when he was a kid and tried to smooth talk his way into a free milkshake after school whenever his mother would have to work late.

"Wouldn't matter. You'd still order that same thing." She cackled and poured him a cup of coffee.

"You sure do know my taste. When are you going to finally give in and run away with me? I'll treat you real nice."

She swatted at the hand he waved in her direction. "Kaleb McMurran, if your mama heard you now, she would have your hide." She leaned across the counter conspiratorially. "But my shift ends in just over a half hour."

As he laughed, she winked. "Hell, Frannie, you still got it in you."

"Well, I must admit, I would have thought your tastes would run in different directions these days." She nodded behind him toward a corner booth. He turned and looked over his shoulder.

She was staring at him as though she had seen a ghost. For a moment, time really did stand still for the two of them. Finally, Kaleb broke the tension.

"Well, little Anna Keller. What a...pleasant surprise."

"Hello, Kaleb."

He knew he would be faced with her again soon, but he had hoped it could be under better circumstances. He had been trapped under a lighthouse for the better part of a day and was sure he not only looked it but smelled it also. Dirt and grease streaked his entire body, and he suddenly became very conscious of the grime under his fingernails. He stood and walked to her, shoved his hands in his pockets. He hated that she could still make him that self-conscious.

"When did you arrive?"

The way he was looking down at her made Anna realize she had not been safe returning home. "Couple of days ago." They continued to eye each other. "I see some things never change."

She had gestured to Frannie with a slight shake of her head, but he was not sure she was speaking entirely of his exchange with her moments ago. "Yeah, well, some of us still consider this place home."

He saw the light in her pale blue eyes dim and cursed himself for the pleasure he got from knowing he had been the one to dim it. "Yes, well some of us know where we belong while others try to hack their way—and still can't come out on top." She knew what she was doing was hateful and still could not stop herself.

He leaned a bit closer. "Must be real comfortable to be able to say that from your position."

"Anna. I am ready to go."

Kaleb raised his head in the direction of her mother. She was looking down her nose at him the way she always had, and damned if he was going to let her see how much she intimidated him.

"Hello, Rose."

He knew how much she thought it inappropriate for him to refer to her by her first name, but she would not give him the satisfaction of seeing that—not today. "Mr. McMurran. How lovely of you to say hello to my daughter upon her return home. Now, if you will excuse us, I need to take Anna home with me. Come along, dear."

Kaleb watched with some concern as Anna rose from the booth slowly, as though she were in slight discomfort. Her mother shielded her body on the way to the door.

"Thank you, Frannie. This was a lovely lunch."

Once they exited, Kaleb simply stood staring after them. It took Frannie clearing her throat to get through to him again. "You want to eat this here at the counter?"

He looked at the plate of food he no longer wanted. "No, Frannie, I'd better take it back to the house with me. I think I'll be staying there tonight." After he settled his bill with Frannie, he grabbed the paper bag with his sandwich and stalked out.

Frannie watched his retreating back and prayed for anyone in his path.

* * * * *

Anna Keller studied herself in the vanity mirror in her old bedroom. She was still awed over the fact that her parents had yet to change the room into something else. Everything looked the same—the pale violet walls, the islet white covering on the bed with matching curtains hanging from the large windows that looked out onto the river, her doll collection in the glass cabinet standing tall in the corner, as though they had stood the test of time to await her return. Only the reflection that gazed back at her seemed different and uncomfortably the same.

She had never really seen what Kaleb had seen in her. Her hair was a dull light brown, her eyes almost too close together, and her mouth appeared to be set in a permanent pout. But Kaleb had always said it made her look sexy— womanly. Whenever he had run his fingers through her hair, he had talked about the way the light would reflect off of it—

Turning abruptly away from herself, she chastised her thoughts. She would not allow herself to think of him that way. Not now, not later. She had not returned from New York to revisit the times they had shared. It had been obvious at the diner that he certainly wanted nothing to do with her either. In fact, if she really thought about their encounter, he had appeared almost grateful that he had had the chance to irritate her. And before New York…well, before New York was a different lifetime.

Her mother knocked on her door and, without waiting for a response, let herself in, along with their maid. She was a middle-aged woman this time, someone her mother had only recently hired to clean their house twice a week. She nodded at Anna and went straight to dusting.

"Are you comfortable, dear?" her mother inquired as she brought in a tray with tea and cookies.

Anna studied the afternoon treat that she did not want, knowing her mother would give her no privacy until she sampled it. "Yes, Mother. I'm fine."

Rose looked at her daughter and saw sullen, tired eyes, a face that was distressingly too thin, and hoped to God that neither had a thing to do with Kaleb McMurran. She had dealt with that issue years ago and would do so again if need be.

"Anna, you barely ate anything for lunch today."

She had known the conversation would go in this direction eventually, so she took a nimble bite of a cookie and sipped gingerly on the honey and lemon tea. Her mother smiled at the gesture.

"Mother, I barely got into town two days ago. I just need rest." She waited a beat, saw her mother was not going to let it rest, and delivered the ace up her sleeve. "Besides, your father's funeral was only a month ago, and I was on tour, not exactly available for you. I can be here now."

Her mother's eyes softened for a brief second, and only a veteran with experience in the many moods of Rose O'Connor Keller would have spotted the change. She was back in control once again when she spoke.

"I greatly appreciate your sentiment, dear, and yes, it was terribly difficult to arrange everything on my own. But you were available for the funeral, and that is really all that matters." Anna knew this to be very true. As long as the people within the community saw a unified front, that was all that really mattered—ever.

She did not want to mention the ring but knew she would need to do so soon. "Mother, if we are to find the ring—"

"Anna, let us not worry over that now." Rose smoothly interrupted her and walked to her daughter's childhood bed, turned it down. "Why don't you take a short nap? Then you will be rested for dinner later this evening with your father and me."

Anna let the disagreement slip from her lips silently; they could discuss the ring later. "Will Adam and Ian be joining us for dinner?" she asked as she crawled under the covers, thinking of her two brothers with warmth. Having not seen them since the funeral, and only one time a year prior before that, she missed them terribly.

"I have notified both of them that we will be dining tonight. If they choose to come, so be it." Rose fluffed the covers around her daughter's face, touched it softly for a moment, before she left Anna to her thoughts.

Anna tried to recall the last time her mother had touched her like that. Not being able to pinpoint the memory made sleep very restless.

* * * * *

Kaleb sat in the dark of the lighthouse, drinking a warm beer, his sandwich of earlier only half-eaten. The river was calm tonight on this evening in early March, and the wind picked up just a bit, enough to have him pulling the sweatshirt he had packed over his head. He was always prepared to stay the night where he worked; he liked to think of himself prepared for anything.

But he had not been prepared for the scene in the diner. He had not been prepared for how thin she looked or how tired. Her hair had been slightly disheveled, and that was not at all like Anna. She had always taken the utmost care of herself. She had never been terribly vain, no more than any other woman, but she certainly had been put together well. That was why his brother had joked with him so often. Why would Anna Keller take a liking to him?

He had yet to figure that out.

No, he thought, standing. He was not going to take the time to figure out anything. If she had changed from the girl he had known years ago, so be it. What did he care? He had certainly moved on with his life; he had plenty to keep him busy. And if the people around here had thought he had moved west to get away from flapping tongues and prying eyes after her departure, let them. He spent the better part of seven years sweating her out of his system on that ranch in Colorado. Had certainly entertained enough women to fill the hole, too. So what if he had come back. His brother was here with his wife; his parents were here. Family had always been important to him.

And if the family he had imagined creating with Anna had disintegrated like dust the day she flew the nest, so much the better. He saw the distress his brother was experiencing right now with a woman who was ready to deliver. He liked his independence.

And if none of these thoughts comforted him as he tried to sleep, he simply ignored the gnawing in his gut and concentrated on the night air.

Chapter II

Dinner had gone relatively well, considering the looks her brothers had given her throughout the meal. She knew what they were thinking...too thin, too pale, too shaky. She had tried to mask her unease with stories of New York, her dancing, her demanding schedule. Of course, her mother had not allowed her to linger terribly long over the real reason for her visit. *Yes, she was tired, but that was all. She would be back on the stage within a month, she was sure of it.* Her mother's sentiments echoed around inside her head.

Well, Anna was not so sure. As she lay in bed staring at the ceiling that night, she began to give serious thought to what had been niggling at the back of her brain for some time now. Dancing with the company had been a dream of hers ever since her parents had taken her to her first ballet when she was six. Immediately begging for lessons, she was sent to the best teacher in the area. When Mrs. Martin had noticed real God-given talent, she informed her parents that she should be sent to a private coach. And so the madness had begun.

Anna could not count the number of times she had not been allowed to attend a sleepover, a high school dance, a birthday party, all because she had to rehearse. Whenever she had complained, her mother simply reminded her that this is what she had wanted. Reminded her until Anna no longer needed reminding, until she understood that she had duty to fulfill and a promise to keep. Reminded her until she no longer knew what she had been complaining about in the first place.

To dance the ballet had been like breathing for her—second nature and life-giving. But recently, she had felt it suffocating her and could not figure out why. How could something that had given her so much joy drain her so completely? If she really allowed herself to answer that question, only one moment came to mind.

Six months ago she had been training hard for the new production, and this time she was the lead. Her waif of a figure had certainly allowed her to be

17

considered, but it was her strength and dedication that had gotten the producer's attention. She rehearsed longer and harder than any of the other dancers, knowing that when all was said and done, her mother would finally get her wish.

But all Rose had said was that it was about time her daughter had been noticed for her true talents, and now she could always be in the lead.

Always.

She expected nothing less.

Anna began to grow tired then. Just thinking about striving for that position each and every time for the next several years made her feet burn. After fourteen and sixteen hour days, she could no longer find the strength to get out of bed. Until the director asked for her help with the school.

Then she had begun to shine once more. Anna had thought no more time could be taken from her already busy schedule and given to anything else but sleep. Yet, once she had started teaching as an aide, she could think of no other place she would rather be. And if she had not had that breakdown...

Well, the doctors had been too polite to call it that; they simply termed it exhaustion. But Anna knew that she had really run her course on the stage, and at twenty-five, that was not so bad. But as her mother saw it, she still had a couple of good years left.

She would need to find a way to tell her that the stage was no longer a part of her life, and a new phase was about to begin.

* * * * *

The sun was shining almost too brightly the following morning as Kaleb hung up the phone from the contractor. He would need to put a rush on today's work and get over to the other end of the island. Apparently, someone had commissioned his work for the front of their home, and it was enough of a profit that he would need to put the museum on hold for about three days until he finished fixing the elderly couple's private lighthouse on their property. He understood that it was a much smaller version of the one he was currently fixing, but at least he was making a name for himself.

That was something that still shook him at times. Here he was restoring lighthouses to their original shape and texture, and people were paying him real money to do so. Grosse Ile had been written up in the paper so many times over the community's love for its landmarks, and Kaleb had always had a personal yen for them. Now he could share his love with others and leave something behind in his wake.

Not a bad way to make a living.

18

As he stepped out of the base of this lighthouse to view his latest progress, he saw Anna get out of the car she had driven up the drive. If he had not been so engrossed in his own thoughts, he may have heard her coming and been prepared. He was getting damn tired of her throwing him off his balance like that already—and she had only been here for three days.

"Something I can do for you, duchess?" he asked as he swaggered in her direction.

Anna tried not to let the glint in his eye or the steel in his voice get the best of her. "I was told to come here to rent a paddle boat for the day."

He studied her for a moment. "Who told you?"

"Frannie."

He smiled inwardly. Dammed old bird should mind her own business. "There are other places around here to rent paddle boats. You may want to try them instead." He started to walk away, but she only stepped into his path and blocked him. He glared down at the hand she had laid on his arm.

She tried not to shake visibly at the sudden drop in temperature. "Kaleb, please. I need some privacy, and this end of the island provides exactly that. Plus I knew you wouldn't batter at me with questions." She removed her hand, and he could feel his tongue again.

He studied her another minute. She shifted on her feet and waited for him to turn her away. He did not oblige. "It's ten an hour or forty-five for the day."

She smiled, and if she had not seemed so fragile and grateful all at the same time, he would have snarled at her. "Well, that price has certainly gone up some."

"Yeah, well, a lot happens in nine years."

He knew it was a slap in the face, and truthfully, he did not care. Let her see what her leaving had done to him.

"I'm not sure I deserved that."

"No. You deserve worse."

She snapped. "What was I supposed to do, Kaleb? Not follow my dream? My goal?"

"Are you sure it was yours to follow?"

He said it with such an icy calm that she could all but see the breath flowing out of his mouth. Because he had hit too close to the mark, she needed a defense and quick. "I'm sorry that some of us have goals, Kaleb, and dreams. Not everybody just floats around town, picking up skirts, and running off to play cowboy."

She could tell by the look in his eyes that she should have swallowed the words instead of speak them, but of course, it was too late for that. He decided to take the conversation into a new direction.

"So…you've been checking up on me, have you?" He stepped closer, and when he did, she involuntarily backed away. The movement did not get past him.

"Yes—No. I've just—heard things."

"Why, Miss Anna Keller, I don't believe I've ever heard you stutter." He smiled with the knowledge and again took a step closer. Again, she retreated.

"Look, Kaleb, I just need the boat. Please."

"Are you sure that's all you need?" He flicked a piece of stray hair from her cheek and tucked it behind her ear.

They both tried to ignore the shudder the small gesture had sparked.

"Yes. For now."

She stood her ground, chin up. That was something he could never fault her for—she could hang on to her last nerve if she really needed to do so.

He walked away from her toward the boathouse. Anna let go of the breath she had not been aware she had been holding and followed him.

She watched him tug at a smaller paddle boat and would not acknowledge the pool of saliva that had formed at noticing how his muscles bunched as he worked. She waited until he faced her.

"Will you accept a check?" She clutched her handbag as though her life depended upon it.

He thought this over. Looking at her, he began to notice the dark circles under her eyes, the red rims as though she had not been sleeping well. Her cheeks were sunken, and she had lost too much weight. He supposed dancers were supposed to be light, but if he could meet the person who told her to weigh only this much, he would do more than just talk to him.

He stepped closer in a softer way. "Anna—"

"I'm sorry, but checks are all I have with me right now." She had seen the way he was looking at her, and she did not think she would survive the questions. Not yet, not now.

He stepped back. "Consider this your welcome home present. Just have it back by dusk." With that, he stalked back inside the lighthouse and left her to stare after him.

* * * * *

"Damn woman, coming back and doing this to me again. I won't have it." Kaleb stormed into his brother's house. "Evan!"

Michelle came around the corner. "Must you yell for him every time you come over?"

He smiled the way he knew would win her over. "Michelle, you look amazing." He hugged her and swung her in a circle.

"Don't you try your charming ways with me, Kaleb McMurran. And put me down. You're going to make this baby come sooner than it should." She was laughing as she said it and stepped back to study his face.

"Where's Evan?"

"He is at work, which, I'm assuming, is where you should be."

He went to the refrigerator and grabbed the milk. "Why aren't you at the school?"

"I was feeling a bit tired today. Thought I'd stay home and rest a bit." She eased herself into a chair.

Instantly concerned and paling at how uncomfortable she looked, he went to her side. "What's wrong? Are you sick? Should I take you to the doctor?" The thought of the baby coming right now while Evan was nowhere to be found danced up and down his spine.

Michelle tried to suppress the laugh at the utter look of fear in her brother's-in-law eyes. "Kaleb , I'm fine. I'm just tired. It happens toward the end before the baby comes. In another six weeks, I'll be right as rain." He felt her forehead just to be sure; she swatted at his hand. "Pour me a glass of that, would you? I don't feel like getting up again."

He went to the cupboard for two glasses. "What time can I expect him home?"

"Oh, I'd say about 4:30. He's been pretty much right on the dot these days. Doesn't want to miss out." She winked as she took the glass of milk he offered.

"You think I could have him this evening?"

Michelle thought about the crib that had yet to be put together. Studying her husband's brother, however, helped her to decide. "Yes. Please take him out. He is practically in my lap every night, waiting for this kid to just come shooting out. I could use an evening alone."

"Thanks."

There was a pause, and she watched him shuffle his feet, look around the room nervously. She was pretty certain she knew why he was giving off this kind of energy.

"So, what's new with you? I hear the museum trust fund has commissioned you."

"Yeah. It's going okay. I need to spend a couple days at the Harrisons', though. They want me to fix up their art work in their front yard."

"Is that what they're calling it?"

He smirked.

She decided that with Kaleb, it was just better to come right out and ask. "Have you seen Anna?"

He almost bobbled the glass but recovered nicely. "She just stopped by to rent a paddle boat. Frannie sent her."

"Ah." Michelle smiled into her glass to hide the pleasure in that. "So how long's she staying?"

"Hell if I know." He walked the space of the kitchen. "I saw her first at the diner yesterday. With her mother."

"Oh." The mention of Rose brought a shiver to even Michelle. "And how is dear old mom?"

He could always count on his sister-in-law to side with him. "As nasty as ever. I had the pleasure of making her uncomfortable."

"Honey, you make a lot of women uncomfortable."

"Not the right one." He said it before he realized the thought was there. Before Michelle could leap onto the comment, he continued. "We haven't said much to each other. We've done our best to irritate each other a bit the two times we have seen each other so far. That's all I know."

Irritation's a good start, she thought, a wicked gleam in her eye. "Well, just keep your head above water, for now."

"I'll be keeping it above water for always." He set his glass in the sink. "I should go to the Harrisons'. Have Evan meet me at the Inn. Thanks for the milk." He kissed her cheek absently and left.

Not one to leave all the work to the fates, Michelle decided a phone call was in order.

* * * * *

Madelaine Murphy worked with Michelle at the high school and simply could not wait for spring break to begin the following week. After receiving Michelle's phone call earlier, she tried to bury the hurt that Anna had not phoned to say she was back. She and Anna had been friends since she could remember but had not seen her since her grandfather's funeral a month ago. Before that, she had saved every penny she could from her teacher's salary to attend Anna's last ballet, and Anna had been impeccable. But even though her friend had shone under the stage lights, she could still sense that something was amiss. Now that she had returned home without any notice, she wanted to get to the bottom of things as soon as possible.

Pulling into the drive of the Keller Residence was like driving up to visit royalty. The long stone driveway was lined with trees and rhododendrons. The house, itself, was large and picturesque, but it was once she was inside that would count.

She used the large brass knocker to announce herself. Coming over to Anna's house had never been easy, except to see Anna and perhaps get a quick peek at her older brother, Adam. Whenever Madelaine's friends came to visit her, they were always allowed to just barge right in, clamor into the kitchen for a quick treat or a playful shooing from her mother. They could kick off their shoes, flop down on the sofa, and change the TV station that Madelaine's father would surely have programmed at the time. Her friends were allowed to argue about something in the news with her parents or explain their dislike about a policy at school. They could stay for dinner without an invitation, and on more than one occasion, bunk in the basement with Madelaine rather than go home.

But not at Anna's house. At Anna's house, there were procedures and policies and rules that needed to be followed. She dreaded them now even as Anna's mother opened the door.

"Well, hello, Madelaine. What a lovely surprise. Please come in."

"Hello, Mrs. Keller. It is lovely to see you again. You look well."

Indeed, she did. The woman was aging rather gracefully, her light blonde hair pulled back into a sweeping and elegant bun. Her ivory skin sprouting only the most appropriate wrinkles when she smiled. Her dress of choice for this cool spring afternoon while she lounged around the house was a pale pink linen pant suit and casual tie-back sandals. Her fingers were adorned with only her wedding ring, which was positioned on almost wrinkle-free hands. She smiled pleasantly at the expected compliment.

"Oh, dear, I was just reading out in the sun room. Our new maid, Cindy, was just finishing the upstairs, and I thought I should give her the space to work. Is Anna expecting you?"

She said it in such a way that Madelaine knew Rose was quite aware her daughter had not told many people about her return home. She smiled like a school girl.

"I thought I'd surprise her. I hope that's all right."

"Of course it is. She's probably up from her nap by now. I'll get her for you."

Rose left the room, which gave Madelaine the time to gawk at her surroundings without Rose's knowledge.

The wide sweep of windows across the back of the house gave a beautiful view of dense trees. The pine floors shone immaculately under the Chinese rugs that Madelaine was certain were actually from China. She gazed longingly at the art that hung on the walls, the vases that stood proudly on tables, and wondered how any normal person could afford such niceties. Of course, since Anna's father was in the import/export business, she could see the possibilities.

She began to shift toward the wall-size fireplace when she heard him come through the door. Turning, she used her best smile on him. "Hello, Mr. Keller.

"Maddy Murphy. How good to see you!" He crossed the room with large strides, setting his newspaper on the table as he did. He embraced her in a bear hug. "Does Anna know you're here?"

"She will. Your wife went up to get her from her nap."

"Ah, well…" He stood back to look at her. "You're looking well. How's that high school treating you?"

"Good enough. Spring Break is just around the corner." She laughed.

"Ah, that's my girl."

When Anna stepped into the room, that was how she found them—her father's arm draped casually across Madelaine's shoulders, Madelaine laughing up him. She was so grateful for that.

"Maddy."

They turned, and for a moment, no one spoke. Then Madelaine swooped in her direction and knocked her breathless with a hug.

"I've missed you! Oh, I've missed you!"

"I've missed you, too."

Madelaine could feel Anna's grip around her—tight, as though she were drowning. Underneath Anna's baggy sweater, she knew the girl was skin and bones.

They pulled apart, each studying the other. Anna began to speak tremulously. "I'm sorry I didn't call you sooner. I just—let time get away from me."

Madelaine waved off her remarks as though they meant nothing because she was very aware that was exactly what her friend needed at the moment. "Nonsense. We're both busy. I'm just glad you're back."

"Well, don't get too comfortable, Madelaine. Anna's only here for a short break. Then she'll be off and running again to the ballet." Rose crossed over to her daughter and patted her shoulder.

"Is this true, Anna?"

When Anna did not respond, her father stepped closer. "Rose, why don't we let these two catch up with each other? It's been too long for two raving beauties to be apart. I'm sure they have a lot to discuss." He gave a knowing look to Madelaine and led his wife away.

The two of them stood there for a moment in an awkward silence. Then Anna said, "Forgive me, my manners. Would you care for something to drink?"

Madelaine only stared. Then she laughed. "Manners? Honey, it's me. Maddy. Let's go crack open a beer and sit on the swing. You've got a lot to tell me."

Once they were seated with their drinks—beer for Madelaine, iced tea for Anna—on the swing under the trees in the yard, Anna inquired, "How did you know I was home?"

"Michelle called to tell me."

"Michelle?"

"Michelle McMurran. Evan's wife. I work with her."

It took a moment for it to sink in, but Anna found the connection. "Yes, she would know I was here."

The girls sipped in more silence. Madelaine began to swing gently. "What's going on, Anna?"

At that simple statement, Anna felt her eyes fill and turned away. Madelaine reached out for her. "I just need a minute to compose myself."

Madelaine gave her two as she held her shoulder. Anna gulped down the rest of her tea, wiped her eyes, and turned back. "I rented a paddle boat today…from Kaleb." Madelaine nodded knowingly but said nothing. "I spent a couple hours on the water by myself trying to figure out…just trying to figure out. My mother doesn't know. She thinks I went to do some window shopping. I don't know how to explain what's going on inside of me, but I know it's something big, and I think I just am going to need time." She met her friend's gaze directly. "Can you please bear with me?"

The desperate plea squashed all thoughts of her demands for answers. It was obvious that Anna needed a real friend right now, and being given the chance to do that for her again was something she could not pass on.

"Yes. I will give you as much time as you need. As long as you make me a promise." Anna waited. "You come to me when you're ready to talk, and we'll battle any demons you're facing together."

"Oh, Maddy!" Anna leaned forward in another fierce hug and held on for several long minutes. Madelaine stroked her hair. When Anna sat back, she continued.

"Promise number two—"

"You sure are being demanding."

"Hey. My best friend is back in town; I get to be as demanding as I want. You need to stop taking naps and go out with me tonight." As Anna shook her head in protest, Maddy stopped her. "Look. When we were kids, you always had a rehearsal, a recital, a something or other that had to do with dance. Now…you're on a break. Let's live it up a little. Let me at least take you to dinner. You can catch me up on the scene in New York."

Anna thought about this offer for only another second. Then she shook her head, and for the first time since she had come back, smiled sincerely. "I think that would be great."

"Okay. I'll pick you up at seven." They stood. "And, Anna, please wear something a little more flattering than a big ol' baggy sweater."

She did. After taking a long hot bath, she decided to spruce up a bit. If anything, the ritual of being female would raise her spirits.

She sprayed light citrus perfume and chose a white cotton dress shirt tucked in to her favorite snug blue jeans, which really accentuated her small waist. She accompanied the look with chunky glass-blown jewelry she had purchased at a street market in New York. She left her hair down and casual, and it softened her eyes. Not being one to wear too much glamour, she opted for a light blush and pale pink lipstick. As she was putting the finishing touches on, her mother came into the room.

She studied her daughter, none too happily. "Do you really think it is a good idea to be going out so late, Anna? You did just get here."

Anna waited a beat before responding to her mother. "Mom, I'll be fine. Madelaine is picking me up in just a few minutes, and she'll bring me home safely."

"I am not worried about Madelaine. I am worried about you." For that moment, Anna hoped she was really worried about her daughter rather than about her dancer. She was proven wrong. "You will be back in New York soon, and you would not want all that hard work gone to waste—should I say, to your waist. Your body cannot survive too many nights on the town."

Anna stood, smoothed down her blouse. "How do I look?"

Before her mother could say anything, her father swooped in to her rescue. "Anna, you are a peach among pits." He crossed to her and kissed each temple. "Maddy's here. She's waiting for you out in her car. Now go have fun and break some hearts."

"Thanks, Dad." She kissed her mother's cheeks and left.

"Gregory, you should not encourage her. She needs to be careful."

"Rose, she's been careful all her life. It's time our girl let loose a bit." With that, he walked out of the room and down the stairs.

* * * * *

The Lighthouse Inn had not changed much over the last fifty or so years. As Kaleb looked around at his surroundings, he was grateful some things remained the same. Evan walked back from the bar with two beers in his hands and settled in next to his brother at the far booth.

"The pool table's ours next. When I win, you are buying me dinner."

"Well, I sure hope the menu's expensive, then, because I brought quite an appetite." He raised his bottle in a toast.

Kaleb continued to scan his surroundings. He had been coming here ever since he donned his first fake I.D., which, he now knew, was incredibly stupid, considering the bartender had watched him grow up. Now that he was "of age" by about eight years, he could smile at the memory.

He saw Lindsey Aaron and Mike Demillimister dancing to something slow on the makeshift dance floor and wondered when she had grown up. They would be getting married next month. He only knew this because his mother was doing the flowers for the ceremony. Rita McMurran owned the most successful shop on the island.

He saw Mr. Collins seated at the bar, drinking what was mostly likely an imported beer, and flirting with Melanie Wilson as she tried to balance a tray, talk with him, and catch Kaleb's eye.

"I didn't know Melanie was working tonight." He raised his bottle in a slight toast to her that she acknowledged with a nod of her head.

Evan caught the exchange and winced. "Please, I beg of you. Don't get involved with her. Michelle can't stand her." He guzzled the brown liquid quickly.

Kaleb looked at his brother. "Too late. I already had me a taste, and I think I'd like another."

"Ah, Kaleb…"

They continued their conversation, good-naturedly. Anyone observing from the outside would have seen a pair of attractive brothers, the kind who break women's hearts. Evan was every bit as handsome as Kaleb, but his eyes were a bit softer, kinder. As was his heart. The only woman to have ever put a scratch on it had been Michelle, and he saw to it that she never did so again by getting her to marry him six years ago. The thought made him smile.

"You're thinking of Michelle, aren't you?"

Evan, realizing he had been caught, tried a sheepish grin. "When a man's got as good as I do…"

"Yeah, yeah, I know. She had me worried today. I thought I was going to have to deliver your baby."

"She's been pretty tired, but according to everyone down at work, I'll know when it's really time. Hey, looks like the table's open."

They stood, shook hands with the two giving the pool table over to them, and proceeded to play nine ball. Kaleb took the first game easily. Then Anna and Madelaine walked in.

He was bent over the table, taking his time on his favorite bank shot, when they came through the door. Madelaine's almost auburn, curly hair, long legs, and full lips certainly got the attention they deserved from every red-blooded male in the place. But Kaleb's eyes never left Anna's face.

She looked a little more relaxed as she gazed around for a table. She had some color in her cheeks, and she tucked her hair behind her ear, much in the same manner as he had done earlier that day when she had come to rent the boat. He reached for his beer, saw that it was empty, and waved down Ed behind the bar for another round.

His mouth was, quite suddenly, very dry.

Evan missed none of this. "You gonna shoot today, pal, or should I help you out?"

"Kiss ass." Kaleb took his shot, missed when he heard her laugh at a joke that someone had come over to their table to tell. He swore under his breath and turned the balls over to his brother.

Anna was well aware that Kaleb was there, watching her. She did her best not to look at him or his brother. "Maddy, Kaleb McMurran is here."

"Really?" Maddy asked, all innocence. "Where?" She strained her head to see.

"Don't make it so obvious." Anna pulled her friend back down into her seat as two men, both strangers to Anna, made their way to their table.

"Hey, Maddy. Who's your friend?" Josh smiled easily at Anna, causing her to blush.

Madelaine felt the hairs on the back of her neck stand up from the holes she was certain Kaleb was boring into her neck. "Hi, Josh. Tom. This is Anna Keller. Anna, Josh Bunker and Tom Hamlin." They all shook hands. "Anna just got back from New York. She's a dancer." Their eyes bugged out of their heads, and Maddy laughed. "Sorry, guys. Not that kind of dancer. Anna is a ballerina."

The group of them laughed, and the two men offered to buy them a drink.

"Actually, it's girls night out, so I think we'll be on our own."

Josh moved in closer to Anna, toyed with the ends of her hair. "You sure? I'd hate to see what could happen to two pretty things like you without a chaperone."

Anna tried to shift, but Josh kept his hand right where it was. "I think we can handle ourselves, Josh. Now go play somewhere else." Maddy waved them away.

"Tom just wanted to sit near you, Maddy. And I just want to get to know your friend better." He leered down at Anna.

"I believe they said no."

Kaleb had snuck up behind them, quietly, like a snake. His mouth was set in a grim line, the long line of his body primed for a fight.

"McMurran, I don't believe this concerns you."

"Actually, Bunker, it does. The ladies have spoken. Why don't you take Hamlin and go sit on the other side of the bar?" He inched closer. People nearby began to speak in hushed undertones. Evan took another step closer as well, pool stick in hand.

"This lady here ain't said a word, have you, sweetheart?" Keeping the piece of hair twined around his finger, he looked down at Anna once again. "As soon as she tells me she's not interested, I'll back off."

Kaleb kept his eyes on Josh throughout the entire exchange. "Anna, please tell Bunker you're not interested so that he may remain in walking condition tonight."

She tried to find her voice; the intensity of the moment was making her head spin. Eventually, it came out in a whisper. "I'm not interested."

"Thank you. You may now let go of her hair."

Josh held on another few seconds to prove that he could and began to back away. "Sorry, McMurran, I didn't realize you were dipping your pen into this ink well, too." He spared Anna a glance. "She didn't look the type." Josh and Tom walked off.

"Hey, Kaleb," Maddy said once the guys were gone. "Thanks."

Kaleb watched them until they were seated at their own table. Then he finally laid his eyes back on Maddy. "You're welcome. Let us know if you need anything else." With that, he turned back to the pool table with Evan.

Anna let out her breath. "He looked pretty steamed."

"Well, I thought it might do him some good to see another guy interested in you, but I certainly didn't see Josh turning into such a jerk. Are you okay?" She laid a hand on Anna's unsteady one.

"Yeah. I wonder why Kaleb came to our rescue like that."

"You're serious?"

"Well, yes."

Maddy bit back an oath. "Anna, I don't think he's ever stopped thinking about you."

"He seems to be thinking about her just fine."

Maddy looked over her shoulder to where Melanie was flirting wildly with Kaleb. The exchange Melanie had just witnessed between all of them had not been lost on her.

"It's not real. Whatever they have, it's not real. I've never seen Kaleb protect someone like that. I think he's still got it for you."

With a shake of her head, Anna looked back at Maddy. "Let's just order something and get on with our own evening. I might even drink a beer tonight, Madelaine."

"Well, my goodness, Anna Keller, you never stop!"

The two of them ate dinner and laughed a lot. All the while, Kaleb played pool with Evan, lost, bought dinner, and tried to avoid Melanie's advances as nicely as possible. He wondered when everything had gotten so complicated.

"If you keep staring at her, she'll never begin to relax."

"What?" Kaleb looked at Evan, snapping out of his daydream. "She doesn't appear to be un-relaxed."

Evan tossed down his napkin. "Kaleb , I know I was pretty moon-eyed over Michelle when you two started dating, and maybe I didn't pay much attention since I am the younger brother. I don't know Anna that well, but what I do remember is that she's pretty hard on herself. She works hard at whatever she does. Doesn't it seem a bit odd that she's back from New York for no apparent reason? That can't please her mama too much." He swallowed the last of his water, something he had switched to an hour before. "Again, I don't know her that well, but she doesn't look right. She seems edgy, tired. I don't think you should add to that."

Kaleb knew he was right; something about Anna had not been right since her return home. He gestured to Melanie for the bill as Anna approached their table. Madelaine stood protectively behind her.

"Hi, Evan. It's been a while."

"Hi, Anna. It's nice to see you."

"Congratulations. I hear you and Michelle are expecting your first baby."

"Yeah. Just a few more weeks to go."

She smiled and turned her focus to Kaleb . "I wanted to thank you. Maddy said a guy like you didn't need thanks; that's just the sort of thing you do. But I thought I should mention it."

"Well, don't."

The silence was awkward until he could stand it no longer.

"Did you return the paddle boat?"

She nodded yes.

"You should know to expect that from guys like him. You come in to a bar, all dolled up, what do you think is going to happen?"

Anna looked down at her blue jeans and then back at Kaleb . Once again, the light in her eyes had dimmed. "Maybe Maddy was right. There was no need to thank you. I'll see you around, Evan."

She turned and, without a backward glance, walked out.

Maddy let him know just what she thought of him at that moment and then joined her friend.

"Way to go, ace. Nice way to end the evening." Evan stood and threw money down on the table. "If you're in the mood for company, I think Melanie will wait for you."

Kaleb watched him leave. He rubbed his hands over his tired face.

Chapter III

Four days later, Kaleb entered the lighthouse just after sunrise and found an envelope tacked to the door. Upon opening it, he withdrew a check in the amount that would cover an entire week's rental of the paddle boat he had lent to Anna the previous week. There was no note of thanks, only her signature on the check. When he went to the boathouse, he saw she had already taken it out. Swearing mildly, he returned to try and get some work accomplished.

He had not slept well in the days following their incident at the bar. True he had had the job at the Harrison house to keep him well occupied, but all in all, he kept seeing Anna's face in his mind after the way he had spoken to her. No matter how he played it out, he knew that when it came right down to it, he had hurt her feelings.

And why shouldn't I have? he thought now in disgust. It was not as though she had always been terribly considerate of his feelings. She had taken off for New York without so much as a backward glance, danced her way into fame and fortune, never gave him a call or wrote him a line. He knew because he had tried to follow her progress throughout the years since she had been gone. He would go online to read the articles that were written about her in the New York papers, and when she had that one article done on her over in Europe, his heart could not help but swell with pride. He had tried valiantly to ward off those feelings of pride regarding her accomplishments, but in the end, he had even bragged to his brother and Michelle about her.

Now here she was back in his life, and so far, he had screwed up every meeting they had had thus far. He knew he was being spiteful, pathetic, cold. And it was painful to admit it, even to himself, that there was a chance he had never really gotten over her.

He had tried—first in Colorado, then here in Grosse Ile. Melanie had certainly been a warm and willing body over the last few months, but even after he had finally given in and allowed her to come back with him to his apartment, her touch had felt odd, to the point that he feigned illness and sent her home. She had been none too pleased, and frankly, he had not cared.

Evan had been trying to contact him, but he avoided his calls, too, by claiming he was overworked. He knew Michelle had not had the baby yet, so there was no pressing matter in needing to see his brother. His mother and father had both called to invite him to dinner, but again, he made no time. He knew this was probably better all around, considering the bear he had become.

As the first dusky moments of twilight began to settle on the river, he cleaned up his tools and looked—again—toward the water for any sign of Anna. She had been gone now for over twelve hours. All he could imagine was that she had gotten lost or shipwrecked and could not find a way to call for help. What if she were unconscious, lying in the paddle boat, a victim of sunstroke? Or worse? If she did not return soon, he would have no choice but to—

The sound of light splashing had him whipping around to the front of the lighthouse. There she was, pretty as a picture, just now coming to shore, a small basket at her side. He was going to kill her for making him worry that way.

He strode up to the shoreline to help her drag the boat in.

"I can manage, thank you," she said stiffly.

"Too bad. I'm helping." He pulled at her arm, tried to ignore the shock that danced up his fingers from contact with her skin.

"I said I can manage." She jerked away.

"And I said too bad." There was a storm rolling in; they could both feel it, although the sky was a clear and misty blue.

"Why are you so angry? Did I not leave enough for the boat rental? I wrote you a check. Didn't you get it?"

"You think this is about money?" he spat at her. "You could have been killed out there, spending the entire day in the water like that. Did you tell anyone how long you would be?"

"I told you I'd need the boat for a week. I didn't think—"

"That's right. You didn't think. What if you'd capsized? What if you had gotten burned out from heatstroke? What then, duchess?" He knew he was being ridiculous, but he was on a roll now and could not stop.

"Kaleb , I took a life vest and my cell phone. I had bottled water and food in my basket."

"Yeah, well…" was all he could manage. "It's not like you know your way around here. You've been gone too long. I think you could have easily gotten lost."

"Stop throwing that in my face!" she yelled, and he was taken aback. "Yes, I left! I went to New York to pursue something! I wanted to dance, and by golly, dance I did! I'm sorry if you don't like it, but I guess I'm the kind of person who actually needs to go after something rather than just sit by and watch the world move past me!" She tried to leave, but he blocked her way.

"Stop throwing that in my face!" he tossed back at her. "Do you like those words, Anna? Do you? I'm sorry that I wasn't gutsy enough for you! I'm sorry that I liked my comfort zone or whatever you would like to call it! But I'll tell you this, duchess; I sure as hell got out of Dodge after your boots hit that pavement. There would be no looking back for me either!"

They stood there, toe-to-toe, neither one knowing what to do next. Her ponytail was slightly dampened from a day in the rising spring heat, and her cheeks were now flushed from excitement, nerves, adrenaline. He was still sweaty and dirty from the day's efforts at the lighthouse; he hadn't bothered to shave recently, which only added to the intensity of his eyes. They held heat—and a lot of it at the moment.

She cleared her throat; he released her arm. "Well, now that we've got that out of our system, perhaps we could actually manage a conversation while I'm here in town."

"Oh, so this time you plan on staying?"

She turned abruptly, and he wanted to cut out his tongue. He raced to her over the gravel, grabbed her arm again. "Anna, I'm sorry, I'm sorry. You were really trying to be nice, and I blew it—again. Seems I've been doing a lot of that lately. With you."

Considering him, she asked, "What do you mean?"

He exhaled audibly. "I should never have said the things I did to you at the Inn the other night. Those guys were the jerks, not you and Maddy. You deserved someone who really was more gallant. I'm sorry." When she said nothing, he released her arm and turned toward the lighthouse.

Anna lengthened her strides to catch him. "I accept your apology." That stopped him. "But only if you'll accept mine. I've said some things that—friends should never say to each other. I mean that."

They studied each other again. He stuck his hand out; she took it. "Truce?" he asked, and they shook. She smiled. "That's something I haven't seen you do enough of since you've been back." At her confused look, he elaborated. "Smile." The light dimmed in her eyes, only a little this time, but he was not in the mood to be responsible for it. So he changed the subject. "What is so interesting out there on the water that you would need to keep the boat out for fourteen hours at a time this whole week?"

Neither of them acknowledged she was the one to let go of his hand first. "It's rather complicated. And you look like you've had a long day. I should probably let you shower, eat, sleep." She began to walk away. "I should get home now. I'm sure my mother's worried about me."

"Hey, don't go on my account. I can get cleaned up here with the makeshift tub I have inside. If you stay and tell me your story, we could pick up a pizza, eat it on the shore. I could build a fire. If you remember correctly, I build pretty amazing fires."

He was smiling at her, trying to get her to relax the way he always could. This would be her first chance at friendship with him—real friendship. And it had been so long since she had anybody real she could talk to.

"Okay. Sounds great. I'd really like that. But I'm paying for my half."

"We'll see."

She waited inside the lighthouse while he washed. At the island's only pizzeria, he would not allow her to pay, but she won at the party store when they picked up a bottle of wine. He even gave in and allowed her to choose the bottle.

They situated themselves on a bed sheet near the river's edge, partially on the grass, partially on the sand. He poured wine into plastic cups, and they dove into the pizza. Neither had realized how hungry each was.

"So tell me the great mystery behind your latest hobby," he stated over a mouthful.

"You'll think it's silly."

"Probably. But I'd still like to hear about it."

She could see he was sincere. The light from the small fire he had managed shadowed his face, which would make telling the tale that much easier.

"My grandfather, my mother's dad, as you know, died last month."

"I know. I'm sorry I wasn't at the funeral." He paused. "I could try to cover with a lie, but I'll tell you straight out. I wasn't sure I could face seeing you, especially under those circumstances. I knew you'd get back on a plane right away, and well…" He did not bother to finish his sentence.

"It's all right. I didn't mind. I had enough to deal with in my own family at the time. My grandmother, my mother…She's an only child. Somehow I think that makes it harder, made her harder." Anna surprised herself with this comment, not just because it had obviously been buried deeply but because she had shared it with Kaleb. Kaleb had his own opinion of Rose but decided against talking about it just then. The wine was obviously loosening her tongue, and he did not want to stop her. "He left clues in his last letter to us. My brothers and myself. There's a connection between us and this ring. Apparently, there are three pieces of a ring, a ring with Irish symbolism, that each of us needs to find in our own time. The Claddagh. He was pretty specific about that. We are not to help each other, but we are allowed to reveal when we've found our piece. My piece deals with friendship. Once I find it, I can either keep it for myself or join it with the other pieces. It will be my decision."

Kaleb thought this over for a few minutes, staring at the flames as they lapped at the wood. "What are you going to do about it?"

"I am not entirely sure."

"So why have you been in the river so much?"

"Because he said the pieces were connected to things, people, or places that brought us our part of the ring. I've always had a feeling of—comfort near the water, near the lighthouses. I thought I should start there."

He decided not to comment on the depths of the comfort and friendship she had explored with him during their youth inside the very lighthouse where he now worked. "As good a place as any. So…when would you like me to begin helping you?"

Just like that, she mused. If there were ever anyone who could help her, it had always been Kaleb . "Thank you. You know, this could all be some ridiculous ruse the old man is playing on us, one last gig from the beyond." She stared up at the early evening stars. "But most of the time, you just believe an old Irish man's tales. They're too intriguing not to."

He raised his plastic cup to her then in a toast to her grandfather and his tales— tall or true remained to be seen. Then he put his foot in his mouth. "Why are you back now, Anna?"

She shifted, uncomfortable. This was an area she had obviously not wanted to discuss tonight, but Kaleb could not help it. He needed to know, but more importantly, he was beginning to see that he needed to feel trusted by her.

She rose and walked to the water's edge. He stayed where he was and watched her in the moonlight. When she turned, her eyes were difficult to read. He tried to blame the minimum amount of light.

"Kaleb, you and I—you and I have a history. Although most of it is good, I'd like to really try our hand at being friends. I don't think we ever really knew how to be friends—before. Can we do that?"

His throat had gone bone dry, his chest felt swollen, his palms were sweaty. At that moment, with the way she was looking at him, had she asked him to walk on the water and crow like a chicken, he would have agreed.

"Yes. I think we can."

"Then, as my friend, I need you to leave me be about that for a while. Just— let me figure out some things, and I promise you, as soon as I do, you'll be the first to know."

She seemed more relaxed, more at ease at this moment. So he let it go. For now.

"I'd better get home. I'm very tired." She began to clean up their mess.

"How did you get here?"

"I rode my bike. My parents still had it in the garage," she managed with a chuckle.

"Well, it's too dark for you to ride back now. We can throw it in the back of my truck, and I'll take you home."

He saw the worry come over her face, the little waves of panic at the idea of her mother seeing them together, but she closed that thought off, almost visibly to him, and hopped into his truck a few minutes later.

When he drove back to his apartment that night, he slept soundly, shapes of Celtic blessings floating through his mind, images of a pretty girl laughing up at him from her spot near the river.

* * * * *

Rose was on her the minute she walked through the back door. "Where have you been?"

Anna jumped a little; she had known deep down that this would happen. She felt the quiet solitude of the evening draining out of her. "I've been on the river." She started toward her room.

"All day?"

"Yes, Mother, all day. I had my cell phone with me. I'm sorry if I worried you."

"Was that Kaleb McMurran who dropped you at our curb?"

The icy tone in her mother's voice had Anna turning and facing her head-on. "Yes, it was. He didn't want me to ride home on my bike in the dark. He was being kind."

"Yes, I am sure that was the foremost thought in his mind tonight—kindness."

"You're being ridiculous, Mother. I'm going to bed."

As Anna tried to go up the steps, Rose stopped her. "Do not take that tone with me, young lady. You have obligations to fulfill, and I will not have—that man ruining them for us—you." She was almost seething.

"I'm well aware what my obligations are, Mother. You rarely allow me to forget." With that, she stalked up the stairs and slammed into her room, locking the door behind her.

* * * * *

Anna decided that rest was in order the next day. She would admit to no one but herself that she had overworked herself yesterday under the circumstances, so grabbing an old favorite from her family's library, she headed out to the hammock in the late morning sun. Slipping her jacket over her shoulders to ward off the slight breeze, she did not get past the first two pages before she drifted off to sleep.

That was how her mother found her an hour later. She tried to cover her without disturbing her but failed as Anna sat up abruptly.

"I am sorry, dear. I did not mean to wake you. You looked very peaceful but a bit chilled. I brought you out this blanket."

Anna rubbed her eyes and tried to focus. "How long have I been asleep?"

"I would say an hour or so."

"I guess I was more tired than I thought."

"You probably worked yourself too hard yesterday."

"Mother—"

"Anna." Her mother spoke with such finality that Anna chose to be quiet and listen. "I should never have spoken to you that way last night. Your father overheard and replayed the conversation the way he heard it, and even I have to admit, I sounded awful."

She was so dismayed that all she could was stare at her mother for several long seconds. Rose continued. "I am just so worried about you. When you arrived at the airport last week, you looked so distraught and tired. I do not want you to look that way."

"Oh, Mother." Anna stood and held her arms out to her mother. They hugged while Anna apologized. "Mother, I'm sorry, too. I should not speak that way to the woman who has done nothing but care for me and worry over me."

"And then to see you come home with Kaleb McMurran—"

Anna pulled back at that, and Rose knew she had pushed too much. "I did not come home with him; he gave me a ride to my home. There is a difference."

"What if the neighbors had seen? Imagine the talk. How you have barely been home, and already you are gallivanting around town with him. I know about the commotion he caused the other night at the Inn."

"Kaleb did not cause any such commotion. He helped Maddy and me to fend off a couple of jerks that wouldn't leave us alone."

"Well, it seems like his kind has a tendency to bring those sorts of people around."

"And what kind is that, Mother?" Anna folded her arms over her chest.

Rose could feel that she was losing ground and had no idea how to regain it. "His kind. You do not belong with that type, Anna. You are a Keller, for goodness sake. You are a ballerina. Kaleb McMurran does not appreciate what you have to offer. This is where you belong. On the stage is where you belong."

"How do you know where I belong when even I don't?" Anna waved off her mother's response before she could speak again. "You and Dad always taught me to respect people, and I respect Kaleb. He has really made something for himself, and if that means working with his hands, well, I guess then we'll all have to live with it. Kaleb and I are going to be friends. Friends. Please don't stand in my way in this matter." She began to cross the lawn on her way back to the house. "Oh, and another thing. He'll be assisting me to find my part of the ring. Don't look so surprised, Mother. I know he's the one who is supposed to help me. If you don't like that, I'm sorry. It's just the way it has to be." She went into the house, leaving Rose staring after her.

Patrick O'Connor had been very right about one thing before he had died—his daughter did not like the direction any of his nonsense was taking.

* * * * *

Kaleb and Anna met the next morning for breakfast. She needed to get her footing in this phase of the adventure her grandfather had left for her, so she thought she would begin the day with a sensible meal. As Kaleb watched her over the rim of his coffee cup, she outlined her plan.

"I know it seems foolish that I would spend all this time on a river in a paddle boat, searching for a ring—or worse, a part of a ring. But my grandfather—well, you should have seen my grandmother's face when I told her I was looking into all of this. It was as though I had given her the best gift ever."

Anna never babbled, and although her end of the conversation appeared to have direction, Kaleb could sense that if he did not get hold of the reins soon, she would begin babbling. And that could only mean worry for her.

"Anna, tell me what's bothering you."

He had reached for her hand across the table, held it there, without realizing that had been his intention. Frannie, spotting this new moment of intimacy from across the room, stopped halfway to their table with a fresh pot of coffee. She busied herself with another table nearby.

Anna worried her lip in a way that made Kaleb's mouth water. She tucked a piece of hair behind her right ear and looked hard at the tabletop. "It's my mother."

She heard him suck in an involuntary breath, but he still did not let go of her hand. She kept hers in his and would not think about that until later. When he said nothing, she continued.

"I know you've never been a—fan of her, Kaleb, but she's still my mother." At his arched brow, she continued. "She is quite unhappy about this ring business, so every time I leave the house now to go looking for it, she makes me feel very guilty."

"Why?"

His response was so simple that she almost felt a tear escape with gratitude. "Because I think she feels cheated. I mean, after all, he was her father. If there was some kind of family heirloom, then she should be the one to get it, not her children. But I got the idea from his letter that this heirloom needs to be passed on to a generation of three."

He considered this for a moment. Then he simply could not help himself. "I think it's very selfish."

"Kaleb—"

"No. Don't interrupt. Think about it. Your grandfather leaves a ring to you and your brothers, albeit in a very unusual fashion, but let's just pretend he's having one last bit of fun before he passes on. Now your mother, who claims to have your best interests at heart, is upset because she wants the ring. I think that's selfish."

Anna sipped her juice. "Well, she's not too happy that you're involved with this whole thing either."

I guess she'll have to get used to it. The thought had entered his mind so quickly, he had not had time to catch his breath before allowing himself to think it. Now he had to figure out what to do before he said it aloud to Anna.

"Of course, she certainly didn't hide her feelings from me the other night. Or yesterday morning."

He was brought back to the task at hand. "What do you mean?"

"I mean she really gave me a piece of her mind about allowing me to be seen dropped off by you so late that night. What would the neighbors think? I basically told her…tough cookies." She tried, unsuccessfully, to hide the smile.

Kaleb almost choked on his toast. "You did not say that."

"Not in those words…but close enough."

After a full minute of disbelief passed, he let out a laugh that had a table of truckers looking at them. "Anna, you still have surprises in you. Come on, let's get this paid up, and we'll get to work."

He drove her in his truck to the river. He first needed to take care of some items inside the lighthouse, so she took a few minutes to walk along the water's edge.

From her vantage point, she could see the park where Kaleb had given her her first kiss—not just their first kiss but hers altogether. She thought it would do his ego too much good to know that each boy—or man—that had kissed her since always left something to be desired. There had been times in New York, after she had left to pursue her dreams—or had her mother sent her away?—when she could still feel the moisture from his lips if she closed her eyes and brought herself back to this place. In fact, the more thought she gave it, the more she began to see that her grandfather must have known how special this area was to her and that she would never stay away for long.

Time was quite unforgiving in Anna's mind. How she had managed to stay in New York for even this long befuddled her brain. She had missed out on too many family celebrations, not that her family had thrown block parties, but they had certainly had their share of get-togethers. Adam, her oldest brother, had just recently completed his Masters degree in business and was already the youngest manager the island's country club had ever employed. And Ian, the middle child, was beginning to sell his wood sculptures on the island. Plus, a client had made some noise about him to another art aficionado inland, and he might just have his share in the art world sooner than he had hoped.

That leaves me, she realized. Yes, she had made a name for herself in New York on the stage, and before she had left, she was just beginning to make a dent in the papers, to the point that people recognized her when she went to certain restaurants.

And still she felt lost, as though she had yet to contribute something. She had a feeling that Kaleb, of all people, would be the one to understand. He had needed to contribute, too, and he was doing exactly that. She felt the unexpected surge of pride well up inside of her and knock her breathless. She tried to regain her bearings at this new feeling for him, and as she turned, he was there, looking at her—or rather, studying her. She could not take her gaze away from his, and neither one of them could move. The connection was so fast, so powerful, that it clamped down hard around her heart like a tight fist and propelled her to take one step toward him. That was all the invitation he needed.

He came to her, put his arms at her waist, noted that it was still too small; she was still too fragile. His own heartbeat was telling him to go easy; he knew he could spook her. She was looking up at him, expectantly, her mouth open just enough that the breath she pushed in and out wavered. He brushed a lock of hair aside and wanted, truly wanted, a woman for the first time in a long time. He bent his head to her, waiting to brush his lips over hers.

She turned her face into his shoulder and held on.

Not knowing what to do next, he kept his hands at her waist and hugged her closer. Then he brushed a hand over the back of her head. The only sound was of the water moving passed them, her breathing, shallow and deep, and his blood roaring in his ears. He wanted to be able to tell her.

"Anna, what's happening here?"

She was too afraid to speak. Knew that if she did, she would break. He had come to her with such tenderness, such longing in his eyes and in his stance, but there still was nothing she could do about it. She held on to him tighter.

"Anna…"

She sighed. "Kaleb, do you remember how it used to be?" At his shudder, she smiled into his chest. "I think you might be offering me that again, and I—"

"No. I'm not." He pulled back to look at her face. "Not that again. Better."

She knew what he wanted, and it was just too much for her. She tried to pull back a bit more, but he held on tight. "I can't handle—better just yet. I need you, Kaleb, I do. As my friend."

At his quiet oath, she curled into herself for protection. The fire that had once turned her to jelly was there again in his eyes, stormy grey and rocky. His eyes had always intrigued her, and even now as she felt the tremors of what she knew he could do to her, she held fast to what she had come here to do for herself.

"Okay. Then let's get started." He began to walk to the boat.

"Kaleb, please don't be angry. I'm sorry."

He turned to her in one swift motion. "Don't. Don't apologize. Just let it be, and let's get on with this. I told you I would help you, and I will not let you down."

As he climbed into the paddle boat, she had a feeling that would not always be the case.

Several hours and several mosquito bites later, Kaleb and Anna pulled back to the shoreline, neither feeling terribly successful in any area. She knew he was irritated with her but was not certain she had really done anything to promote that. Had she not been honest? She had made him aware of her needs at this time; the ring had to be top focus. It was all that was keeping a taut string on her sanity at the moment. If she had told him all that had happened while she had been in New York…but that would need to wait. She was not ready to tell him; she was not even ready to face it herself. And the worst possible thing she could do right now was to start anything but a friendship with him.

He could tell she was thinking hard. She had not said much on their way back from their picnic area. Anna had wanted to keep searching for the ring, the part that was hers. But he had made her sit down on some level ground and eat. Having thought ahead, he packed his famous hoagie sandwiches and felt a bit more relaxed when he saw her polish off more than half. She had even dipped into the potato chips and fruit salad that she had made, so all in all he figured she had eaten better today than she had in a while. She had even joked that she may have a difficult time getting back into her costumes if he kept feeding her this way. He had silenced that kind of talk with a look and had not spoken himself in quite some time.

He was beginning to realize that it was difficult to imagine her going back to New York and leaving him. Although, she would not exactly be leaving him. It was not as if she had come back home to be with him, to see him. She had come—well, he supposed partly for the ring. But the other reason…He knew there was another reason, and she would not tell him. By the time he finished tying the paddle boat down for the evening, he had worked himself into a nice mad.

Anna quietly packed up their things and retied her shoes. She could sense he was close to boiling now and was not really in the mood to deal with it. She was already beginning to anticipate going home to her mother. If her father was home, she could play the part of coward and remain by his side until her mother went to bed. But he had left that morning for an overnight business trip, so Anna would be on her own—something she did not enjoy.

Kaleb tossed some of the contents into the picnic basket and walked toward the lighthouse. He stopped at her voice.

"I don't expect you to drive me home. You've done enough for me for today, and I'm sure you have other things you could be doing now anyway."

He turned to face her. "That's just it. You don't expect anything from anyone. You just say 'please' and 'thank you' and figure people ought to be satisfied with that. Well, I'm not."

"Kaleb, I don't know why you're so angry—"

"Of course you don't! You're probably not expecting it! Well, then, I can still surprise you maybe with this."

Before she could stop him, he had crossed the distance between them with two strides, hauled her up on her toes, and covered her shocked mouth with his.

The kiss was hot, hungry. It sent waves up her spine that she tried to deny were there. His hands were gripping her arms as though she were drowning—or perhaps it was he who was in trouble; she could not tell for sure. He shifted just enough so that their bodies grew closer together. He feasted on her mouth, her neck, and back to her mouth again. She knew that if he continued this assault to her system he would devour her whole. She could not stand the pressure that was certainly building inside of her chest, and as she tried to push him away, she felt her arms winding their way around his neck, pulling him to her. She could sense them falling to the ground, rolling over each other, but no—they were still standing. It shocked her to the core that she could envision it so clearly and want it so much.

Kaleb felt the panic begin to rise. He knew he was hurting her, and he did not care. He was certain the panic was from her, but as the moan escaped her lips, he was no longer certain of anything. He shoved back and looked at her.

Her lips were swollen from the possession of his. Her eyes had glazed over, and she pressed a trembling hand to her face. He fisted his hands at his sides and tried to think. He closed his eyes and concentrated on breathing.

"I'd better get you home."

Nothing he could have said could have pierced her quicker or finer. She could only stare.

"Come on, Anna. You're shivering. It's almost night time."

Snapping herself back to the moment at hand, she looked away before he could see how he hurt her. "I had said that I'll get myself home." She took great care to ensure that her voice did not reveal the turbulent emotions inside.

He wiped at his face angrily. "You didn't ride your bike this time. I gave you a ride from the restaurant this morning. Remember?"

This morning. Had it really only been this morning since she had eaten with him, since he had looked at her with such tenderness before they began their adventure on the river? She moved quickly to avoid further contact with him.

"I'm well aware that you drove me here. It's a lovely night. I'm in the mood for a walk. Good night, Kaleb."

As she moved toward the road, he touched her arm. "Anna—"

"Don't you touch me!" The rising sharpness of her voice surprised them both. He stepped back. "Not now, not ever. I've had enough from you to last me a lifetime, Kaleb McMurran. Now, if you'll excuse me…" She quickened her pace as the first tear fell.

Kaleb kicked at the ground. Then he went inside to his makeshift overnight home and worked on getting very drunk.

Chapter IV

Anna really needed to talk. She was so frustrated, she could hardly see straight. But she realized that other than when her mother had picked her up from the airport, she had not spent much time with her. They had eaten a few cursory meals together, but she felt the guilt and knew it was foolish. She also knew it would not go away until she did something about it. So she allowed her mother to take her shopping and treat her to a day at the spa.

It really was not a terrible life when she thought about it. It just seemed so superficial, and Anna needed so much more than the surface right now. Her mother sensed none of this. Anna could see that Rose was simply grateful her daughter had decided to set aside two full days for just the two of them.

At the spa, Rose bragged about Anna's accomplishments. Even though Anna knew she meant well, she did not want to spend all that time talking about the dance. Rose would not hear of it, of course. She showed them photographs and news clippings until Anna's head began to swim. Eventually, she stopped trying to control her mother's efforts at charm and sat back to enjoy them.

But Rose could sense that all was not well with her daughter. At supper on the evening of their second day together, she sipped her after-dinner coffee and asked, "So, I suppose you will go back to looking for the ring tomorrow."

Anna knew it had been too much to hope for that Rose would not discuss the ring. She decided to keep talk of it simple. "Yes."

Rose set her cup on its saucer. The waiter refilled it immediately. "Anna, why do you insist in searching for such nonsense? I thought your father and I had raised a more sensible girl than this."

Anna merely raised a brow at her mother's tactic. "You did, Mother. Therefore, I need to check out all the angles. That's something I've never really done for myself."

Sensing trouble, Rose motioned for the check. "It is just that your grandfather was not always—with it, if you know what I mean." She slipped her credit card into the bill holder discreetly. The waiter whisked it away.

"I can't believe you would say something like that about a dear, sweet, old man just because you're jealous he gave this task to us instead of you."

Rose's ice blue eyes came up at that and held. "It has really been a lovely couple of days, Anna. Do not spoil it."

"I'm not. You are." She rose from her seat. Her mother hissed at her to be seated, and she did.

"Now you listen, young lady. I have known your grandfather a lot longer than any of you. He does—did this sort of thing all the time. Do you know that when I was a child he promised me a circus in my backyard if I kept my room clean all week? And after I scrubbed and dusted and polished, all I got for it were some of his lousy friends in stupid costumes parading around like fools. My mother thought it had been a kind gesture, but I saw it for what it was—nonsense. Thank God I grew up sensible."

"Mother, you describe yourself like Dad would a pair of shoes he likes to wear to meetings."

"And what is wrong with that? Why is it so awful to be sensible and dependable? Why is it so terrible to do what is expected?"

Anna knew this, too, was coming. "Grandfather expects us to look for the ring."

"And your father and I expect you to return to New York."

"I don't think I'll be doing that, Mother."

Saying the words out loud was so much easier than she had ever imagined. Her throat was just beginning to tighten, and her palms had gone damp, but she remained steady—in her voice and in her movements.

"I do not believe I have heard you correctly, Anna."

"Yes. You did."

"You needed a break; you have taken the time that was necessary. Now it is time for you to get back up on your feet and finish what you have started."

"I didn't start this, Mother."

"Well, do not say I did. I simply tried to make the opportunity more available to you." She paused thoughtfully as she considered her daughter's actions as of late. "Does your decision have anything to do with Kaleb McMurran?"

"You say his name like it's a curse."

"Call it how you see it."

Anna felt her temperature rise. "You were right, Mother. This really had been a nice couple of days. Let's not spoil them by trying to have a real conversation." She got up and stopped at Rose's question.

"You think I do not see? You spent one day with him, and then suddenly you are willing to be with me? I will bet he hurt you again just like he did when you left to pursue your dreams, Anna. And now you think you can just spend the day with Mummy, and everything will be the better for it. Well, I will not be used, certainly not by my own daughter." She stood, regal now in her evening suit of mint green. "I will take you home, and then you can decide how you want to spend your evenings." She walked out of the restaurant, leaving Anna to handle alone the stares from the people at the nearby tables.

* * * * *

"I can't believe she said those things to you, Anna." Maddy scooped her feet under herself as she sat on her couch in her living room. She and Anna had been talking for the better part of an hour, listening to music, and drinking wine. Maddy reached for another cracker with cheese as Anna considered her comment.

"I can. I'm sure she's been waiting to say them to me all along. Let's face it, Maddy—I haven't been my usual self in so many ways. And then again, maybe I have. She probably feared she was losing ground. She needed to say those things to me now or lose the chance. Besides, she may not be too far off about Kaleb."

"Hold the phone." Maddy leaned forward and forced her friend to look her in the eye. "You just finished telling me how Kaleb kissed you brainless, and now you think your mother may have a point? Wow, you really are giving in to her too much."

"Now that's not fair. I didn't give in. I just—" Anna stopped in her defense long enough to notice the wicked gleam in Madelaine's eye. "Very clever, Miss Murphy, very clever."

She smiled in a mock toast to herself. "Thank you."

Anna sighed. She had come to Madelaine's home because she knew her friend would take her in, no questions asked. Now here she was spilling her guts without batting an eyelash. This was one of the many reasons Anna appreciated Maddy so much.

"He really did kiss me brainless." Anna smiled and gulped down more wine.

"Tell me the part again about how he picked you up off your feet."

"Mmm…"

"Like an animal."

"No, no…like a Neanderthal."

Both women laughed at themselves.

"You know," Anna continued, "I'd forgotten how good he could kiss."

"Hells bells, Anna, he kissed you first when the two of you were kids. I don't know that Kaleb was ever a kid, but you sure as hell were."

"We did more than kiss." It was out before Anna knew it and saw Maddy's eyes widen in shock.

"That night? The night he kissed you, you—"

"No, no, no. Back when we were dating. All those years ago."

A sly smile crossed her face as Maddy realized what Anna was saying. "Oh my…you two…back when you were just…"

"Sixteen," Anna finished for her. "He was nineteen. My mother would have killed him if she knew. She'd kill him now." A shaky thought flew through her mind. "Maddy, you can never tell her about this. She'll—she'll never forgive me."

Maddy found it to be curious that Anna would be so rocked over her mother discovering that Anna was a normal woman with normal needs, but she decided to let that pass for now. "Anna, do you even know me? Yeah, I plan on calling your mom tomorrow. It'd go something like this: 'Uh, Mrs. Keller, yeah hi. Listen, Anna and I knocked back a bottle of wine last night, and right in the middle of everything, she revealed the most amazing thing to me. Lost her virginity, she did, when she was sixteen. And you want to know to whom, you ask? Why, none other than Kaleb McMurran!'" Maddy peeled over in laughter as Anna smacked her on the knee.

"Oh, my mother would just die! The horror!"

"Honey, I lost mine so long ago, I think it's back!"

They both howled with laughter.

"Please. Tell me. Who was the lucky stud?"

Maddy paused for dramatics. "Steven Pascuzzi."

"Huh! Oh, Maddy, I thought you had better taste than that."

"I do. I had been hoping it could be your brother."

"Which one?"

"Adam."

"Oh, now there's an image I'd hoped to never have in my head, thank you very much."

"Tell me. How is dear Adam these days?"

"He's fine. Working like a hound at the club, which, of course, pleases Mother to no end. Last I knew, he was dating Hillary Swan for a few months, but I don't think it was serious."

"I hope not. She just married Ed Campbell right before you came home."

For no other reason than the wine, the girls laughed uncontrollably again at that until they both became quite somber at the same time. Anna finally spoke.

"Maddy, is it true?"

"Is what true, Anna?"

"Did we really polish off a bottle of wine?"

Madelaine reached for the bottle—and held out two. "Nope." They laughed themselves into the rest of their evening.

* * * * *

Kaleb worked until his fingers bled. The interior of the lighthouse was being completed in record time. He spent as much time as possible sweating it out to hard rock—Zeppelin, Metallica, Vaughn. If he ran out of beer a little quicker than he usually did, so much the better. The days were beginning to warm now that Spring Break was just about over, and he knew the kids in the area would be even more restless than ever as they waited for summer vacation to arrive. This would, of course, bring the tourists, and that meant more money in his pocket. He would be able to build his clientele for boat rentals, which would make him feel better about bringing money in from more than just his current renter.

She had dropped another check off to him the day before in a discreet envelope under his door.

Swearing as he hit his finger with the hammer, he cursed Anna. She was getting in the way of his thinking and construction. He had tried to stay away from her and so far had been very successful. They had not laid eyes on each other since that evening when he had been foolish enough to touch her again. How could he have thought that touching her would have been easy? Even when he had been in Colorado, those women had left his bed and left him aching for her touch, her scent. If he closed his eyes and concentrated, he could bring her lips back to his in seconds.

Swearing again, he tossed aside the hammer and stood to go to the refrigerator. His mother snuck up behind him.

"Hello, stranger."

He hit his head on the overhang, swore one last time, and turned. She only raised an eyebrow at his choice of language. "Sorry, Mom. Hi." He went to her and kissed her lightly on the cheek to avoid wiping any smudges on her face. He stepped back to study her and let out a low whistle. "Wow, Mom. You clean up nice." She had pulled her chestnut hair up into a sweep that framed a wide face with clear eyes, had brushed some color onto her cheeks and lips, and stood in crème sandals that complemented her yellow linen pant suit.

"Well, I wish I could say the same about you, Kaleb." She set the bag she was carrying on the counter and looked at her son. He was grubby, short on breath, and obviously preoccupied if what she had heard as she had approached was indicative of where his thoughts were. In any case, she intended to find out.

"What did you bring me?" He nosed into the bag.

"Sandwiches. Sylvia took over for me at the shop for a while, so I thought I would come have lunch with my son. Seeing as he doesn't have time for his mother nowadays." She smiled quietly at his wary look.

"Ah, the master of the guilt trip. I think all I've got is beer. Oh wait." He nudged some items aside. "I have one bottled water."

"I'll take the beer."

"Mom, you're working. What if you mix up someone's wedding flowers?"

"Then maybe I'll get my face in the paper. More advertising, better for business."

He laughed and set up paper plates on the slab of particle board that lay flat on two work horses. He dug into the sandwich greedily, poured chips out of the bag she had also brought with her. "I didn't realize how hungry I was."

"I can see that." She could also see the dark circles just beginning to form under his eyes, the restlessness that simmered around him and never seemed to fully leave him. She wanted to curse Anna for putting that hunch in her son's shoulders, but she honestly could not. She liked the girl and was relatively certain it was not Anna's doing in the first place. Thinking of Rose only made her spine stiffen, and if she wanted Kaleb to talk to her openly, then she would need to remain relaxed.

"So, how's it feel to become a grandma in a matter of days?"

"I can't believe it's almost time. Michelle went to the doctor's earlier this morning for her check up, and she said that it could be any day now."

"Evan's a lucky guy. She'll keep him in line for years to come."

"Evan doesn't need to be kept in line, but he'll remain there nonetheless. It's you I worry over."

He chugged back some beer. "No reason, Mom. I really don't see myself giving you and Dad grandbabies any time soon."

And therein lays the problem, yes? But she thought it better to keep those thoughts to her for the moment. "I'm not wishing you anything you don't want, Kaleb."

He paused, the bottle halfway to his lips, and missed the expression in her eyes. "Well, there's nothing I really want right now anyway."

They ate in companionable silence for a while. Rita decided he was not going to make this easy, so she began to lay the groundwork.

"I hear Anna Keller's been by to see you."

He met her direct stare with one of his own, and Rita was reminded why she had fallen for her husband all those years ago. She made a mental note to remind Marcus later.

"News sure does travel fast around here."

"Kaleb, she's been back for almost a month. You came over for dinner once in that time and never mentioned it. Now I hear from Michelle—"

"Aha! The gossip vine continues." He smiled at her.

"Your brother tells her things, and she fills me in on what's pertinent."

"I'm so grateful to have all of you looking out for me."

"Kaleb, don't be wise with your mother. The point is…I just don't want to see you hurt like you were the last time you two became involved."

"There isn't going to be a 'this time.' Mom, she's made it painfully honest that what she needs right now is a friend while she's here, and then she'll be off to New York again, doing her dance thing. All I do is rent boats to her. She's looking for some silly ring. Or part of a ring that her grandfather left her."

Rita could see that her son was already almost lost. Almost could be saved, and she thought she might be able to help him there, but she still needed to address the issue here with him now. "Are you helping her?"

He sighed. He knew when to give in and give up the information she was asking for. "I was. I don't think I am now."

She decided not to press any more, which surprised Kaleb, but he let it pass. "Okay. Well, now that you're finished with lunch, give your mother a tour of this place. Show me how my hometown is going to attract tourists."

As she began to clear their mess, he could sense that she wanted to say more but was holding back, which was very unlike her. So he gave her the opening. "What is it, Mom?"

She turned to him, saw that he really wanted to know. "Kaleb." She walked to him and placed her strong hands on his face. "Sometimes people aren't strong enough to make their own decisions. Others, like you, don't understand that. You were lost some time back and found your way again. If Anna's lost, I don't think it's her doing. And you may need to think about that. She has an easily bruised heart." *Just like you*, she wanted to add. "Handle it the way I know you can."

With that, she walked to the stairs and waited for him to join her for the rest of her visit.

Chapter V

Rose O'Connor Keller was worried. Things were not progressing as she had hoped. Anna had been home now for a little over a month, and there was no sign that she would be returning to New York any time soon. When she and her husband had first investigated a dance instructor for Anna, she had great visions of her daughter living a life on the stage, taking in all the glory she deserved in the newspapers and on the television. Then, when the time came, she would marry the right kind of man and perhaps have two children, who would grow up in the kind of life to which Anna had become accustomed.

Instead, her daughter was back here in Grosse Ile, hanging around with people like Madelaine Murphy…and Kaleb McMurran…and looking for some foolish treasure she was certain had been her father's final joke.

At least her sons were doing what they were supposed to do and had ignored the old man's last ridiculous request. They had good solid heads on their shoulders and worthy jobs at their disposal. Any woman would consider herself quite fortunate to become involved with either Adam or Ian. The right kind of woman, of course.

And the right kind of man for Anna was not Kaleb McMurran.

She could feel the direction her daughter was headed, and it worried her down to the bone. How could Anna even consider for a minute giving up all that had been done for her to live a life with Kaleb McMurran? Not that her daughter was dating him or—Heaven forbid—falling in love with him, but Rose could sense the other night when they had gone to dinner that Anna was beginning to feel something for him again.

Just like she had been when she had been younger before she and her husband sent Anna to New York.

Rose had found a way to block their relationship then, and she would do so again without batting an eyelash.

And now her father added more trouble to the mix, even from beyond the grave. He had Anna looking for a ring that she was certain did not exist. And if it did, then she should have been the one to whom the ring was given. Instead, he sets up all three of her children, making them believe that the ring was only good for a generation of three, that it would provide them with the guidance needed to find whatever was missing in their lives and set it free for them to take ownership.

Her children.

Well, she had birthed all three of them, had she not? She knew what was best for them, did she not? If her mother wanted to buy into the nonsense, too, that was her business, but she would not allow him to interfere with her plans for Anna. Anna would return to New York soon and follow her goals, get back on the right track, and leave the ring and the McMurran man in her dust.

Her husband, Gregory, saw her sitting on the chaise lounge in the sunroom. He could tell she was in rare form. Deciding against his better judgment, he called to her.

"Rose, what are you up to?"

She turned to him, flashed a lovely and innocent smile. "I'm just reflecting on—things. Our children. Our life. I have one quick phone call to make. I won't be long. Then I'll join you for dinner."

He left her as she picked up the nearby extension.

* * * * *

Anna spent the next several days in the library doing research. She had known what the Claddagh ring had represented in its basic form most of her life since her mother still wore the one her father had given her when he had promised to propose to her one day. It was actually a very nice story, one that she was certain her parents had long ago forgotten to think about over late dinners and quiet moments by the fire. She wiped at eyes that became unexpectedly misty.

And came across a picture, one that stole her breath.

It was drawn of a woman sitting amongst Ireland's greenest hills, wearing flowers in her hair and laughing up at the artist. She was throwing a light toward the center of the picture, and in the center of that light was the Claddagh. Anna could study it clearly—the heart in the middle of the ring that represented love, the crown at the top that stood for loyalty, and the hands that held it all together on either side of the ring that meant friendship.

Her part in this journey.

But that was not what had shaken Anna. Holding the book closer to her face, for the painting was a replication, and it was cracked and old, she could just about make out a familiar face…

Grabbing the book and her purse, she raced to check it out on loan and drove like a madwoman to her next destination.

* * * * *

Her grandmother's home was at the far end of the island, settled just a bit off the main road, but it still allowed easy access. Anna knew her grandmother would be baking something warm, allowing the breeze to flutter at kitchen curtains she herself had made when she was a blushing bride of seventeen. She knew she would be welcome here anytime, day or night, as would her brothers. In fact, as Anna pulled up her drive, she recalled the countless hours she had spent at this woman's kitchen table, telling her stories about her day at school or about her latest recital.

She ached for those moments again, quite suddenly, but pushed them aside as she had a mission for this visit.

She knocked once on the door and walked in. It had never been necessary for any of the Keller children to knock when needing entry into their grandparents' home, but Rose had ingrained in them such manners that Anna could not quite break the habit.

She found Olivia Hudson O'Connor bent over a recipe book, leaning on the counter and wrinkling her forehead in great concentration.

"Hello, Grandma." Anna spoke determinedly so as not to scare her. Olivia's hearing had recently begun to slip, and although the old woman would admit to no such thing, she did not want to cause her any embarrassment.

Olivia turned and welcomed her youngest grandchild with open arms—and flour on her face. "Well, well, look what the cat dragged in." She hugged her tight. Anna breathed in her scent and felt her cheeks grow wet. Olivia pulled back to study her. "What's this? Anna, darling, why do you bring me such a sad face on this visit?"

"Oh, I guess I just missed you, that's all. And—him." Anna retrieved a towel from the rack to wipe at her face.

"I know it's hard to come over here and not see your dear old grandpa tinkering with something in the yard. Just the other day, Ian stopped by to see me. I think he had an awful time being here without Patrick because he's the one that taught Ian about his art." She was referring to Ian's wood sculptures.

"Oh, well, I'm glad you've had company recently then."

"Anna, I'm lonely for him, but I still find time to do things for myself. Come on, darling, let me fix you a cup of tea. And I'll get these cookies and tarts into the oven, then we can have ourselves a nice little visit."

She guided Anna into a chair in the center of the kitchen. Holding the delicate China in her hands, she looked around at the familiar room and felt comfortable. They had redone the cabinets a couple of years ago while her grandfather had still been alive, but the tile remained the same as did the atmosphere. Her grandmother washed her face off in the sink, poured a cup of lemon tea for herself, and sat with Anna, held her hand.

"So what brings you by today?" Her eyes sparkled with mischief, making Anna wish she had some sordid story to tell.

"Maddy and I got a little tipsy the other night."

Olivia laughed, and it was gravelly in its sound. "Good for you girls. I haven't done that myself in ages. Used to be able to hold my own where your grandpa was concerned, but he could still out drink me almost until the day…well, the day he went home." Her own eyes misted over, and she carried on. "Were you drinking over a man?"

"Oh, goodness, I should hope not! I'd never want a hangover because of some man!"

"That's my girl!" Olivia laughed and sent some flour dust floating into the air.

"Although, I had been spending some time with Kaleb McMurran up till then."

"I see."

"Now you sound like my mother."

"Girl, don't go comparing apples to sour grapes." At Anna's shocked expression, Olivia cackled again. "Anna, your mother is my pride and joy. But somehow she grew to be too serious for my taste. I'll bet she's not even letting you have any fun searching for your grandpa's ring."

"You must be able to read minds, Grandma."

Olivia chuckled. "How is she handling it?"

"Truthfully, she's not. We've gotten into a few squabbles about it, but I'm not giving in. I won't back down. Not this time."

She studied her granddaughter, grateful that she was beginning to see a stiffer spine and a stronger back. "I'm glad to hear that, Anna. I really am. Is this something you really want to do?"

"Oh, yes. I feel—almost privileged that he chose to leave this task to us." Her grandmother welled up at that, and Anna continued. "It's like I have a connection like I never did while he was around. I know I was gone, and I still feel incredibly guilty for not coming home more often…"

"Anna, your grandfather and I were prouder than peacocks knowing that you were doing what you loved and making a life out of it. Nothing pleased him more than to see the three of you so happy and fulfilled." She paused. "You were doing what you wanted, weren't you Anna?"

Because her grandmother was hitting too close to home, she veered the conversation back in her favor, not yet ready to confront the issue. "I brought this book with me. I checked it out today from the library and came straight here. I need you to look at something." Anna flipped to the page she had marked and lay it flat open on the table between them. She waited for a response. When there was none, and her grandmother only stared at the drawing, she pressed further. "Grandma, is that you?"

Olivia brought the book closer to her face, a gesture so like her granddaughter's from earlier that day, the motion was not lost on Anna. She caressed the page like she might a child in need. Her breathing slowed, and her face became almost transparent, as though she would disappear right in front of Anna. So frightened did Anna become in that moment, she reached out to hold her grandmother's hand to keep them both grounded.

"Grandma?"

She looked back to her granddaughter then and smiled wistfully. "I'd forgotten I'd posed for this."

Relieved at the sound of her grandmother's voice, Anna leaned back in her chair. "It is you then."

"Yes. It's me. But I don't know that you were supposed to find it just yet. In fact, I don't know that *you* were supposed to find it. But he must know what he's doing…"

"Who? Why shouldn't I have found this, Grandma? When did you pose for this?"

Olivia released her hand and sat back, knowing the questions her granddaughter had raised deserved to be answered. "Anna, you brought me such pleasure when you told me you would take your grandfather's letter seriously and look for your part in the ring. I knew it existed, but I had no idea…"

"No idea about what?"

"This story goes back quite a long time ago. Your grandfather was trying to court me. I was barely fifteen…" She glanced at the artist's rendering again, stroked it lovingly. "He painted this, Anna."

"Grandpa did? It's lovely."

"He saw things in people that not everyone could, or, in some cases, not everyone wanted to see. When he found me walking through the countryside picking flowers, he begged me to paint my portrait. At first, I was taken aback. Here I was, a young English girl, on holiday with my family, and this stranger—

this man—wanted to paint my picture. I should have been afraid, but something about him told me not to worry. So I let him. I was terribly nervous; I felt naked with the way he was looking at me. We agreed to meet every afternoon that week while I would be there with my family, but I could not tell my father. An Irish painter would not be good enough for his daughter. So we met in secret, and soon I understood he wanted to be…intimate with me. But I would not allow that to happen. I was waiting for my wedding night as most good girls in that day did." She sipped her tea, even though it had turned cold.

"Anyway, when he finished the painting, he would not let me see it unless I promised to see him again. I explained how that would be impossible since I would be traveling on throughout the rest of Europe with my parents and sisters. Your grandfather would not budge. I begged him until the point of tears, but even that did not work with him. I left to tour another country—France, I think—but my mind came back to that painting and that magical week I had spent with him. I could barely function—until I was seventeen. That's when I saw him again, only this time it was in England, my homeland. He was painting street art near my neighborhood, and when he saw me look upon him with my mouth hanging wide in shock—not very ladylike, I might add—he walked right up to me and said, 'Do you still wish to see the painting?' Just like that, as though we had never been apart. All I could do was nod, dumbly. He promised to show it to me if I would agree to a cup of coffee with him. Two weeks later, we were married."

Anna dabbed at her eyes. It was the telling of the tale more than the tale itself that had shaken her. "Why have you never told me this until now?"

"You never found the painting until now." She paused, raised a shaking hand to her lips. "And I've never seen it until this moment."

Anna gasped. "But I thought he was going to show it to you if you agreed to see him again."

"He tricked me." She smiled lovingly at the memory. "If I had agreed to that date, surely I would agree to another. And another. Until finally I had agreed to marry him. Then surely I would agree to have a child with him. That took a bit more time than we had anticipated—six years. But after your mother was born, I had become ill. The doctors said I should probably consider giving up any thoughts of having other babies. It broke my heart not to give your grandfather a son. But he really didn't seem to mind. And when I asked him to show me the painting, he said the legacy needed to be filled first. In the time of three. Three parts to the ring, three family members to each take. Since we did not have three children, I knew your mother would. And it seems that everything is going according to whatever plan he was to follow."

Olivia rose to give herself something to do. She went to the oven, pulled out the cookies and tarts, and placed them on a cooling rack. Anna waited until she was seated again to speak.

"So I was supposed to find this picture. But where is the original, I wonder?"

"That is still something that remains to be seen, Anna, darling."

"I'll need to show this to my brothers…and tell them the story. Although you are certainly a better story teller than I could have ever hoped to be. You don't mind, do you, Grandma?"

"Of course not."

"I'll need to tell Kaleb and Madelaine, too." She rose to leave.

Her grandmother rose as well, a bit more warily. "Why do you need to tell them, Anna?"

"Because they are a part of it. I don't know why I know this. I just do."

"Just be careful, Anna. Not everyone will see as clearly as you do with their hearts. Some will bring doubt to the table."

They kissed goodbye, and Olivia watched her climb into her car and pull out of the driveway. She knew the painting was not for Anna but for one of her other grandchildren. She also knew that Anna's piece of the ring would come from an area that none of them were expecting.

* * * * *

Knowing her efforts on the water were futile, she drove there in the hopes of reconciling with Kaleb. It was silly to allow one kiss to anger her so much and disturb what had been developing into a nice friendship. They had never been successful with it before she had left, and now that she was beginning to feel more in control of her life, she thought she should take the first step toward him.

When she arrived at the lighthouse, she was disappointed to see his car was nowhere to be found. She quickly jotted a note on a scrap piece of paper to have him call her later that evening so that they could talk. When she went to tuck it under the door, an attractive blonde pulled it open and stared hard at her.

"Can I help you?"

Startled only momentarily, Anna regained her composure. "Yes, I—I'm looking for Kaleb…" Her voice trailed off as her memory tried to identify the pretty face. "I know you."

"Yeah. We went to school together—until you became too good for the rest of us and split. Can't say I blame you. I'd get out of here, too, if I could."

"I'm sorry, I don't remember your name."

The blonde studied her up and down. "Melanie Wilson. I was also at the bar the other night when you and your friend decided to play hostess to Josh and Tom. That was quite a show." She leaned against the doorjamb, obviously not allowing Anna to enter.

"Well, I wouldn't call what we did 'playing hostess.' Maddy and I wanted only—"

"Your kind never do."

"Excuse me? My kind…"

"You've got too much class to 'play hostess' to guys like Bunker and Hamlin. I'd of thought you'd have too much class to play hostess to guys like Kaleb, too."

Anna arched her brow. "You don't seem to mind."

Melanie laughed, loud and piercing. "Girls like me don't. Kaleb won't be back for quite a while. He went out, told me to meet him here. I let myself in." She allowed Anna to think she had a key instead of telling her the truth—that Kaleb never locked up the lighthouse while he was working.

"I see."

"You got a note for him? How sweet. Want me to give it to him when he gets back?" She held out a perfectly manicured hand, nails pointed and dipped in a glossy pink.

"No. That's okay. I'll give it to him myself the next time I see him."

"Well, he probably won't be available until tomorrow—" Melanie made sure to emphasize the last word—"but I'll be sure to let him know that you stopped by."

"There's no need. Nice talking with you, Melanie." Anna got into her car and drove off.

"Nice talking with you, too." Melanie went back inside to wait.

* * * * *

It had been nearly impossible to get Melanie to leave him alone. Her offer had been quite—interesting and generous, but Kaleb wanted nothing more than to spend an evening alone, at home, with something on the television. He had not stayed at his own place in several days, and after the amount of hours he had been putting in at the lighthouse, he figured he deserved a day to himself. He would take the next day off to relax, maybe go fishing with his father, maybe stop in at one of the shops inland and think about finally buying that motorcycle. Now that he had steady work, he felt he might be able afford it.

He had thought Anna might stop to see him; this was not her usual style. But then again, did he really know what her usual style was? They had been kids when they were last together and had not spoken in more years than he could remember. She had never answered his letters, and after writing to her for over a year, he quit, understanding that she had indeed moved on to bigger and better things.

But why had their first kiss in so long been so very good? It had to mean— something. Unless she had become the kind of girl that could kiss a man like that and not mean it.

The thought was so distressing, he balled his hands into fists and dug deeper into his fried chicken, made special for him by Frannie earlier that evening.

The knock on the door was loud, quick, and urgent. Rising and wiping his hands on his jeans, he hurried to see what could be wrong this late in the day.

Anna was the last person he expected to see standing on the other side of the door.

She marched straight in and planted herself in the middle of his living area. He was so surprised by the intensity of her presence that he did not have time to feel awkward about her standing there in the middle of his simple way of living. He had not bothered to clean in several days, and the dust was growing thick. His one small plant in the corner near the television was desperate to be watered, and the garbage needed to be taken out days ago. Had she bothered to call and not come stomping into the place as though it were hers, he might have cared.

Or, at least, more than he was trying to pretend he did not.

"I realize you and I are just friends. And I realize that you are free to do whatever you want—be with whatever you want. But what I do not understand is how you can tell me so many lovely things, pretend to be my friend, kiss me the way you did, and then get—involved with someone like her."

He could see that she was seething, and although he found this new trait to be quite alluring, he felt he should discover the source of her anger before he became too happy about it.

"Anna, what a lovely surprise. Won't you please come in?" He shut the door and remained where he was.

"Don't take that tone with me, Kaleb. I know I haven't had any contact with you since—in days, but that gives you no right to make me look foolish."

"Anna, I'm really glad you dropped by. How did you know where I lived?"

"I—" The question caught her off guard, as he had intended, and being raised with strict manners, she felt inclined to answer it. "Frannie told me. I went in for something to eat. She said you had stopped by—without a buxom blonde draped over you—for chicken and took it home. She happened to mention where you live, and I decided to come by and give you the note I was going to give you earlier. So here." She tossed it in his face and tried to leave. He, of course, blocked her.

"I'll just bet that good ol' Frannie let it slip where I live. More than likely she would have preferred the fireworks display."

"I don't know what you're talking about."

"This." He gestured around the room. "She would have paid big money to see you so steamed at me." He paused as part of what she had said ran through his head. "What was that about a 'buxom blonde'?"

Appalled that she had let that slip, she tried to recover—unsuccessfully. "Nothing. It doesn't matter. I would like to leave. Please."

He had her blocked from the door and was not going to let her go any time soon. "What note? Earlier today, you say?"

"Yes. It doesn't matter, Kaleb. All I had wanted—"

"Ah." As realization dawned, he moved to the sofa but did not sit. "Okay, I see how it all went down. You can go now if you'd like. I'll look at your note later."

Anna did not know what to make of this man. Here she thought she would be able to get some answers, but instead, he was giving her the brush off. "So, your evening ended a bit early. Not able to play all night, Kaleb?" She wanted to light that fire in his eyes and felt a small amount of satisfaction when she saw that she had.

"Yes, my evening did end early. But not without my own satisfaction first." He saw the disgust cross her features and leave just as quickly as she once again tried to storm out the same way she stormed in. He caught her by the arm. "What's the matter, duchess? Afraid I might still need to be satisfied again tonight, but you're just not up to it?"

She slapped him, hard and fast, across his face. Her palm made direct contact and left his entire left cheek red and pulsing. Although it stung, he made no move to soothe the ache.

Anna gaped at him, horrified at what she had just done. She covered her mouth with her hands, her eyes welling up as she did. "Oh, my, Kaleb, I'm so sorry."

"Oh, God, Anna, don't. Don't cry. You'll undo me." He grabbed her and hugged her hard against him. "It was my fault. I should have never spoken to you that way. Not you. Never you."

He held her as she wept silent tears. He wanted nothing more than to punch himself, but for now, he would take his punishment in the form of her wet face and deal with the consequences later.

"Anna, please, I'll never speak to you that way again. Just please forgive me."

"I forgive you."

Her voice was muffled against his shirt, and he cursed himself for allowing her to make it so easy for him. She pulled back, and when he tried to hold her, she shook her head, explained that she needed the restroom. He pointed down the hall. A few minutes later, she returned, fresh-faced and bright-eyed.

"It's none of my business how you spend your free time. I had come by to give you that note." She gestured to the scrap paper on the floor. "I had wanted to make things right again between us. I wanted you to call me tonight, and when Melanie explained about the two of you—"

"There is no two of us. There never was." At her arched look, he shrugged uncomfortably. "Well, never longer than a night—and even then it was never longer than part of the night." He sighed and faced the window that faced the street. "Anna, I haven't been able to be with any women since you came dancing back into my life. They haven't been able to survive the comparison."

Nothing he could have said at that moment would have turned her heart over more slowly, more delicately, than that did. She had no idea what to do next, so she simply waited for him to guide her.

"I'm sorry I behaved so poorly the other night. You came to me looking for a friend, and I treated you quite the opposite. I should never have kissed you like that—spoken to you in that way…I'm sorry." He faced her now, his courage dwindling with each passing minute she was quiet.

Anna stood there and felt what she must have felt all those years ago. She sensed that he felt it, too, because color washed over her cheeks and warmed her. She understood that she and Kaleb were not to remain friends—not just friends.

As she walked over to him, he saw the change in her eyes, in her mouth, and could feel his chest tighten. His throat suddenly dry, he tried to remember his own name and came up blank.

"Maybe that's how you were supposed to kiss me all along. Kaleb."

She leaned into him, just a fraction of an inch, felt her pulse flutter under her skin. Looking up at him, she saw her reflection swim into the stormy grey of his eyes, and it excited her. He was breathing on her face, as though he was about to breathe life back into her.

"Anna, if you let me, I don't know that I can—be your friend again."

"I think we should try to be both. Don't you?"

She leaned in just enough to brush her lips over his. The first shockwave coursed through his system, and he made himself pull on the reins of control until he could all but hear them snap. He would not rush this; he had waited patiently for too long.

She pressed her lips more firmly, which gave him time to catch up. He wrapped his arms around her waist, pulled her closer yet, and allowed the moment to linger. She was fisting her hands against his back while he took the kiss just a bit deeper.

Angling her head, he could dive into the depths of her. His mouth covered hers fully and completely until she knew this time there would be no turning back. He began to stroke a lazy line up and down her back with his left hand as he gripped her waist with his right. His breathing became labored, and she moaned graciously as he trailed small kisses down her throat and across her jaw line.

He trembled; she shuddered. He moved with her now toward the sofa. He had to get her to a flat surface. As he laid her down, he met her eyes with his. What he saw there frightened him more than when she had first shared herself with him, knowing it was the first time she had shared herself with anyone. He did not want the fear now, only the pleasure and the glory and the pain, the kind that would last with him until she was gone again.

Because he was so certain she would be gone from him again.

He brushed her cheek with his thumb. She turned her head to take his thumb into her mouth, and all the blood drained out of his head and went straight to his loins.

"Anna…"

As he covered her mouth again, even firmer yet, he thought he could hear conversation somewhere deep in the background. As she wiggled beneath him, he thought he would lose his mind.

"Kaleb, your machine…it's Evan speaking on your machine…I think Michelle's in labor." Anna grabbed his face between her two hands to get him to focus on what she was saying.

"What?"

"Listen. Your brother is speaking to your answering machine. Michelle is in labor."

They froze to hear the excited panic in Evan's voice. Kaleb sat up quickly and grabbed the receiver, cutting his brother off in mid-sentence.

"Yeah, I'm here…no, I was sleeping…When?…Okay, okay…mom and dad, yeah…I can be there in twenty minutes…Okay, Evan, go be with your wife…Everything will be fine." He hung up, turned to Anna, and swore viciously.

"Sometimes babies can't wait."

He studied her on his couch, her clothes rumpled, her face swollen and flush. She looked very much like a woman who had been about to be satisfied—and could have done some satisfying herself. He cursed Evan inwardly.

"If this baby turns out to be a boy, he and I are going to have a little talk in a few years about timing."

Anna laughed lightly and sat up. She was quite suddenly very aware of the position they had almost gotten themselves into, and Kaleb could hear those wheels turning inside her head.

"Come with me."

"What?"

"To the hospital. Come with me. We can spend some time together."

Anna sighed. "Kaleb, this is a family affair. Go be with your family, and I'll see you another day. I promise." She held her hands out to him.

He took them in his. Then, inspiration struck. "The Island Fest is this weekend. I want you to be my date."

"Your what?"

"My date. I haven't taken you on an official date since you've been back. I realize I did almost eat you alive on my couch—" to her credit she blushed enormously, and he was rather pleased about it—"but I think I should take you on a date. Rides, carnival games, the whole nine yards. I'll buy you cotton candy." Pressing his forehead to hers, he heard the laugh escape before she could stop it.

"Okay. But I can't do spinning rides."

"Still?"

"Still."

He took her face in his hands one last time, kissed her until she felt it in her toes. "I need to go."

"I know."

Neither of them moved.

"Kaleb…"

"All right, all right. I'll call you tomorrow. You're my date, Anna Keller. Don't you forget it."

It was all she could think about throughout the rest of the night.

Chapter VI

Anna was singing the following morning as she stepped from the shower. She felt alive, light on her feet, happy. She had not received a call from Kaleb as of yet, but she also knew that a woman's first baby could take considerable time. She had prayed for Michelle last night before bed and again this morning when she had woken.

And still, she was anxious to hear from him.

How long had it been since she had been on a date? She thought back to the dancer in New York, Jose Hernandez. He was working his way to making lead in just a couple more years, and Anna had been caught up in him for a couple of months. When she had finally decided to go to bed with him, it had been nothing short of disastrous. He had told her she knew nothing of what she was doing and left her bed cold and empty. She learned a few days later that Jose had simply been interested in making a name for himself on Broadway, and Anna had been one way to get there. The hurt had come, naturally, but she was over it sooner than she had expected. Which made her think she had not really invested too much in him to begin with.

Now as she stared at herself in the foggy mirror over her bathroom sink, she felt the anticipation rise. Kaleb was going to take her to a carnival, something she had never even done as a child. There had been too many rehearsals then, too many obligations. But now, she could sit back and allow herself to be courted.

Would her grandmother not love her use of the term?

She was laughing as her father stepped into the room.

"Everybody decent in here?" he called.

"Yes. Give me just a minute, Dad. I'll be out of the bathroom in a sec."

She wrapped her robe around her shoulders and tightened the belt. Tossing her wet hair into a towel, she came into her bedroom. Her father had planted himself on her bed. He was so striking. Gregory Keller had jet black hair to match Adam's, the same ice green eyes as Ian. What he had given Anna were the dimples. They winked at her now as he welcomed her with a hug and a kiss to the top of her forehead.

"You don't have work today?"

"No. I have the next few days off. Thought I'd take your mother out of town, maybe go to a bed and breakfast for some antique shopping. Thought that would help her to relax a bit."

"That sounds lovely. When do you think you'll leave?" she asked as she ran a brush through her shoulder-length hair.

"Probably not until tomorrow. She's afraid to leave you alone."

Anna paused, mid-brush. "That's ridiculous. With all that's happened lately with grandpa's funeral and such, she should go. Tell her I said so." She smiled mischievously at him.

"I'll tell her."

"Dad, how did you stay so handsome?"

He laughed at her. "I guess I'm just lucky."

"Yeah, so's Mom."

"Thank you. I'll take that as a complement." He paused to watch her begin to apply her make-up. "Kaleb McMurran called while you were in the shower."

He saw her almost bobble her eyeliner as she gaped at him in the mirror. "I didn't hear the phone ring."

Interesting, Gregory thought, *she's trying to stay composed but can't.* "I guess Michelle had the baby."

At her father's questioning look, she explained, "Evan's wife. Kaleb's brother."

"Oh."

When he continued to provide no further explanation, she whipped around to face him. "Well? What did she have? The suspense is killing me!"

"He didn't say, and I didn't think to ask. But he did say that he would fill you in on all the details tonight when he picks you up for the carnival."

Anna could not hide the smile this time; it was full and lovely, just like her, and it was a father's duty to ask her about it.

"The two of you are seeing each other again?"

She met his eyes in the mirror again. "Dad, don't start."

"Start what? I think I have a right to know. As your father."

Anna stood and went to her bed, sat down next to him. "I think we are. I don't know. He's taking me to a carnival. I've never been to one."

"I know."

She laid her head on his shoulder. He put his arm around her.

"I don't know what's going to happen, Dad, but I would really like to enjoy it like a normal person for a while. You know?"

"Yes, I do know. Anna…" He shifted, so they could face each other. "Did we screw up?"

Quite surprised by the question, she only stared at him. "What?"

"Your mother and I. Did we mess things up for you?"

"How?"

"With your dancing. Just a second ago, you're telling me you've never been to a carnival. That is so sad. I should have taken you but—"

"There was always a meeting in France or Libya or Algeria, and I was too busy dancing on a gym floor or in a dance school or here at home until my feet were purple and bleeding." She touched his face. "Dad, I wanted to dance. You wanted the import/export business. That doesn't mean you and I grew apart. I still have a lot of your letters you used to write to me while I was away."

He sighed. "How fortunate for me. Kaleb can give you memories of carnivals, and I gave you letters."

"Dad…"

"Ah, I know, bygones be bygones. I just—I just want you to be happy."

"I am. Or at least, I think I'm getting there."

He stood, hugged her again, and went to the door. Before he left her room, he told her, "You make sure Kaleb treats you right. I've always liked that young man. He has a kick to him. But if he hurts you, he'll have to deal with me."

Anna laughed and got dressed.

"Madelaine Murphy, you look wonderful! Now would you please come with me!" Anna was dragging at her friend's hand across the parking lot of the country club.

"I cannot believe you tricked me into coming here for lunch. What if your brother is working?"

"I'm sure he is."

That stopped her. "Anna, I am not going in there like this. I barely have anything on my face!"

"Which is exactly how Adam likes his women." At Madelaine's vicious oath, Anna chuckled. "I'm teasing. Look, if you come have lunch with me, then I can tell you all about how Kaleb mauled me in his living room and how we have a date tonight."

"Ooh, that's low, Anna, really, really low. You think you're going to get me in there on the promise of a hot sex story? Well…you're right. And I want all the details."

The two of them settled into a table that overlooked the water. Anna said hello to several of the employees as well as the patrons. She contemplated the menu.

"Well, you certainly know the right crowd." Madelaine fidgeted in her seat.

"Maddy, are you uncomfortable here?"

"No, it's just that—oh, God, here comes your brother." She tried to straighten and fluff her red hair before he had a chance to see.

He headed right for their table. "To what do we owe the pleasure of two beautiful women dining here today?" He swooped down to kiss Anna's cheek and patted Maddy on the shoulder.

Since Maddy seemed to have trouble finding her tongue, Anna spoke first. "I'm glad you stopped by the table, Adam. I need to meet with you and Ian. It concerns the ring."

At the mention of the ring, Adam's hazel eyes glazed over. "You're not seriously looking for it, are you, Anna?"

"Our Anna here's been on quite a search." At Anna's pithy glance, Maddy sipped her water.

"Adam, I know it seems ridiculous, but you and Ian need to see some of what I've discovered. It's all beginning to make sense."

Adam studied his sister and saw that it meant something to her. "When?"

"Thank you, Adam. I knew you'd come through for me. I still need to talk to Ian—"

"How about tonight?" Maddy interrupted, and Anna glared at her. She ignored her friend and kept on. "We could all meet at my place, order a pizza, I'll provide the beer." She smiled helpfully.

"I told you, Maddy, I've got plans."

"Oh, that's right, and who are they with again?"

Anna knew exactly what Maddy was doing, and because Adam was staring at her and waiting for an answer, she obliged. "Kaleb and I are attending the Island Fest tonight."

At the mention of Kaleb's name, Adam pulled up a chair. "Do you really think that's a good idea?"

"Well, Adam, I've never been to a carnival before, but I bet I'll catch on as to how one behaves at a carnival."

"That's not what I meant, and you know it."

"Yes, I know. Why are you so concerned about Kaleb?"

Adam looked at Maddy's expectant face and then back to his sister. "I don't really know. I just want you to be careful. That's all."

Anna studied her brother in his suit and tie, noted how very much like their father he was, and on impulse, threw her arms around him. Taken aback, he tried to stiffly return the hug. "You are terribly sweet, Adam. I'll be fine."

He tried not to get caught up in the moment. "I'm really glad you're back, Anna. I've missed you."

She began to well up inside, and he stood. Maddy dabbed at her eyes, discreetly. "We'll plan an evening for all of us. Just let me know when. I'll fit it in to my schedule." When he was called away by an employee to deal with a matter in the kitchen, he kissed Anna once more, patted Maddy's cheek, and left.

"Is it any wonder I'm crazy about him?" Maddy asked.

"You just want to get into his—"

"Be that as it may," Maddy interrupted, "I still think he's got something real to offer."

"Yeah, he does."

They ordered lunch and talked the afternoon away. Anna wanted to tell Maddy everything her grandmother had revealed to her, but she knew she should wait until she could speak to all of them at once. Kaleb would need to hear the story, too, and she was trying to avoid contact with him until later that night.

"So tell me about the hot and heavy with you and Kaleb," Maddy said over a mouthful of spinach salad.

"Well, we almost...you know. But his brother called. Michelle went in to labor, and he had to go to the hospital."

"Bummer."

"I know. But I also think it was good that it happened that way. Maddy, I practically let him maul me to death on his couch. I think I am the one who started it."

"Good for you, Anna."

"No, not good for me. I'm not exactly—experienced in that area. I haven't really had rave reviews over previous performances."

Madelaine studied her friend. She knew this was an area that had to be dealt with gently. "Anna, when it's the right guy, he's the one who will make it 'your best performance.' Besides, if you look at it as something that you need to do well at, then you won't. Just be yourself, and let Kaleb guide you. I have a feeling he could do that well." She chuckled.

Anna blushed. "What should I wear to this thing?"

"Are you serious? Something flirty, I think. Maybe a sundress."

"I don't have one. Here. I have plenty back in New York. But I don't think I'd planned on staying this long."

"How long had you planned on staying?"

Anna pushed the food around on her plate. "I don't know. I didn't have a plan. I just needed to get out of there."

They sat in silence for a few minutes, the only noise coming from the bustling around them. The sun was at its peak over the water, which glistened like new diamonds on a woman's hand. They could see the trees bending just slightly in the breeze. Maddy wanted to ask so many questions of Anna, but she knew Anna needed to be the one to come to her in friendship. She waited, giving her the time she was almost certain Anna needed to compose her thoughts.

"It was opening night of the new ballet. My mother and father came, along with Ian. Adam had to remain behind to work. He's always working—so much like my father. I was nothing but a bundle of nerves. I finally had the lead. You want to know the sad thing, Maddy? I didn't care. Here I was at the epitome of my career, and I didn't care. All I wanted was to leave that stage, never perform again. I had sweated and bled for this part, and none of that crossed my mind as I waited in the wings that evening. I just wanted out. But I knew my family was there. And I couldn't disappoint them."

She drank more water. As Anna looked back into Maddy's eyes, she could tell the rest of the tale would be easier to tell. "The music swelled and then softened, and that's when I was to make my first appearance in the production, discreetly, so that the audience would be surprised by my sudden appearance. And they were. I pulled it off beautifully; everyone said so. And then afterward, I met with my parents and Ian backstage. Their arms were full of roses, and their faces were all smiles. My father and Ian left to allow me time to change. That's when my mother told me she was proud...but could I just hold my head back a few seconds longer in the third movement? Then all she said was to keep doing my best, and she couldn't wait to see me as the lead in the next one. That's when I lost it."

"I don't blame you, Anna. I don't think anyone would."

"I cried. Sobbed was more like it. At first, she thought I was just overreacting. But then she really could not get me to calm down. It was as if the floodgates had opened, and Noah would arrive shortly." She laughed at her attempt to lighten the situation. "My shoulders were wracking, my head was held down. My eyes became so swollen and red, and I remember that I began to—moan. Howl. She was mortified. My director called for an ambulance, and I was whisked away to the hospital. My parents left two days later."

Maddy demonstrated her shock by the sharp intake of breath. "They didn't stay to make sure you were okay?"

"They did. Mother was pretty steamed at me. She thought I was making things up for attention. My dad really got into it with her over that. After they spoke with the doctor and me, they knew it was okay to leave me. I did better without them there. I could barely handle the way she kept looking at me."

"Anna, I know you wanted your privacy, but I would have been there for you. All you would have had to do was ask."

Anna smiled wanly. "I know that now. But back then...I was completely alone. Or at least I thought I was. When I was released, the first thing I did was go back to my apartment and shut myself in for three days. My understudy was having the time of her life. The producer called me over and over...and eventually gave up. They sent a service over with things they had collected from my dressing room in the theatre. That's when I called home, to ask to come home. My mother was so against it that I had to promise I would return to New York as soon as I had regained my composure. But my father...he was eternally grateful that I was coming back. You should have seen his face when he picked me up at the airport."

"So, they let you go from the ballet company?"

"No, not the company, just this particular ballet. My mother doesn't know, and she doesn't need to know yet. In fact, Maddy, you're the only one I've told so far."

"Oh, Anna..." Madelaine raised her glass in a toast to her friend. "I think you're amazing."

"Maddy, don't make me cry."

"I do. And you are going to have an amazing night. Come on. We'll finish lunch, and then you and I are going shopping for a sundress for tonight."

"You said you have papers to grade."

"They're nothing that can't wait until tomorrow. Or Monday. Besides, it's almost the end of the year. These kids are more concerned about summer right now than some grade on an assignment."

They paid their bill, waved to Adam from across the room, and floated out into the balmy spring air.

* * * * *

Kaleb was nervous. And this made him even more perplexed than he could ever remember feeling in his life. Women did not make Kaleb McMurran nervous. At least, not any that he had bothered with before—well, before.

He tugged at the collar of his shirt as he pulled into the Kellers' driveway. He had decided to keep it casual for tonight; after all, they were only going to a carnival. But he still figured Anna would like something different, something besides a t-shirt and blue jeans. So he opted for a linen dress shirt and khaki pants. Kept the shirt open at the collar. Brushed his hands through his golden hair. And swore. He wanted a cigarette to settle his nerves, but he also wanted to appear relaxed, carefree. And he knew her mother would spot his unease at ten paces if he had something in his hands to fidget with while she was around. So he got out of the car and walked the steps with a swagger, prepared to do battle.

When Anna, herself, answered the door, he was, at first, relieved. Then, as he really began to look at her, his nerves unraveled again, and he found himself shoving his hands into his pockets, for fear of smudging the picture of perfection he had standing in front of him.

"Hi."

"Hi."

She gestured him inside. He took three steps in and looked at her again. His mouth watered.

"Anna, you look—you are…"

"Really?" She turned in the pale green and summer blue sundress, causing the skirt to flutter around her legs. He reached out to touch the tendrils of hair that had escaped from the twist. She smiled at him. "Tell me about your brother's baby."

"Marissa Eileen McMurran arrived earlier this morning. Eight pounds exactly, twenty inches long. Both mother and baby are fine. Dad is a wreck."

"I'll bet. What a lovely name. Have you seen her?"

"Yes. She's got a head full of Michelle's hair, and her middle name comes from Michelle's mother, who is deceased. And her eyes are little duplicate's of my brother's. Poor kid." He laughed and twirled more of her hair around his finger. And her mother came into the room.

"Anna. What's this?"

Both Anna and Kaleb turned to greet Rose. "Mother, you remember Kaleb."

Rose eyed him coolly. "Of course. How do you do, Mr. McMurran?" She nodded, quite obviously not offering her hand. "Where are you off to, Anna?"

"Kaleb and I are going to the Island Fest. You and Dad enjoy your trip."

"Anna, it will more than likely get cold later. Are you sure you'll be all right in that dress?" Kaleb asked.

"I'd better get my sweater." Anna went to the front closet, only a few steps away.

Gregory entered the room. "Kaleb. How nice to see you again. It's been quite a while." He extended his hand to him, shook.

"Mr. Keller. Likewise."

"Gregory," Rose interrupted, "did you know that Anna and Kaleb were going out this evening?" She kept her eyes firmly on her husband's.

"Yes. I did. Now if you don't hurry, Rose, we'll get caught in terrible traffic. I already tossed your bags in the car." He tried shooing her along but to no avail.

"Anna, I'm not sure I should leave you alone this weekend." Rose was looking deliberately at Kaleb. "You may still not be—fully recovered."

Anna tried to ignore the worried glance Kaleb sent in her direction. He spoke with his eyes on her. "She won't be alone, Mrs. Keller. She'll be in good company. Ready, Anna?" He held his arm out for her.

She kissed her mother's cheek, hugged her father, and went with him. Rose rounded on her husband.

"That boy is nothing but bad news, Greg. And you know it."

"I have a tendency to disagree with you, Rose. Now, let's get moving."

She pulled at his arm to get him to face her again. "No. I will not get moving. You planned this trip for us so that they could have their little rendezvous'. Well, I will not stand for it. I am not going away with you." She started passed him, but he gripped her this time.

"Listen, Rose, I've respected you as a mother and stood by your side as your husband. But I will not allow you to prevent our daughter from some form of happiness while she is back. She was never allowed to be a child while she was a child, and if Kaleb McMurran can offer her that for a small while, then so be it. You and I are going away as husband and wife for a few days. I thought it might be nice for us. If you should decide to stay home, I'm still going." He picked up his briefcase and walked out of the room.

Meanwhile, Kaleb opened the car door for Anna, which made her smile. Once he was seated behind the wheel, she commented. "You certainly are going all out for a little carnival."

"It's not just some carnival, Anna. It's your first carnival. Tonight, you get the works, the best treatment I can offer." He started the engine. "And by the way, may I please tell you that you are prettier than a late spring evening by a night side fire. I can't believe you agreed to be with me tonight. Thank you."

She had no idea how to respond, but it appeared her heart did, as it once again rolled over slowly in her chest. She realized this was quickly becoming a dangerous habit for her, allowing herself to be swept up by his words. She sat back in the seat and enjoyed the view the late spring evening had to offer as they drove through town.

Once they arrived, Kaleb immediately treated her to her first caramel apple. He had to get it started for her since she was truly clueless as to how to eat one, but she soon got the hang of it and dove in greedily. She was laughing uncontrollably as he tried to win some pittance of a stuffed animal at one of the games. That is how her brother found them as he strolled casually—or so he thought—with Madelaine.

Adam could not believe he had allowed himself to become convinced to take Maddy to this festival. But here he was, her arm slung through his, eating cotton candy and trying to keep his hands in his pockets. She did smell awfully good, and he kept reminding himself that she was still his sister's friend.

"There they are." He quickened his pace.

Maddy sighed. She was hoping desperately that Kaleb would have just taken Anna straight to his bed so that they would never find them, and she could have Adam all to herself. But, fate stepped in to turn the cards against her. She waved to a group of her students from the high school band.

"Adam, she appears to be quite safe. And happy. Let's just leave them be. Let's go on the Ferris wheel." She tugged on him, but he was already waving to Anna, calling out to her.

"Adam!" Anna tugged free of Kaleb and ran to give her eldest brother a fierce hug. "Maddy! What are you two doing here?" She was all smiles.

"Your brother felt it necessary to ensure that you were having a good time." Maddy rolled her eyes, and Anna laughed at the exasperated look her friend gave her.

Kaleb finished the game, without a victory, and strolled over to join them. "Hey, Maddy." He faced Adam. "Hi, Adam."

"Oh, sorry. Adam, do you know Kaleb?" Anna asked.

"Yes. We met, Anna, before when the two of you—well, before." Adam reserved his right to shake his hand until later.

The gesture was not lost on Kaleb since he found it to be so like his mother's of only an hour ago. "Good to see you again, Adam."

They nodded.

"Okay, if you boys are done displaying whose property is whose, I think Adam and I will be on our way."

"Madelaine, if it's all right with you, I think we should hang together tonight with Anna and Kaleb. That might be fun, right, Anna?" Adam smiled forcibly at his sister, who did not seem to have a choice in the matter. The four of them began to walk amidst screaming children, exhausted parents, and flirting teens.

They found their rhythm, and soon the girls were talking about a variety of topics while the boys kept a close eye on each other, weighing their options and trying to figure out the other's intentions.

When they finally did approach the Ferris wheel, Maddy became giddy. 'I haven't been on one of these in years! You boys go buy us tickets, and we'll wait in line. Go on." She shooed them away as they almost snarled at each other.

Anna let out the laugh she had not been aware she was holding in. "Madelaine Murphy! You are savvy! How did you convince my brother to escort you this eve? I thought he was supposed to be working."

"He switched his shift when I gave him the brilliant idea of keeping an eye on you." At her friend's arched eyebrow, she continued quickly. "Please don't be mad at me, Anna. It was the only way I could convince him to be my date tonight. But don't use the word 'date' around him. I think it really makes him nervous." She giggled. "Besides, I figured I did such a good job selecting that dress for you that Kaleb would never have let you out of the house. He's a much slower mover than I would have thought."

"Shut up, Maddy, they're coming."

The two of them straightened up their act when Kaleb and Adam arrived with tickets for the ride. They entered the four-seated bucket, Adam and Madelaine on one side, Kaleb and Anna on the other. As the ascended into the air, Maddy's confidence wavered.

"I remember now why I haven't done this is so long." She turned green in seconds.

"Maddy, are you going to be sick?" Anna leaned forward in concern.

"For God's sake, don't do that!" she shouted, and a group of teens in the bucket behind them began to laugh and call out to her.

"Oh, for goodness sake, Madelaine, why were you so insistent to ride this thing if it made you sick?" Adam reluctantly put his arm around her shoulders.

"So, Maddy, if I were to, say—" Kaleb began to rock their bucket slightly "—do something like this, would you flip out?"

"Kaleb, please, I'm begging you."

"Ah, that's what they all say."

"All right, leave her alone. Let's just sit here and enjoy the view. We're stuck at the top now anyway."

"Thank you, Anna, that's very helpful." Maddy laid her head against Adam's shoulder, kept her eyes tightly shut.

The three of them continued to enjoy the view and some conversation. Anna could feel the tension begin to ebb as Kaleb and her brother talked about different interests around town, one of them being motorcycles. By the time they were let off the ride—to Madelaine's eternal gratefulness—they were engrossed in a deep conversation about the Harley that Kaleb wanted to purchase.

"I need to rest for a few minutes, Adam. I'm sorry." The color was just beginning to seep back into Madelaine's cheeks, but she was still perspiring profusely on her forehead.

Adam chuckled. "I'll take you to that tent over there. We can listen to the Polish music for while, and then I'll take you home." He swung his arm around her again, companionably this time, and guided her away.

Chapter VII

"Well, that was entertaining."

Anna smiled. "Maddy's not one to bore you for long. Poor thing! Did you see how green she got?"

"Not her best color." Kaleb stepped to her and placed his hands on her shoulders. "Want to walk with me some more around this place?"

He was looking so intently at her that she felt the muscles in her neck spasm in anticipation. "Sure."

He took her hand easily, as though they had been walking this way all of their lives. Anna realized that in some deep corner of her mind, they had.

Kaleb found several booths selling their wares, everything from soy candles to names engraved on large decorative pieces of wood to jewelry. When Anna sighed over some of it, he made a mental note.

Later, he sent her off to buy two tickets for the helicopter ride. Unsure of her footing, she was shaking at the knees as she climbed into the large machine. "I don't know about this, Kaleb. I mean, does this guy know what he's doing?" she questioned, referring to the pilot, who, at the moment, was easing into his seat.

"Anna, I would never let anything happen to you. I swear."

They lifted off for the seven-minute ride, and to Kaleb's immense pleasure, Anna oohed and ahhed and laughed and shrieked, particularly when the pilot decided to dip just a bit dramatically toward the river. He watched her face more than he did the skyline, and when she turned toward him, the late evening sun slanting its rays over her face, her face frozen in a wide smile, he knew.

He was falling in love with her.

When had this happened? Why now? At this point in his life, the last thing he needed was this sort of complication. Anna Keller had been his once—and she had gone away without too much of a goodbye. How could he make himself subject to that kind of pain? And he thought he already had the answer.

He thought perhaps he had never stopped loving her. Although he had never uttered those words to her—or to any other woman—he could see, clearly now, that when he had had Anna all those years ago, he had what he had always wanted but had never the courage to tell her. So he would tell her. This time. And she would accept it.

Even if he had to beat her over the head with it.

No way was he going to allow her to go back to New York without a fight. And even then, she still was not leaving. Anna Keller was going to remain right where she was.

Even if he had to strap her down to keep her.

She gasped as the pilot dipped low again, this time to prepare for their landing back onto the blacktop of the parking lot where the festival was being held. She reached for his hand instinctively, and he felt the rush of it wind through him like wax might flow down a long, trim candle. It was warm, liquid, and pooling at his feet, making him unsure of his footing with her.

He helped her down onto the safety of the ground again, and she wrapped her arms around his neck, laughed against his throat. It was a low and lovable sound, and it made him yearn.

Yearning was something he had never really experienced either.

She laughed up into his eyes and saw the change. Suddenly, the crying children, the screams from the nearby rides, the workers calling out to patrons to try their hands at the next game, all faded as she was lost in the depths of him.

As lost as he was in her.

He pressed his forehead to hers. "Anna…"

"I've missed you, Kaleb. I've missed having you in my life. I didn't know I did. Not until now."

"You're going to undo me right here in front of everybody. Then what will they say about me? I have a reputation to uphold."

She pulled back to see him. "Maybe this will just add to the mystery that is you."

"Anna, why would you agree to be on a date with me?"

"Really, Kaleb—"

"I'm serious. I just don't know how I got so—lucky."

"Now whose undoing whom?"

She began to walk, and he caught up to her. "I'm serious, Anna." He stopped her with his words. "I really do want an answer."

Anna chewed her bottom lip thoughtfully, and the simple gesture turned his insides to quivering. "Could we go someplace else and talk?"

He nodded, and taking her hand in his, led her back to his truck.

They arrived moments later at the lighthouse. Anna had known all along that they would come here, back to here, back to the place where she had first turned her heart—and her body—over to him. She now understood that this was where they had been headed once again. He opened her door for her and went to unlock the lighthouse. Once inside, neither knew where to begin.

"I might have something to drink."

"A glass of water would be fine."

"All right." He went to get it for her.

She understood that he was giving her time to compose herself, time that she needed to prepare herself for whatever the evening might bring to them, for them. As Anna walked around this humble room, she saw the potential for what could be great. Kaleb had been hard at work, toiling endless hours to make this lighthouse as special for tourists as it had once been for him, for her. For them.

She wondered if it could be that special again.

She decided she did not want to wait anymore to find out.

When Kaleb walked back into the room, he almost bobbled the glasses of water he held. His hands tightened on them, and he sucked in air greedily, as a man might while drowning.

Anna had found a blanket and some candles. She was now lying on the blanket, looking at him, with what appeared to be a smug smile on her face while low candlelight burned at the edges of the room. He could hear nothing but the water lapping at the edge of the sand—and the blood rushing to his ears.

"Hi."

"Hi. Anna…" He took two tentative steps forward, found his legs shaking, which humiliated him, so he stopped where he was. "What…is this?"

"I thought you wouldn't might if I made things a bit more comfortable for us." She sat up. "Is that all right with you?"

He found he could stare into the pale watery depths of her eyes for as long as she would allow. He came to the blanket, set the water on a nearby table, and faced her with false courage.

"Yes. But…"

"But what?" she prompted.

He let out a sharp breath. "I don't know how you can lie here on this blanket and expect me to think of you as only my friend."

She knelt and reached out to him. He took her hands and knelt with her. "Maybe I need more from you now. Maybe I want more."

"Anna, I want you. I won't deny it. When you and I were at my apartment the other night…I would have been satisfied to have you right then and there.

But I don't know that it would have been enough. I want you, Anna, but only if I can have you again."

Had sweeter, more demanding words ever been spoken, she wondered? As the smile began to form on her lips, Kaleb bent his head to touch his lips to hers—lightly at first. If he allowed the need to control him now, it would all be over in a matter of seconds. And he knew he wanted to give her what he could not give her when they had been young.

So he brought his hands to her face and allowed the kiss to linger. He tipped her head back and trailed his mouth down her face and her throat. He found her pulse there to be wildly unsteady, which gave him the confidence he was currently lacking. He pressed his body to hers as she gripped his waist. The hot ball of need curled its fist around his gut and urged him to take and take and take until this burning inside of him was quenched, and he could move beyond this fiery greed.

But as he had spoken the words only moments earlier, he knew once more would not be enough.

Her thoughts wandered for seconds only back to the night they had come here all those years ago when she had bravely asked him to make love to her before she left. She recalled that he had not really believed she was leaving, and he had been tender and sweet and kind, keeping in mind not to hurt her during her first experience. He was being tender and sweet and kind this time as well—and it was driving her mad.

She could feel the thunder clawing its way through her system until she was weak from it. As she pulled him down on top of her, she stopped the meeting of their mouths long enough to look into his eyes. The storm was back in them—grey, deep, swelling with the hunger all these years had caused them to put away. He rose above her to unclasp the tie at the front of her dress. As she helped him to remove it, he murmured such loving words, Anna almost forgot that she was with Kaleb. This was a new and different and exciting discovery. Kaleb McMurran was showing her a side to loving, the likes of which she had not experienced before, not even with him.

He looked down at her, her face reflected in the moonlight and the light of the candles. She was his, and he was going to make her his once again. He pressed his lips to her now bare shoulders; she arched in response. Her hands went out to her sides to grip the edges of the blanket. He traveled down the slim lines of her body with his hands, followed by his mouth, undoing her garments along the way. When his hands and then his mouth found her, she cried out to him. Her hands went from gripping his hair to lying limply by her sides once again.

And still she wanted more.

He would oblige. He raised himself to look into her pale eyes once again. Her skin was flush from the wonder of loving already, her lips swollen, her eyes dazed and giddy. He sat back to remove his own shirt and pants, and she knew.

This is what she had wanted—his skin on hers, the thrill of him pressed onto her own exposed body. She reached out to spread her fingers lightly over his chest, and he groaned from their feathery touch. This new knowledge brought her a kind of power, one she had not known had been inside of her. She sat to run her hands up and down his bare chest and his arms. She pressed her lips to his skin, already moist from anticipation. The light of the evening flickered momentarily over his face, his hair, until she wanted to cry out everything she was feeling in that simple moment. But she knew she should show him first. It would not do to speak of it now, only allow this union to demonstrate the turmoil she had locked away for so long.

Keeping his mouth on hers, he laid her back on the blanket, positioned himself above her. She opened for him. He entered her slowly, and while they kept their eyes locked on the other and their hands gripped in the other's hands, he allowed the fall to consume them both.

* * * * *

Kaleb held her nestled against him in the crook of his arm as he watched the breeze from the tiny open window flutter her hair. He thought she was sleeping already, so still was her body, so steady was her breathing. He kissed the top of her head and tried to shift so that he could look at her face more easily. She surprised him by rolling over the top of him and pinning him beneath the weight of her own body.

He studied her face in the pale light. "You look—smug."

She smile lazily and nipped his bottom lip. "I don't recall it being that way the last time."

"That's because the last time we were too young to know what the devil we were doing."

"You seem to have done an awful lot of growing up since then, Kaleb McMurran."

He could sense the playfulness in her now, and he felt it stir his senses again. Anna noticed this also. "You seemed to have a better handle on things this time, too."

Her eyes clouded over for only an instant. He wanted to question her, but she reversed their positions once again and fought back a grin instead. "Maybe you'd like to show me one more time how this is done."

"Are you sure you need the lesson?" He stroked her hair with one hand and cupped her bottom with the other.

"Mmm, I'm quite sure, Mr. McMurran. I wouldn't want to forget everything I've just learned now, would I?"

She was laughing as he became the teacher.

* * * * *

When she awoke the next morning, Anna was slightly disoriented until she remembered the events of the previous evening. She found herself wrapped in a blanket on a small couch—alone. She sat up to look around for Kaleb and thought she heard him wandering somewhere outside. She stood to pull her dress from yesterday back on and went looking for him.

Kaleb was outside watering a group of pitiful looking flowers near the base of the lighthouse. Upon seeing her, he set the hose down and grabbed her for a kiss that sent her head spinning, her toes curling, and all thought draining out of her head.

"Good morning."

"Good morning yourself," she answered back.

He went to the hose and shut it off. "I've been forgetting to water these."

She nodded toward the plants. "I can tell."

"Well, I've had—other things on my mind." He allowed his gaze to drift down the length of her body and back up into her eyes until she could feel the heat rise to her cheeks. He found that simple notion that was so completely Anna to be quite endearing.

"I woke up without you."

"I moved you to the couch so that you'd be more comfortable. I didn't want to disturb you while I putted around this place, so I let you sleep. After all, you kept us awake into the wee hours of the morning, duchess." His smile was quirky and devilish.

"I don't believe I made the efforts completely on my own, Mr. McMurran."

"No, I don't believe you did, Miss Keller."

They stood there, eyeing each other, until Kaleb stepped forward and put his arms around her again. She leaned into him while he sniffed at her hair. "This is so much better than the last time, my pretty, Anna."

"Why?" came her muffled reply.

"Because last time you were gone in the morning. I lost my heart to you that night, and in the morning, I never had a chance to tell you."

She pulled back to stare at him in disbelief. "I'm—sorry, Kaleb. I'd told you

I was leaving, and truthfully, I couldn't stand to say goodbye to you after the night we'd had. I just wouldn't have—"

"Shh, shh, Anna." He pulled her close for another hug, terrified by the panicked look he had seen in her eyes, mostly afraid because he had been the one to put it there. "I know. I wasn't complaining. I just wanted you to know that back then I had dreamed of this moment—of waking up with you. Now, it's come true, and it's better than I could have possibly imagined. Don't be upset with me, Anna, please."

"When I never got a reply from my letters, I just assumed that—"

"What letters?" he asked so swiftly that she was nearly knocked off her feet.

"The letters I sent you the first year I was gone to New York." At his blank stare, she pressed on. "How could you possibly think I could share myself with you and then not have any further communications with you? That's not who I am, Kaleb."

"No, it's not. How could I have thought it was?" he said, almost to himself as he walked back inside the lighthouse. She followed him.

"Are you saying that you never received my letters?"

"Yes, Anna, that is what I am saying."

"That's not possible! I wrote you every week, telling you about my teachers, my rehearsal schedule. I never stopped until a year had passed, and I'd heard that you left...for Colorado."

"Anna, I left for Colorado because—" oh, how could he tell her? "—because I'd never gotten a reply to the letters that I'd sent you."

Her face paled as realization sunk in. "Kaleb, I never received a single letter from you."

"I sort of guessed that."

They stood there in the silence of the lighthouse with the smells of the river so close by and waited for someone to speak. Kaleb finally did.

"This isn't important now. You and I have found each other, and that's really all that matters. Those letters—"

"How can you say they're not important? It's obvious who kept us from writing to each other, Kaleb! I'm certain it was my mother, and I think you are, too!" She stormed around the small room, looking for something to throw, not finding anything adequate.

This was a new layer to Anna Keller that Kaleb McMurran had never before witnessed. Now that he had, he was relatively certain he did not want to be on the receiving end of her anger—ever. He could see that she was livid, and Kaleb was as well. He would keep his anger in check, though, while Anna spewed enough for the both of them.

"Anna," he began without daring to touch her, "if your mother did have something to do with it, there is nothing we can do about it right now. Not at this moment. You and I can figure this out later. Right now we're here. This is our place, and we shouldn't allow anyone to take it away from us."

"Aren't you mad? She kept us from each other, Kaleb! She knew that I was lost without hearing from you, and still she did not care! How can you be so calm about it?"

"I am not calm, Anna." And she could see that he was not. The storm was back; it began in his eyes and vibrated from every part of his body—his rigid stance, the fists at his sides, the determination in his jaw line. She should have been paying closer attention. "I would love to confront your mother about this, but now isn't the time. There will come a time when you and I will both be able to do exactly that." He cocked his head to the side. "Are you hungry?"

The sudden change threw her off balance. "What? I suppose—"

"Good. I'll take you home for a shower. Be ready in an hour. We'll go back to my apartment, and I'll make you breakfast. Then I'd like to show you something."

Now it was her turn to hide the devil inside. "Kaleb, haven't you already shown me enough of that?"

"Ah, duchess, with you it's all about sex." At her shocked and playful gasp, he pulled her to him. "Come along, Anna. I have a few surprises in store for you."

* * * * *

And indeed, he did. That was what she was thinking as he opened the door to his place an hour later. She was clean, refreshed, and a bit more settled. And, she supposed, she had Kaleb to thank for that. Even through the haze of his own anger, he had seen to it that she was able to let out some steam and still remain in control so as not to do anything foolish. She was very grateful since she was never one to be foolish for too long.

As she toed off her sandals, she noticed that Kaleb had tidied up quite a bit since the last time she had been over to his home. Everything was freshly dusted, the carpet had obviously been recently vacuumed, and there were flowers on the table in an old glass bottle, most likely from the milk store the island boasted. Those little touches warmed her heart.

"How do you feel about eggs benedict?"

"I don't believe I've ever had it."

"Well, make yourself comfortable because I have been complemented many

86

a time on my specialty. Besides cereal, it's really the only thing I can make in the morning that's any good."

"That's a pretty complicated dish, Kaleb. So…" She wandered around the front room. "Is this something you make for all of your women the morning after?"

He walked quickly from the kitchen to Anna, grabbed her shoulders, and made her look at him. "No one else has stayed long enough for me to make her breakfast. They all pale in comparison. Understand?"

Was it any wonder that he could not see what that did to the heart in her chest? Could he not see the words written plainly on her forehead? Should she speak them now? No, he would not want them now, no matter how badly she needed to say them. But she could feel the honesty in what he had spoken to her, so she smiled and said, "Yes."

With a nod of his head, he went to a cupboard to retrieve a champagne glass in plastic. "This is the best I had on such short notice, but I thought I'd make mimosas. I thought that might be something you're used to drinking in the morning."

The amount of trouble he had gone to for her was not lost on Anna. She accepted the glass and asked, "So what is it you wanted to show me?"

"All in good time, duchess. We'll eat first. You really wore me down last night." At her cough that she tried to conceal with a chuckle, he continued. "Did you enjoy the carnival?"

"I did, yes. I'd like to go back—next year."

He clamped down on the hope that she would be around for it. "Maybe I'll take you."

"Maybe you will."

"Won't you miss the dance?"

Taking a seat at his table so that she could watch him while he prepared their breakfast, she considered the question. "You know, I never did answer your question from last night. About why I would agree to be with you on a date. I'd like to start there. I think it's all connected."

Kaleb listened well while he rummaged through the kitchen. He thought perhaps his keeping busy made it easier for her to talk about her moments of panic in New York, her efforts, the blood and sweat, the homesickness. How she had felt alone and lonely and without any worthy friends. When she got to the part about her mother, Kaleb smashed the eggs with a bit more fervor than was required. The gesture did not go over Anna's head.

"I will miss the dance," she continued over her second mimosa, "but I will not miss the stage." This was where she needed to be brave. "I'd like to train young people to dance like me—well, not like me, but like themselves, only with professional training. I've learned from some of the best in the business, and I think it only right that I give back to my roots. There are a lot of young women—and men, for that matter—who have real talent. I have real connections. I think I could help."

"I think you could, too." He checked the pot of coffee he had brewing. "What about your mother, Anna? What do you think she will say?"

She knew they had both been deliberately trying to avoid the topic of her since he dropped her off at her own home earlier that morning, and she could feel the muscles in her neck tense. She wrung her hands under the table in her lap.

"I can't care about her like that anymore. I know what I want. I'll start looking for a building next week." She sipped again and sounded as though she were trying to convince more than him.

"Well, breakfast is served." He made quite a deal out of the eggs benedict and coffee. They ate as though it had been days between meals and enjoyed idle chatter over some memories in New York, memories in Colorado, and things that had changed here at home. Kaleb spoke about his new little niece with wonder.

"Marissa is really lovely. I never thought I would speak about a baby that way. You know, my mother is lovely, you're lovely…but Marissa—that's really the only word to describe her."

"That's a wonderful thing to say, Kaleb."

"I bought her a toy as a welcome home gift. Not a toy so much as—her first baby doll."

"Oh, Kaleb, that's adorable!"

"Just don't go telling everybody I've gone soft."

"Your secret is safe with me." She toasted him as she played footsies with him under the table.

He shifted in his seat. "I've got a present for you."

She sat up straight. "You do?"

"Yes. Would you like it now?"

"I would."

She began to squirm just a bit as he went to retrieve a plain white box from his bedroom. "I didn't have time to wrap it because I bought it last night at the festival. I was going to give it to you then, but we—you know." At her blush, he smiled and presented it to her.

When she opened the tiny box, her eyes filled with something dreamy and soft. Kaleb wished desperately at that moment that he was a painter, for he would have liked to have captured her emotions on paper in watercolors and hung them in their lighthouse.

Funny how he had never thought of the lighthouse as belonging to anyone but them.

"Oh, Kaleb, I love it." She removed the Claddagh necklace and held it up. He went to her to help her put it on.

"I thought it might help to inspire you while you search for your part of the ring," he told her as he fastened it around her neck. "You were looking at it yesterday, and the woman who made it said that it would be the perfect length on you. Let's see if she was right." She released her hair back down to her neck, and he turned her to face him. "Yes, that's perfect. Now you look lovely."

"Thank you, Kaleb." She pressed her lips lightly to his. Before he allowed himself to get swept up in the heat, he abandoned her mouth to ask her something.

"Now would you like to see what I brought you here to show you?"

"Oh. This isn't it?"

"Of course not. I had that on me all last evening. This is something that I've kept here for a while. I'll go get it." He was up and away from the table before she could bat an eyelash, leaving her to sip at her coffee and allow her thoughts to linger, warm and dewy in the late morning light. If she was not careful, she would lose track of her goal—to find her part of the ring—before long. She would always be grateful to Kaleb for his part in their new adventure, but she could feel the ring pulling at her now more than it had when her grandfather's last wishes had first been read to the family. Back then, she had almost considered his letter to be the thoughts of a foolish old man; she had known her brother, Adam, had thought them nonsense, and her mother was angry. Ian had not said much at the time; he had kept quiet, which was his usual modus operandi, but after a time, Anna had begun to grow fond of the idea of an adventure so different from anything she had tackled in New York. In fact, as she looked back on the moment of her decision to come home for a short stay, she realized her grandfather had played a part in saving her.

Kaleb bounded back into the room with a box. Upon seeing the lost look in Anna's eyes, he set the box on the table to snap her out of her reverie. As she looked at him, he asked, "Everything okay?"

She smiled, the worry and anxiety draining so quickly, he pondered if he had imagined it. "Yes. Everything is better than okay. Because of you." She reached out to take his hand. "So, what have you got for me?"

Kaleb motioned to the box and sat next to her. "After you left for New York, I tried very hard to keep busy. I tried very hard to—forget you. Kind of difficult to do when I opened the paper to find these almost every week." He removed the lid and pulled out a stack of old articles, some laminated, some stapled together. He held them out to her. "Every time I turned around I got an eyeful of you. People around here were pretty proud, local girl turns star and all that junk. So, I collected little bits of you over the course of time and kept putting them in my box. Until I left for Colorado. Then my mother kept sending them to me, and although I wouldn't read them right away, I still stored them here." He studied her in silence for another few seconds. "What? Could you please say something?"

Anna looked at the unorganized mess in his hands, in the box. The tears were so sudden, strong, and unexpected that she got up from the table to walk to the little window for air. Kaleb said nothing while she gathered her thoughts.

Crossing her arms over her chest, she continued to gaze out onto the street as she spoke. "When my parents flew in to see me in my first show, I was sixteen. I had a bit part, was only really onstage for a total of twenty minutes out of a three-hour production. Which, at the time, was a pretty big deal to me. After they saw it, my father gave me a bouquet of roses. He said they were from both of them, but I knew better. My mother would not have thought to buy me flowers for such a bit part. The next day I found the article in The Review, where my name was mentioned toward the end, and it was spelled incorrectly. But I did not care. It was my name, in print, and it showed people that my hard work had paid off. When I took it to my mother and father that day at the hotel, my father was in the shower. My mother told me to set it aside because there was no use in keeping it. After all, my part was so tiny, and my name was barely mentioned. She would ask me to send articles once I became—bigger." Anna straightened her shoulders and faced Kaleb. "And now I see that you kept even that article. When it didn't matter."

Kaleb remained standing where he was. He knew that if he were to touch her now she might pull away, even further into herself. He had to tread carefully. "Anna, it's always mattered."

She let a single tear slide quietly down her cheek. "I guess I had thought that it had always mattered only to me."

Now he did go to her, wrapped his arms around her, and held her close, brushing his hands over her hair, kissing the top of her head. "Now I suppose you know better."

They stayed like that for some time, and Anna could feel Kaleb's strength and friendship seep into her. Was this not what she had been longing for all along? Was this not the sense of security and loving she had needed for as long as she could remember? Her mother had never been friend to her, only disciplinarian and guardian. Now she had Madelaine back, a stronger friend than she had ever allowed her to be, and here was Kaleb, holding her as though his life depended upon it. She thought now would be the time to show him how grateful she was to him for feeling so whole once again.

Anna pulled back just enough to look up into his eyes. He smiled down at her and began to say something, but she placed her finger over his mouth and told him in silence that she wanted him to be quiet. When he tried to control the situation by leading her to the sofa, she reversed their positions and began to knead her hands on his shoulders and slowly down his arms to his waist.

Was this what it was like to be seduced, to be taken under by someone? Kaleb wondered. Although there had not been as many women in his life as people may have thought, he had always been the one to decide the when, the how, the where, the why. He had never turned the controls over to any of them, but he could feel that Anna needed him to do so now. He opened his eyes just enough so that the late morning sun slid in through the window slats and formed a slight halo around her hair, the color of chestnuts not quite finished roasting over an open fire. From his vantage point, he watched her light but nimble fingers shake a little as she undid the buttons of his linen shirt one at a time. He reached out to rest his fingers on the pulse that hammered steady and swift in her throat. As she parted his shirt to wrap her arms around him and pull him closer, he bent his head to kiss her back.

Anna allowed herself to become dizzy in the moment, to become as lost to Kaleb as she had a few years ago. She forgot, albeit momentarily, that she was the one who would seduce and charm. She tipped her head back to give him access to her slender neck as she removed her light sweater. He cupped her breasts through the flimsy material of her bra, and a moan escaped. Neither knew who set the sound free.

Kaleb sat with her on the sofa, and Anna tipped herself above him, unhooking his jeans as she did. Naked now beneath her, she allowed her eyes to linger over his taut form. The appreciation Kaleb caught in the tilt of her head and in the crook of her smile was a whole new layer to seduction he had never before experienced. She ran her hands over his torso slowly to the point of sweet torture. He closed his eyes and allowed himself to be treasured by her. She straddled him and quietly bent to nip along his shoulders, his chest, and his fingers. The blood drained out his head, and he gripped her wrists. She smiled at him as his eyes flew open, shook her head, and continued on a lazy journey of sweet intentions and explorations. Anna could feel the pulse in her own head throb and threaten to explode, but she pulled in the reins of control as she traveled back to his face once again and locked him in searing kiss that had his hands gripping for support.

He forced them both to sit back again, and he removed her slacks without much finesse. Naked and slick, they wrapped themselves around each other and kissed for what felt like hours. Anna laid him back down once again.

Rising above him, she took him in slowly, arched her back, and allowed the pace to build on its own. Taking his hands in hers, she tossed her head back with a light laugh. Before Kaleb closed his eyes on the pleasure, he saw her as he imagined so many had before this moment—as a graceful dancer, one who was surprised by her own strength and power. She belonged steeped in her own desires and demands now and always.

This was the final thought to leave him as she took him up, up, and over the edge into nothing but light.

Chapter VIII

"Had I known the articles would please you so much, I certainly would have shown them to you a lot sooner," Kaleb said as Anna lay on top of him in his small living room.

She laughed and picked up her head to gaze into his face. "Somehow I think you would have found a way to write some of your own."

"Even better." She laughed again, and he shifted her so that her breasts lay comfortably against his skin, her head resting on his chest.

"Why don't we just stay here today? I don't have to work on the lighthouse. We could remain here until we feel the need to refuel, and then after..." Kaleb trailed his fingers lightly along her skin from shoulder to waist and back again.

"Because I need to actually get somewhere in my search for the ring." She tried to sit up, but he would not let her. "Kaleb, there is nothing I would like better than to stay here with you, but I feel as though I've let other things get in the way of my search. I really need to refocus."

"Your part of the ring is friendship, right?"

"Yes."

"I promise if you stay here with me today I'll be the best friend you could ever hope for."

Anna laughed quicker and louder and succeeded in propping herself on her elbows. "No." She was firm in her protest and sat up to retrieve her now-wrinkled blouse. "But if you help me a bit more, I might spend the evening with you."

He wrinkled his nose at her rejection. "Promises, promises." Sitting, he reached for his jeans and pulled them over his legs. "Oh, sh—shoot," he amended after seeing the arched look Anna was sending in his direction.

"What?" She smoothed her blouse.

"I promised Evan and Michelle that I would come over for a barbeque tonight. They're showing off the baby."

"As they should. Well," she began as she tried to hide her disappointment, "maybe you could help me for the next few hours before you go to your brother's house. If you don't mind."

Kaleb caught the wistfulness in her voice and kept the clucking noise he wanted to make in check. "No, I will not do that."

She turned to him, her eyes wide in shock and embarrassment. "Oh—all right then."

He caught her arm as she turned toward the table where the dishes sat still dirty, and the box sat still unorganized. He made her look at him. "I will not help you and then shove off to my brother's house. I will, however, help you and then take you to my brother's house as my date."

Her lips curved involuntarily. "As your date?"

"Yeah. You got a problem with that, duchess?"

"No. As a matter of fact, I don't. Actually, it's something I might be able to get used to."

As his eyes clouded for the length of a second, she wondered what would have caused them to do so. But his response put her mind to rest. "Okay then. Let's clean up and head out."

Anna knew that her part of the ring would be found in the water, near the water, or on the water. Kaleb questioned her thoroughly before they decided where to look. He chose a new direction but still kept them focused on the river after Anna described her grandfather's words in the letter. She had concluded that friendship and the river were connected to her.

As they trudged through an area that was a bit more marsh than either had anticipated, Anna's thoughts wandered to her grandfather's unusual message...

For friendship this one has always sought
And never has been sold or bought
Down to the river's bed
My dear Anna would rest her head
Upon the shoulders of whom she loves
The answer to her needs to seek above
Where in the wood her part will glow and sing
And, thus, she will find her part of the ring

Having memorized her part in the letter from the moment it had been read to her, she tried to understand what her grandfather had meant when he wrote of her part glowing and singing in wood. She could only understand it to mean that she should be searching the trees near the water's edge. After having explained this to Kaleb, he agreed and took her to the place where they now stood.

Kaleb watched her hike over small stumps from forgotten trees and almost lose her balance in the sinking soil beneath their feet. His feelings from the carnival helicopter ride swept down on him again, and he lost his footing. Anna chided him as he had chided her a few minutes ago, and they went back to walking silently with only the sounds of nature surrounding them.

He swallowed audibly as he watched her lift her face to the early afternoon sun and smile at rabbits that jumped across their path. He knew that if she were to look at him right now his feelings would not be hidden well at all, and he was desperately afraid that his heart was writing the message plain and clear across his forehead. His hands began to sweat, and a lovely, dull ache planted itself firmly in the middle of his gut. He would do his best not to beg, but if she were to reject him now, at this moment, he was certain he would not be able to stop himself.

After several hours of tromping through the trees and being bitten by the occasional mosquito, Anna decided they had had enough for one day. Turning to Kaleb, she found herself lost in the depths of him as he covered her mouth with his.

When he drew back, she smiled beautifully, and his heart was lost.

"I love you."

Did he speak the words out loud? Neither could be sure, but yet, they both knew that they had each heard them. Anna stumbled; Kaleb supported. She was gaping at him, her blue eyes wide and huge and disarmingly frightened. Kaleb felt quietly nauseous and wished desperately for the hands of time to turn back the clock. He could not move nor say anything more.

"Kaleb..."

He straightened his shoulders. "I'm sorry—you don't need to say anything more, anything at all. I should never have said—that. Let's just—go to my brother's house. Unless you'd like to just go home for the night. You know, away from me. I'll understand. Why don't we do that? I'll take you right now." He began to walk in the opposite direction, but she stalled him with the plea in her voice.

"Kaleb, don't turn away now. Not now."

He faced her again.

"Why, Kaleb, I do believe you're nervous." She tried—to no avail—to hide the smile.

"This isn't funny, Anna. Let's just forget it."

"Why? I don't want to forget it. I'd really rather have you say it to me again."

"Anna, if this is your way of humiliating me further, no thanks. Like I said, let's just go."

"Tell me why you're so nervous."

"Anna—"

"Kaleb, please."

He stuck his hands on his hips, then into his pockets. "I've never said those words to anyone before. And when I thought about saying them to you, I had a much better plan than suddenly blurting them out to you in the middle of a marshy wood after having spent the better part of the afternoon with you looking for some mystical ring. I never wanted to say those words before, and I knew that when I did, I wanted them to mean something."

"Are you saying that you do not mean them?"

"Of course I mean them!" he shouted, loud enough for a mother duck to scurry her flock of little ones away from the scene.

"And why do you think they mean nothing, Kaleb?" Anna stepped up to him and placed her hand against the warm flush of his cheek.

"Anna, when you look at me that way, I wish I could explain the things I want to do to you. With you."

"Answer my question, Kaleb."

"Because you deserve better than this. Better than me." He gestured around them.

"What I deserve is honesty. Don't you think?"

"Yes. Yes, of course."

"Do you love me, Kaleb McMurran?"

He let out a short and huffy breath.

"Kaleb…"

"Yes."

"Then please tell me again, and this time, look at me when you say it."

He swallowed and braced himself for rejection. "I love you."

"Say my name." She nipped lightly at his jaw.

"Anna Keller."

She brought his forehead to her lips and then whispered into his ear. "I love you, Kaleb McMurran."

As they stared into the depths of each other, her family's legacy began to pulse closer to them than either could have thought.

* * * * *

The noise level in the backyard of Evan and Michelle McMurran could not have raised another octave without alerting the local police. As Anna was escorted up the driveway, she could hear rock music pouring out of the garage along with a steady stream of young people. They found Evan grilling an enormous amount of meat on the back patio while Michelle sat nearby with the baby in her arms. Evan spotted them first and handed the spatula over to Michelle's younger brother.

"Hey! I'm so glad you guys could make it!" He slapped Kaleb on the back and turned to Anna. "Nice to see you again, Miss Keller." He kissed her cheek, and she flushed.

"Anna insisted on bringing something." Kaleb shrugged toward the bags he carried.

"I figured what's a backyard barbeque without fruit salad. And I brought the baby a little something." She smiled in Michelle's direction.

Upon hearing this, Michelle carried her snoozing infant over to the small group. "Presents! Did you hear that, Marissa? We have presents! Although it was really unnecessary for you to bring anything at all. We just threw this together at the last minute."

"I could not visit a new baby without bringing something. Besides, if my mother were to find out, she'd have my hide." Anna leaned over to look at Marissa. "Oh, she's just lovely."

"Funny, that's what Kaleb says about her, too." Michelle winked at her brother-in-law.

"Come on, big brother. I'll buy you a beer. They're over here in the cooler." Evan nudged him in the ribs.

"I need to say 'hi' first to the most beautiful women in my family." He kissed Michelle's cheek and then bent to brush his lips lightly over Marissa's head. "Hello, Sleeping Beauty. Nice to see you again." The two of them trotted off to fetch beers and sodas and set the fruit salad on the table. Three young children whizzed by, almost knocking them on their feet.

"We're really glad you could come, Anna. Why don't you come join me over here in the shade? It's warming up late in the day." The two women walked to where Michelle had been sitting when she had first arrived. She watched Michelle sit and nestle Marissa comfortably again in the crook of her arm.

"How are you feeling? You look wonderful."

"Oh, well, thank you. Other than tired, I am doing quite well. Evan has been terrific, although I would prefer that he not know that yet." She chuckled.

"She is really quite a prize. Kaleb and I spent the day together, and she dominated the conversation."

Taking this as the best cue she would get, Michelle prepared to interrogate Anna. She justified this by thinking it was the best a devoted sister-in-law could do. "That is so sweet. He was at the hospital as soon as he could get there. And how nice that the two of you have been spending so much time together. What did you busy yourselves with today?"

Kaleb walked up with a large plastic cup filled with ice and soda and saved her from answering. "We made sweaty love in the park and were arrested but released in time for the party."

"Kaleb!" Anna flushed scarlet.

Evan and Michelle laughed while Kaleb continued. "Even in the jail cell, she couldn't keep her hands off me."

As Anna tried to regain her composure, she corrected him. "We spent the day in the marsh looking for a piece to a puzzle."

"He mentioned something about your grandfather's ring." Evan sipped his beer and sat on the arm of Michelle's chair to gain a better view of his infant daughter.

"Yes. My grandfather left us—my brothers and me—a letter that told us we needed to search for pieces to a ring that apparently belongs in the family. I don't really understand why he was so mysterious, but I can only figure it's because he liked little adventures. In this way, even though he has already passed, he still gets to be a part of our lives for a while longer yet."

"That is so sweet," Michelle commented as the baby began to stir. "I think someone's hungry." She began to make adjustments and then realized where she was. "Will it make you uncomfortable if I breastfeed here? I cover with a blanket."

"Oh, you go right ahead. I'm fine with it. Kaleb?" Anna asked as she smiled into her cup.

The color in his face became a bit pasty as he replied, "I think I'll go relax over by the food for a minute—or two. Would you like me to make you a plate, Anna?" He tried valiantly to keep his eyes focused on Anna's face and not wander to the movement under the tiny blanket.

"Go make a plate for her, and I'll send her to you in a minute." Michelle laughed as he made a quick escape. She dismissed her husband as well to tend back at the barbeque.

"Kaleb says you're really enjoying being a mom."

"I am, yes. It will be harder when I go back to work in the fall. This was a pretty smart plan to have her in the late spring so that I could have a few months with her first."

"I would imagine so."

Michelle allowed the silence between them to linger for a few seconds before she continued with her intended points. "So, how is New York? I hear you've been quite successful on the stage."

Anna tried out a smile, but it did not meet her eyes. "I suppose you could say that. It certainly has been an adventure."

"I would imagine. How long have you been back now?"

Anna had to think about this. She realized it had been nearly three months and told Michelle so.

"How long will you stay?"

The question was asked so quietly that Anna almost missed it. She turned to meet the vibrant eyes head-on. "I wish I could answer you. I just do not know." She looked down at the cup in her hands and saw that the dark liquid was shaking slightly inside the plastic.

"Anna." Michelle leaned forward just enough so that her knees bumped companionably against Anna. "I know you and I don't really know each other that well, so you are welcome to tell me this is none of my business. God knows that is exactly what my husband would be doing right now if he were here listening to us talk." She shifted the baby and began to burp her. "I love Kaleb. He was so supportive to me when my mother died." Her eyes welled for a moment and then subsided. "He's been much more than a brother-in-law should have to be. I know that he and Evan are terribly close. So I know him— well. And when I see him look at you, I see a man who won't let you go back to New York as easily this time."

Anna had known this, too, but had been too afraid to share her thoughts with anyone. Michelle went on.

"All I ask is that you do your best by him. And if that means letting him know your doubts now as opposed to later, then so be it. Just do so gently. He's never brought another woman to one of our little backyard barbeques."

"Never?"

At her astonished look, Michelle decided to go easy on her. "Never. I can see why that surprises you. So be careful."

The two women shared a look of understanding as Madelaine bounded into the yard. "Where's my favorite new baby?" she called as she rounded the corner onto the patio.

"She is finishing her feeding, and then she'll go down for a late nap. Don't argue with me, Maddy. I need some time to hold my own plate and eat some food. This kid's sucking me dry!"

"Ah, you're so poetic, Michelle. Well, let me have her for a moment before you take her in." Madelaine settled her into her arms and finally saw Anna. "Oh!

Your stupid brother would not accompany me to this tonight. Said he had reading to catch up on. I'm a teacher for goodness sake, and I can still find the time to hang with friends."

Anna laughed as Kaleb brought her some food. "I'm sorry, Maddy, but he's quite a workaholic." She forked into the pasta.

"Well, it's nice to see that someone around here besides Michelle is happy with a man. You two look pretty content."

Suddenly all eyes were on Anna and Kaleb. He struggled to calm his nerves. "What? A guy can't bring an incredibly beautiful woman to a party?"

"Sure, but you've never done so before, that's all. Ow!" she exclaimed as Michelle kicked at her ankle. "I'm holding your baby, nitwit."

"Yes, you are, and I've barely had the chance today, so I'll put her to bed." Evan swung her into his arms like a veteran, and Michelle tried not to correct him. Instead, she spotted the decorated bag sitting at Anna's feet.

"Can I open it now?" she asked sheepishly.

"Oh! My goodness! Of course you can! It's nothing, really." She wrung her hands as Michelle pulled out a soft yellow sundress with ladybugs dancing across it. The matching bonnet caused Michelle's eyes to water.

"Oh, dear, look what this outfit's made me do!" She wiped her face with the baby's burp cloth. "Thank you, Anna. This was kind of you."

"It was my pleasure."

And the remainder of the evening felt like exactly that. Anna and Kaleb were content to send each other smoldering glances from across the yard time and again while the women looked on with envy, and the men elbowed each other knowingly in the ribs. All of this activity inspired Evan to drink a little too much beer and toast his wife in front of the crowd as she tried to hide her head in embarrassment. Madelaine sulked at her own loneliness, and Anna did her best to console her. By the end of the barbeque, Maddy and Evan were both delightfully plowed, and Marissa had awoken from her late nap.

Kaleb drove past Anna's house and pulled to a stop a few driveways down. "I'd like you to spend the night with me, Anna." He took her hand in his and nibbled at her fingers.

Anna's insides turned to water. "I'd like that, too, but my mother…"

They both glanced at the lights in the house. Obviously, her parents had returned from their trip and were waiting up for her.

Kaleb sighed. "Anna, you're a grown woman. I don't think you need to ask for their permission."

"Kaleb, you don't understand—"

"I understand that I want to be with you in the morning light. I understand that I want to hold you in my arms tonight after I've made love to you for hours. I understand that I love you. What else is there?"

She let out a heavy breath. "You certainly know how to leave a girl unnerved."

"You're the one who makes me nervous." At her glance, he faced her more directly in the truck. "Anna, ever since I first got up the courage to hold your hand, I cannot tell you how nervous you make me. You knock me flat."

"Oh, Kaleb…"

"I'll come in with you to get your things for the night. We'll say 'hello' to your mother and father, and then we'll come back to the lighthouse. I like you best in the moonlight there."

As her knees were shaky, Anna took the front steps gingerly, knowing the task that lay ahead of her was going to be anything but easy. She unlocked the front door and pushed into the room. Her mother greeted her right away.

"Anna, dear, it is so nice to see you after—oh." Upon spotting Kaleb next to her daughter, Rose stopped mid-sentence. "I was hoping to have you for the evening to myself."

"Hello, Rose. How was your weekend?"

"Fine. Now if you will excuse us, Mr. McMurran, Anna's father and I would like to have some time with our daughter. Alone."

"Sorry, Mother, but I won't be staying." Anna's throat felt dry, her stomach twisting into knots the size of grapefruit.

"I am sorry, I do not understand. What do you mean?"

"I'll be spending the evening with Kaleb. I just came to get my overnight bag. Welcome home from your weekend." She kissed her mother's cheek absently and went to begin up the stairs to her room.

"You will do no such thing, Anna Keller. Your father and I will not tolerate our names being dragged through the mud by this—this man."

"Whose name, Rose?" Gregory asked as he walked into the room, cup of coffee in hand.

"Hi, Daddy." Anna hugged him fiercely.

"Hello, Mr. Keller. Nice to see you." Kaleb shook his hand as they muttered a greeting.

"Your daughter says that she plans to spend the evening with—Mr. McMurran. I have told her we will not tolerate it."

"Rose, I really do not see as how we have any say in the matter."

"As long as she is living under my roof, I—"

"She's not living here, Rose. She's renting space until she figures out what to do next. Anna, go get your things." She left the room, reluctantly abandoning Kaleb in her wake. "Let the girl have some fun, Rose. You're only young once."

"I will not have our good name dragged through the dirt by this—"

"Easy, Mrs. Keller. I'll be kind, but even that will not last long." Kaleb stood, hands at his sides, ready to do battle. He almost salivated at the idea.

"Stand down, Kaleb, no blood will be drawn tonight." Anna reentered the room with her shoulder bag stuffed to capacity as her father continued to speak. "When can we expect you back, honey?"

"I—I'm not sure. I'll be busy tomorrow at the lighthouse and the river again."

Rose rounded on her. "Looking for that stupid ring? You are just playing into a foolish old man's hands."

"Better to be foolish once than to play serious always."

"Well said, Kaleb," remarked Gregory.

"And spoken like a fool."

"That's enough!" Anna spat the words, and all three heads turned to look at her in quiet awe. "Yes, Mother, I am going to spend the night with Kaleb. A man. And I know you'd rather have me twirling the stage back in New York. Well, I don't know that I want that anymore. And before you even suggest it, this has nothing to do with him. But I am finally in love with someone, and I will not allow you to spoil it for me ever again!" Having said her piece, Anna stormed from the room with Kaleb trailing behind her.

On the drive to the lighthouse, neither Anna nor Kaleb spoke. They kept focused on the road ahead of them. Kaleb held the wheel in a death-grip while Anna wrung her hands in her lap. Each wished they could read the others' thoughts.

As he pulled up to the large wood and brick building, Anna hopped out of the truck and ran straight to the water. She picked up the first thing she saw— a big branch—and lofted it into the river. Then she screamed, fell to her knees, and held her head in her hands.

Kaleb found her like this and dropped to the dirt and grass to take her into his arms to comfort her. He let her cry it out for a long time. Eventually, the moon began to sparkle on the edges of the water, and they could hear the late calls of seagulls in the distance.

Anna sat back and wiped her face. She looked up to the sky and then finally to Kaleb. "I don't know what to say to you."

"You don't have to say anything."

"But I do!" She got to her feet; he remained where he was and let her pace. "She made a fool of herself back there! And insulted you in the process. I don't know how to begin to apologize to you."

Kaleb gave this some thought. He could see the trouble brewing in her eyes, in her shoulders, in her fists. He wanted nothing more than to go back to her mother and let her know exactly what he thought of her. But it was Anna who needed him now, and he would be there for her.

"Please. Say something."

Kaleb rose to his feet, came to Anna, and pulled her tight against him. "I love you, Anna. And no amount of insults from your mother is going to change that."

She began to weep silently. He trailed his lips over her face to clean up her tears. When they pulled apart to look into each other once again, their wants and needs were plain in their eyes.

"I want you, Anna Keller. Stay with me tonight. Let me show you how much I want you, how much you're loved."

She allowed him to lead her into the lighthouse. As she awakened throughout the night, he would pull her closer to him, and the fears gradually subsided.

Nearby, a circle embodying friendship pulsed with barely a flicker of light.

Chapter IX

The days flew by and turned into a week before neither Kaleb nor Anna noticed that they spent every day together. But this was not missed by the community or by the members of their families. It was on such a day that Kaleb's mother decided she needed more information. She had already gotten information through Michelle during her last visit with her new grandbaby—God love her!—about Kaleb bringing Anna to their barbeque. Now she wanted something straight from the horse's mouth, but she knew this would not be easy. So when the call came in to her husband's real estate that Anna Keller was interested in looking at some property, she jumped at the chance to help. Marcus had too many bookings that afternoon, and Rita did not need to be at her florist until the next day, so she volunteered to assist Anna with her needs while Kaleb worked on the museum lighthouse.

She pulled her compact into a small slot at the opposite end of the island and got out of the car. Anna was already waiting in front of the locked building. Rita offered her best smile and met her hand for hand to greet her.

"Well, my goodness, Anna Keller, you look marvelous!" she beamed at the girl's chestnut hair and pale blue suit. She thought she was still a bit too thin for her own good, but if talk around town was right, then her son was feeding her well enough.

She hoped talk was right; Marissa should not grow up without any cousins.

"Oh—Mrs. McMurran. I was expecting your husband." Anna wrung her hands nervously on the strap of her ivory purse.

"Yes, I'm sorry, dear, but Marcus overbooked his afternoon. He already had two showings scheduled for the same time, and with you being the third, there really was no way for him to do it. I volunteered since it's my afternoon off." She searched for keys inside her bag.

"You didn't have to do that. I could have rescheduled."

"Nonsense! Marcus would never have forgiven himself if he had allowed you to change your mind. You want to see this building, he'll find a way to show it to you." She went to the front door and jostled the key into the lock. "Well. That wasn't too difficult. Let's have a look inside." She gestured Anna into the room, and both women coughed. "Looks like someone hasn't been here in quite a while to do any dusting. Let me pull out the folder." She shuffled some papers. "Marcus will be very upset with me if I don't give you the correct stats on this place. It used to be a bakery. Went belly-up about seven years ago and has sat empty ever since." She put small glasses on her attractive face and continued to look at the notes her husband had gone over with her just that morning. "Seems like much of it wasn't updated, so you'd probably need to have it inspected before you took occupancy." Rita closed her folder and peered through her glasses at Anna. "If you don't mind my saying so, dear, I'm sure you're used to living in better conditions than these. Why would you want to live here?"

Anna took a few tentative steps forward, mortally afraid that she would smash right through the floorboards into whatever lay underneath them. "I don't want to live here. I want to run my dance studio from here."

"Oh! Well, that sounds terrific! I'm sure your parents will be thrilled to have you back all the time."

Rita could sense the girl's pain before she had finished her sentence. Anna replied, "I think it will thrill my father. And my grandmother. I'm sure my brothers will enjoy having me around, too." She ran her hand along the door trim.

"And your mother?"

Anna turned to face her. "Mrs. McMurran, was if hard for you to let your two boys—become their own people?"

Rita had never seen such quiet discontent in such lovely eyes before this moment. She shifted silently from foot to foot as she pondered how to answer her. "First, call me 'Rita.' Second, I think each mother has her own idea of what her children will do with themselves. All one can hope for is that they will be happy doing it. I'm very proud of both of my sons. Knowing that Kaleb is more settled than he once was brings me a real sense of peace. To see him building and restoring for a community that I have loved since I was a child makes me—misty." She stepped closer to Anna. "My children are happy, which makes me happy. But then, I've always had things for myself. I never had the need to live through them."

Because it felt as though this woman could see directly into her soul, Anna walked to the grimy window again. She looked out of it as she spoke. "My mother says she wants me to be happy. But then she tries to take away that which makes me happiest."

Rita decided to go out on a limb. "Anna, does Kaleb make you happy?"

Anna chuckled slightly. "You certainly don't mince words."

"It's never been a problem for me."

Anna smiled when she looked at her. "I'm in love with him."

Rita felt her heart flutter in her chest. "Oh dear." She pressed a hand to herself. "Should I not have told you?"

"No, that's not it. I am glad you did. It just catches a mother off guard, that's all. You'll understand someday when your son falls in love."

"He's told you then that he loves me?" Anna's eyes took on a healthy different kind of glow.

Rita sighed, remembering the first stages of love, the unease, the torment of not knowing all, the fear of rejection. "He hasn't had to say the words. But I can see that he has said them to you."

"Just last week. It was very unexpected."

"Then I imagine that is how your mother is feeling. Anna, she's probably had it in her head that you would *be* someone! She figures you'll dance your way into stardom and then fall in love with the right man. You'll marry, have children, and live in some glamorous city, where people on the street will recognize you. Not here where you grew up, and now you're with an overstated carpenter." At Anna's offended look, Rita laughed. She placed her hand on Anna's shoulder. "I don't mean that in a negative way. I am simply trying to show you how your mother might see it."

"For the first time in my life, I feel grounded. Secure. I finally have friends. And your son is rapidly becoming one. He means so much more to me than—just a boyfriend might."

"Anna, if you feel that what you're currently experiencing is something important, and it gives you the sense of longevity, then I don't see how you couldn't go with the flow."

Anna gave this some thought all the way back to her home. She had not told Kaleb that she was looking at that piece of property, and she recalled the serious pledge she made his mother take so as not to tell him anything about it. Her own parents did not even know that she was interested in opening a studio; in fact, only Maddy knew what her desires were at the moment, and even what she knew was very basic. But the prospect of Anna remaining here for good had made Madelaine more than happy.

She realized abruptly that Rose O'Connor Keller and Rita McMurran were two very different people. While Rita might hold her children's happiness above all else, Rose would see things in an opposite light. Knowing she would need to face her mother now gave her the chills, but she summoned up her courage as she walked in through the front door.

She found her sitting in the back parlor, reading a book and reveling in the breeze that fluttered the draperies around her. Rose did not acknowledge Anna's presence in the room, so Anna took it upon herself to be heard.

"Hello, Mother."

Rose never stopped reading. "Look what has finally stumbled through my door."

Anna sat on the stool opposite her. "I think we should talk."

Still keeping her eyes on her book, she replied, "You certainly did not have time for idle chat last night."

Anna sighed. "No, Mother, I did not. And this is not going to be idle chat either. This kind of chat serves a purpose. I'm a grown woman."

"And yet you insist on acting like a child." Now Rose did set her book down with a loud thump against the table next to her. Hoping it would cause her daughter to jump like it had when she had been a child did nothing to soothe her nerves when she realized that Anna was unrecognizably calm. She switched to another tactic. "You are a grown woman, Anna, and I would like to apologize for treating you poorly yesterday in front of…"

"Kaleb."

"Yes. But neither here nor there, I do not feel that you should have spent the night with him. What will the neighbors think?"

"I do not care what the neighbors think, Mother. Ironically enough, I think they have other things on their mind besides where I spend my evenings."

"That may very well be the case, but still, Anna, your father and I raised you better than that."

"Raised me better than to want to wake up next to the man I love?"

Both women fell into stunned silence. Anna had not meant to reveal her feelings to her mother, and Rose had not wanted to hear such words from her. Neither woman moved until Rose spoke again.

"When you said that last night to your father and me, I thought you spoke out of anger to make us mad. I had no idea you were serious."

"You should know me better than that. I would never use Kaleb's feelings to hurt you and Dad. I would never do that to anyone."

Silence descended upon the two of them again. Finally, Rose responded. "I suppose this means I owe you another apology. Well, that is all the apologizing you will get from me today. Richard called for you last night."

The sudden turn in the conversation knocked Anna off balance. "Richard?"

Rose had the pleasure of seeing that old familiar light begin to spark in her daughter's eyes. "Yes. He said the company misses you terribly and that your replacement is dreadful. He wants you back—soon, if not sooner. He's writing his own ballet, you know."

"No. I didn't know that."

"He wants you for the lead in that as well. This could really be something, Anna." She paused dramatically to let the information sink in. "But if this does not excite the way it used to, I guess you should call him back and tell him no."

As Rose left to refill her teacup, Anna sank back into the Victorian settee. All thoughts of the studio left her as she saw herself on the stage once more in the lead role.

* * * * *

Kaleb decided that while Anna was out running her errands he should spend some quality time with his brother and his new niece. Which, of course, meant that he would also be spending quality time with his sister-in-law and that meant he would be barraged with questions about his love life. As he whistled his way into their house with a bottle of wine under his arm, he chose to take the questions as they came and to have some fun answering them—at Michelle's expense. After all, she had often told him that he would have driven her crazy had they grown up together—and then she would actually ruffle his hair. He was smirking when Evan walked into the kitchen carrying Marissa.

"Don't you knock? Michelle and I could have been running around naked."

"Not very likely!" came the reply from the back of the house. "I just had a baby!"

"I think your naked days are over, pal." Kaleb set the wine on the counter.

"Oh, you brought Michelle's favorite bottle over. She can't have any yet."

"She's not pregnant anymore." Kaleb took the baby from his brother.

"Breastfeeding." At his brother's awkward look, Evan laughed. "Come on, Kaleb, the word 'breast' has never bothered you in the past."

"That's because it should serve an entirely different purpose than what you are suggesting."

"Ah." The two men moved to the back patio, and Kaleb settled Marissa comfortably against him. "So, where's your girl?"

"She had some errands to run, so I thought I'd come by to see you guys. Well, really to see Marissa." He cooed at her while she shifted around.

"You know, you look pretty natural holding that baby, Kaleb. You'd better be careful. Some people say it's catchy."

"I want to marry her."

Evan took a minute before responding. "I'm sorry, you can't. First, she's way too young for you, and second, she is your niece."

"Evan, you know who I'm talking about. I want to marry Anna." He looked back at the door to make sure Michelle was not going to make an appearance any time soon.

The younger McMurran ran his hands through his hair and stood to pace the small area. "Kaleb, are you sure? I mean, marriage is quite a commitment."

"Who's getting married?" Michelle asked as she combed through her wet hair and tightened the belt on her robe. Sitting on the arm of her husband's chair, she leaned down to him for a kiss.

"Kaleb wants to marry Anna."

Michelle made a sound of shocked glee while Kaleb glared at Evan. "Thanks. I wasn't ready to talk with her about it yet."

"Oh, Kaleb! I won't say anything to anyone! I swear! Come here!" She stood to envelope him and her baby in a strong hug. Marissa stirred, and her mother took her to settle her.

"So you think it's a good idea." Kaleb looked worried and miserable—the picture-perfect combination of a man in love.

"Well, yes. Doesn't everybody?" She looked from Kaleb to her husband and back again. "Tell me how you proposed."

"He hasn't. Anna doesn't even know that he wants to do this."

Michelle was silent a moment before she responded with "oh."

Now it was Kaleb's turn to rise. "Now suddenly it's no longer a good idea? You know, she might actually say 'yes.'"

Michelle and Evan exchanged knowing looks, and then Evan stepped up to the plate. "Yes, she might. And, Kaleb, if this is really what you want, then Michelle and I will support you all the way. But do you think Anna is ready to give up her life in New York? She's pretty well-known out there, and I can't see her family approving of her giving up that life."

"The hell with her family! I don't care what Rose has to say about it. I love her, and in the end, that's all that matters." But he had thought about the sacrifices she would be making by agreeing to marry him and live in their hometown. He considered that he may need to sacrifice as well, and so he turned to them to tell them exactly that. "And if Anna needs me to go with her to New York, then I will." He put his hands in his pockets to keep them from shaking.

"You would leave? You would go just like that?" Michelle placed her hand on Evan's arm to steady his voice.

"Evan, when you proposed to Michelle, if she had said that she would marry you, but she really needed to move away, what would you have done? I'll tell you what. You would have followed her to the ends of the earth. No one could have stopped you from following her to wherever she wanted to take you. We're all just lucky that you married a teacher at the high school who loves this area so that we could all be a part of your lives. I've found a different kind of woman."

For the next few minutes, the only sounds came from Marissa as she sucked on the pacifier. Michelle allowed her thoughts to tumble around inside of her for a time because she knew that this was for them to settle first. Eventually, Evan spoke.

"You're right. I would have gone anywhere to have what I have now." He looked at his wife and child and knew Kaleb was right. "Whatever you need from us, we'll give to you. Just make sure that she doesn't rip your heart out like the last time. If she does, Anna Keller will have the other brother to deal with." Evan stood once again and hugged Kaleb. "I'm happy for you. I'm just sad to see you go. I always assumed my kids would have their uncle around all the time."

"I know. Me, too. But my place is with Anna. I can't be anywhere else, Evan. I just can't."

"I think you two make a lovely couple," Michelle said from her chair. "And at least this way we'll always have a place to stay when we visit New York. I've never been, but I hear it's quite entertaining." She smiled, and Kaleb knew all would be okay.

"I'll go get the chicken for lunch. Only this time, you're grilling, Kaleb, so that I can sit back and enjoy myself." Evan went into the house.

* * * * *

Anna decided that Ian needed a visit from her. Or rather, she was the one who needed to visit Ian. They had only seen each other twice since her return home, and both times had been while they were surrounded by family, so they had not had the chance to really talk. Not that Ian would talk any more if they were alone. Of the three Keller children, he was the quietest. As she pulled into his driveway, Anna reflected on their childhood. Adam had certainly been serious about his studies, but Ian had been quietly passionate. And once he discovered he liked to do something, his mind was set. He would read everything on the topic, watch every type of program about it, and when that was not enough, he would write his own papers and theories. Adam and Anna had often joked that he would eventually be found living inside of one of his creations, and in essence, that is where Anna found him today.

111

She rounded his property to the back of his small home at the edge of the island, where he worked all day and well into the night in his workshop. Ian's sculptures from old tree stumps had created fame for him, but it was not fame he had sought. Ian wanted peace, solitude, and a sense of accomplishment. Even if that meant disappointing their mother.

When that thought entered Anna's mind, she stopped short. Before this moment, this had never occurred to her. Of the three Keller children, Ian was the most independent of their mother. He had followed his mother's wishes and gone to college, and he lived on the island, but he worked in a field that Rose had not dictated. While Adam's field certainly appeared to make him happy, Anna knew that hers was unsettling. As for Ian, the disdainful glances their mother had sent in his direction had ultimately not seemed to affect the decisions he had made. This was certainly worth thinking over.

Anna could hear the instruments of Ian's labor hard at work—the buzzing of saws and sanders, the easy rhythm of man bringing something inside the crumbling old pieces of wood to life. She stood in his doorway watching him and was at a loss when pride threatened to pour out through tears. She held her hand over her heart and called to him once he shut off the noisy machine.

He turned and set the protective goggles back on his head. "Hi, Anna. I wasn't expecting to see you here."

"I hope it's okay that I just stopped by. I wanted to see how your shop was coming along." She edged her way inside and began to look around.

Ian may have been deemed the quietest of the Keller children, but he would also have to be called the most observant. He could sense distress in his youngest sibling, so he continued to work quietly, allowing Anna time to gather whatever she needed to talk to him.

"Anna, you've never needed an invitation to stop by. I have cold drinks in the fridge there. Help yourself." He reached for the manual sander and busied himself for several minutes while Anna poured them both iced tea into Styrofoam cups.

She set one on his workbench. "You've really come a long way with this shop, Ian. You have a lot to be proud of."

He could hear the wistfulness in her voice, which surprised him, but he let it go for now. "Mmm," was his only reply.

"When I was in New York, I would brag about you." At this, he looked up at her in subtle shock. "I did. You sent me that wooden sculpture of the ballerina, and when I had some friends over after a show one night, many of them asked me where I got such a magnificent piece of art. They all assumed that I had purchased it from one of the galleries. But when I told them that you had made it for me, their eyes bugged out of their heads. This one dancer, Eileen, I think, she kept insisting that I tell you to move there so that you could be discovered. She just knew that you were money waiting to be made, especially after I showed her your picture. Then all the girls wanted to meet you."

Looking at him now, she could certainly see why. His hair was a shade darker than hers—mostly chestnut—and it curled at the ends at the base of his neck as though he had long ago given up haircuts. His eyes were a deep green; they were poet's eyes, holding a stillness that understood even when the onlooker did not. Since he towered over her, Anna could put herself in the shoes of the women who had admired him from afar and up close. His build could be quite intimidating if he needed it to be, but when he walked, he did so with an easy gait, one that welcomed people on the most basic of levels. She could feel him studying her now with those eyes and knew that he understood that she wanted more from him than just a friendly chat.

"Ian, how did you manage to do it?"

He set the sander down and picked up the tea. "Do what?"

Anna sighed. "How did you manage to go your own way? Mother had ideas for each of us, and you managed to find your way without her help."

He thought he was beginning to see where this discussion was headed. "Our mother helped me quite a bit. She helped me to see that I did not want to go into Dad's business as much as she wanted me to."

Anna laughed at her brother's candor. "Yes, I know. But that is precisely what I mean. Of the three of us, you've been allowed to open your shop and make something with your hands." She picked up a piece of wood and set it down again. "Somehow I think this is what you had intended all along."

"Except when I was going on a fishing expedition to the Antarctic."

They both laughed at the memory. "I forgot about that! How old were you? Ten, eleven?"

"I believe I was nine, which is probably the only reason why she let me prattle on about it. I think she figured I wouldn't be leaving any time soon, so it was safe to let me fantasize."

"But soon after you began researching sculpture. That has certainly become more than fantasy."

"Yes, it has."

Anna began to pace again. She still was not sure what to say to him, but she knew she had something gnawing at her, and she needed to purge herself of it. Before she could, Ian changed the subject.

"I hear you're still looking for the ring."

"Yes. Only I am looking for my part in the ring. The hands that encompass the sides of the ring. Oh, here!" She pulled the necklace from under her shirt to show him the Claddagh. "I know you know what it looks like, but I thought this might help."

Ian studied it for a moment. "Where did you get this?"

"Kaleb bought it for me at the Island Fest."

"Oh." He stepped back to his worktable. "So are you two serious?"

The question surprised Anna mildly because Ian was not one to meddle in her relationships. "Yes. I think we are."

"Okay." And that would be all Anna would get from him regarding Kaleb. If there was one thing Ian had always believed in, it was to trust those that you love. And he loved his family with a fierceness that even they would never understand.

"When I dated him before I moved away, it was like a child's love. I'm not saying that we did not love each other, but this time…this time, it's more balanced." She laughed at her description. "Yeah, balanced like a roller coaster ride. We've both done some growing up, and I think we may be ready to tackle something bigger."

Ian remained quiet. He could see everything plainly in her face. His little sister was in love, and this was not a joke. She meant everything she was feeling, and that scared him. Would this new relationship affect her goals and dreams? He intended to find out in his way, in his time.

Anna pressed on. "And now I'm not sure what to do about New York. And that has nothing to do with Kaleb." Studying her unobtrusively, he could see that she was telling the truth—both to herself and to him. "I've been so restless for such a long time, and I've not known what to do about it. Then I come home, and he is thrown into my path, and everything turns upside down. I need to find this ring, I need to decide what to do about my career, I need to decide how to handle Kaleb. And our mother tells me this morning that Richard called from my company and is writing a ballet and wants me for the lead. Do you have any idea what that could mean, Ian? The lead in a brand new production…It's unheard of. My name would go in the programs as being the one who started in that production. They would always remember me. Uhh, I just don't know." She sat in a dusty chair.

Polishing off his cup of iced tea, Ian tossed it into the trash can. "Anna, maybe our mother really does know what you want. Maybe this is not such a tough decision after all. You are just allowing these interruptions to block your thinking."

She looked up at him. "No, that's not it at all. But thank you for trying to make it easier. I should let you get back to your work." She rose and went to kiss his cheek. "Maybe you and Adam and I could meet for dinner one evening."

"I'd like that." He tugged on her ponytail.

"I'll see you later."

As he watched her go, Ian thanked his lucky stars that he had never allowed love to muddle in his life. Living at the edge of the city and the island on his own suited Ian Keller just fine.

Chapter X

When Kaleb knocked on Anna's bedroom door later that day, he found her sitting at her desk studying a pile of books. Before long, he was studying her. Her hair was piled on top of her head, and some of the pieces were escaping the knot. She rested her head on one hand while she wrote furiously into a notebook with the other. Her mouth was twisted into stern concentration, and the lust swooped down on him so swiftly that he almost lost his breath. He could already feel her writhing under him on her whiter than lilies bedspread; he could smell her skin against his face, feel her hair on his chest while she slept after loving. He knew none of this could happen at the moment in this room. It had been difficult enough getting her mother to allow him entrance into the house, let alone her bedroom. But her father had agreed easily, and so here he stood.

He snuck up behind her to tuck his chin into the crook of her neck, causing her to jump out of her seat.

"Kaleb McMurran! Don't scare me like that!" Her eyes were laughing.

"I'm sorry, but you looked so studious. Did I ever tell you that my best subjects in school revolved around girls who looked as smart as you do right now?" He was slowly backing her into a corner.

Anna looked around for safety. "I'll just bet they were. Now, Kaleb, I've work to do. You can't just come barging in here and think—" She stopped herself as he captured her in his arms. "Wait a minute. Does my mother know you're up here?"

"Yes." He wiggled his eyebrows and bent to nibble on her neck.

She bit back on the moan. "How did you convince her to let you in?"

"To your bedroom?"

"No, the house."

He looked at her, and they both laughed. "I'm very charming." At her raised brow, he conceded. "Your father said it was okay."

"Ah."

He kissed her, and she kissed him back, each once again lost in the other. He whispered in her ear, "Do you feel what you do to me every time? Imagine my embarrassment while grocery shopping when thoughts of you pop in to play with my libido." He bit her ear.

"I guess you should spend more time in the frozen food section."

As the needs continued to rise within each of them, Anna was forced to think for the both of them. "Kaleb, I don't think this is a good idea here."

"Then tell me where because I need you. Right now."

She could not only feel that he was serious but could see it. She pushed away from him, smirking. "Why don't I pack up my things while you calm down, and we'll go get something to eat?" She moved to her desk.

"I like a woman who takes charge."

She swatted at him playfully as Kaleb looked down at her books.

"What are these?"

"These are research. I went over to my grandmother's house a couple weeks ago and spoke with her about this ring business because I had found something quite interesting. I'll show you over dinner."

"Oh, so we really are going to eat? I thought that was just an excuse to get you out of the house from under the watchful eyes of Rose."

Anna sighed. "I know she frustrates you. She frustrates me, but she is my mother, and I have to believe that she has my best interests at heart."

"Okay. But just for that, you're buying dinner."

"Then I get to pick the restaurant."

They headed down the stairs to say "goodnight" to Anna's parents and were greeted immediately by Rose.

"Anna, you have not eaten yet tonight. Is Kaleb going to take you to dinner?"

Anna noticed the sudden change in how her mother addressed the man standing beside her but made no comment. "Yes. That's where we're headed now."

"Good. Kaleb," she inquired as she stepped closer to him, "did Anna tell you about her offer from New York?" Rose waited only a beat and knew that victory hung in the balance by the expression on his face.

"Not yet, Rose, but she did mention that she had much to tell me over dinner. I can only assume that New York would have been the topic of choice."

"Well, her father and I are beaming. I hope you do not mind, Anna darling, but I took it upon myself to tell your father. He thinks that if Richard Carlyle is writing a ballet and wants you for the lead, then you have received one of life's greatest honors. It is just such good news that I could not wait." She clapped her hands together.

"Yes, Mother, I can see that. Now if you'll excuse us, Kaleb and I are off to dinner." She took two steps to the door and glanced at her mother over her shoulder. "And I won't be back tonight. I'll see you in the morning."

At her mother's slightly irritated face, Anna chalked up one point for her small victory.

Kaleb and Anna drove in companionable silence to the diner. He left the radio tuned in to a country station, and his hands gripped the wheel so hard, his knuckles turned white. Anna could feel the air simmering around them and wondered if that silence would soon erupt.

Frannie waved at them long enough to break away from the factory worker she was flirting with at the counter. They sat at a corner booth and began to read the menu. Frannie brought them each a glass of water, and Anna guzzled it greedily. Still, Kaleb said nothing.

Finally, Anna could stand it no longer. "Kaleb, talk to me."

He looked at her briefly. "About what?"

Anna sighed. The day was only getting longer. "You know what."

He placed his menu on the table with an icy calm that should have fooled no one. "You must be talking about your offer from New York. Funny, I don't recall you mentioning that. Oh, wait, you didn't. I had to hear it from your mother. Did you see how it pained her to tell me?"

"Sarcasm does not become you, Kaleb."

"Really? And what does? Honesty? I seem to recall someone saying she deserved honesty, and I gave it to her." Anna looked down at her hands. "Don't like having your words thrown back in your face, Anna? Well, too bad. They fit."

"I was going to tell you—"

"When? After you'd bought your ticket? Nice timing, as always."

This time it was she who had eyes of cold. "Don't bring up the past now. Not now."

"Why not? It seems rather fitting don't you think? History repeating itself all over again. Right after I gave my heart to you."

"You never gave it to me the first time."

Frannie stopped in her tracks on the way to their table, pad of paper poised, ready to take their order. She eased away slowly.

Kaleb's face distorted, and he looked away. He chose his words carefully as he pondered the parking lot out the window. "You never chose to accept it for all it was." He slid out of the booth. "I think I'll take you home. Tonight may not be a good night for us after all."

Anna stood and met him toe-to-toe. "Yes, you're right. History is repeating itself. We're in the middle of something unpleasant, and you're choosing to run. Maybe not as far as Colorado, but you're running nonetheless." She swung her purse over her shoulder. "Frannie, call me a cab, please." She met Kaleb's gaze with all the courage she could muster. "I don't need a ride from you, Kaleb. Right now, I don't really need anything." She went in to the back room of the diner, and Kaleb stormed out, leaving Frannie to stare after both of them.

* * * * *

Anna found herself on Madelaine's overstuffed couch, sipping coffee she did not want. Madelaine turned on a soft radio station for background noise and sat facing her friend on the sofa.

"That was a pretty low blow for Kaleb to tell you that this was like what you two had gone through before. Even for Kaleb." She tucked a stray piece of her reddish hair behind her ear.

"What do you mean, 'even for Kaleb'?"

Maddy sighed. "Anna, after you took off for fame and fortune, Kaleb worked like a dog and did not exactly remain a very nice person. He was bitter, rude, and angry. He even hit on me and not in the most gentlemanly of ways." She chuckled slightly and drank her coffee.

Anna gaped at her. "What do you mean he hit on you?"

"Oops." Maddy set her cup down. "I just mean that Kaleb needed to burn you out of his system. And one night, a bunch of us were down by the boats watching some guys race. Kaleb got hold of some real good beer—and by that I mean cheap and lots of it—and we all proceeded to drink our underage selves into oblivion. Later that night, we sort of, made out by the fire. But I soon realized that I was just going to be a bandage for the boo-boo he had already named after you, so I told him to back off and sober up. He was none too happy with me at the time, but a couple days later he thanked me, and we've been friends ever since."

Anna gave this some consideration. She stared at Maddy in amazement.

"And by the way, I am insanely jealous that you get to kiss that gorgeous mouth as often as you do. Is he still as good as he used to be?"

Anna could only laugh at her predicament. "Better."

Maddy made a sound of pain. "Don't torment me, Anna. And I suppose he's just superb in bed?" At her friend's little smile, she waved her away. "Here we are supposed to be talking about how sad you are, and instead you manage to make me green over the two of you. Thanks. This coffee will not do. I need wine. Want a glass?" She got up to go to the kitchen.

120

"Sure. Why not?" Anna followed her into the pale yellow room.

"All I want is one date with your brother so that he'll see how fantastic I am, but no, I spend most Saturday nights here at home scrap booking old family photos."

"I'm sorry."

"Anna, I can hear the laughter in your voice. Cut it out."

"I'm sorry."

"And quit saying you're sorry." She handed Anna a goblet of wine. "Cheers. Let's drink to the idiots in our lives." She drank deeply.

"Maybe I should be drinking to myself, Maddy."

"Oh, no, you need to keep the focus on the game. On him. He was the jerk; let's not forget that."

"But I probably should have told him about the offer."

Maddy thought about this. "Yeah, you probably should have. But he could have talked to you in a more civilized way than he did."

"I know."

"You're really hung up on him, huh?"

"Like you wouldn't believe."

Madelaine finished off her first glass with ease and refilled it, pushing Anna's glass closer to her friend so that she would catch up. "I love falling in love. It's once you've fallen that the real problems begin. And what if no one's there to catch you?"

Anna grinned into the goblet. "Maddy, you have such a way with words."

"I probably should have taught English instead of band, huh?"

They drank in silence for a few minutes. Then Anna said, "Thanks for letting me stay here tonight. I'd rather have my mother think I'm with Kaleb than know I'm alone."

"No problem. You can stay here anytime. You hungry?" Maddy got up to rummage through her cupboards.

"Starved. We never got around to dinner."

"Normally, that'd be a good thing, but in this case…I think we need Chinese food. I'll have them deliver."

"How do you eat like this so late in the day and stay so slim?" Anna eyed her friend.

"I burn it off the fun way…when I can. See, now you're making me depressed again, so I'll just need to eat more. Three egg rolls, no less. What do you want?" Maddy asked as she dialed the number from memory.

All Anna could do was laugh.

* * * * *

Kaleb awoke groggy and miserable. He scowled at himself in the mirror above his sink, ungrateful that he had yet to shower before looking at his reflection. He had not bothered to shave in the past few days, and he thought it suited his mood perfectly.

Stumbling to the kitchen, he switched on the coffee maker and slammed his toe into an open cupboard. Swearing with merit, he reached for two mugs—and stopped short.

What was he doing? He only needed one mug for coffee that morning, not two. The other mug was tossed unceremoniously back onto the shelf before he slammed the door shut. He cursed himself for being so foolish. Already Anna Keller had planted herself so firmly in his life that he was getting used to the idea of making coffee for the two of them in the mornings. Well, obviously she did not want her coffee from his kitchen every day for the rest of her life, and he had been foolish to think otherwise.

He sat down at the table to try to decide how to spend his day. He had finished work on the Harrisons' house some time ago, but they were very good advertisement for other prospective clients. He needed to seriously consider starting his own business and taking other families up on their offers.

He would not be able to do that if he moved to New York.

Moving away was no longer an option; Anna's silence over the issue had made that very clear. When the knock sounded at the front door, he cursed whoever was behind it but dragged himself and his coffee to it. Anna stood on the other side, looking fresh and clean in red shorts and an American flag t-shirt. She allowed her gaze to travel up, then down his disheveled appearance and instantly felt sorry for the grief she had obviously caused.

She cleared her throat. "Can I come in?"

"I'm busy."

"I can see that. You and your coffee must be having quite a time in there."

"I'll see you later."

He started to shut the door in her face, but she put her hand on it to prevent him from doing so. "Kaleb, please. Don't be mean. I've come to apologize."

He scanned her face and opened the door wider, allowing her to step through it. Anna went to the middle of his living room and faced him. "I'm sorry. I should have made a point of telling you about the offer before my—before you heard it elsewhere. I already had a nice chat with my mother about that, and although I do not think she is really all that sorry, she still apologized to me for causing me discomfort. I came here to do exactly that. It's obvious you're still angry with me,

122

and I cannot really blame you. Maddy and I discussed it over a large bottle of wine, and she sides with you. Mostly." When he remained silent, she straightened her shoulders. "I've said what I needed to say, so if you're just going to stand there, I'll be leaving."

"You sure do know how to make it difficult to fight with a man, duchess," he told her as he prevented her from making a quick escape. She looked up at him with such trusting and sorry eyes that he could not resist taking her bottom lip between his teeth. "You're right. You should be sorry. But you're not the only one. I should never have thrown the past at you the way I did."

"That's okay. I threw it right back at you, didn't I?"

"I wasn't running, Anna. I just didn't want you to see me beg. You can make me beg. You know that, don't you?"

He was doing something wildly delicious to her ears and her throat, and it was causing her knees to buckle. Sensing this, Kaleb swept her up into his arms and carried her to his bathroom. So dazed was she, she did not realize his intentions until he had the sprayer on and her shirt over her head.

"Kaleb, I've already had my shower today, and my make-up is ready. I don't feel like doing it again."

"Oh, that's too bad, duchess, because I feel like messing you up." He had her naked and hot in seconds. He joined her under the pulsating water and fused his mouth to hers as he pressed her against the cold tiles of the shower wall. The cold did not seem to bother her as she forgot why she was there in the first place.

Hadn't they been fighting? Was he still mad at her? She did not think so as he ran soapy hands over her breasts and up her middle. He allowed his fingers to linger in certain areas longer than in others, and she could feel herself clawing at him, trying to gain purchase to keep from sliding right down the drain. She was aware that some part of her raked her nails over his shoulders, but instead of panicking, she felt only more alive. She grabbed his butt and squeezed playfully as she used her tongue to tease the edges of his mouth and jaw.

Not being able to hold out much longer, Kaleb raised her off her toes. Anna wrapped herself around his waist as he plunged into her, thrusting with her back against the wall until both of them became weak from the effort. As the tension built, and the water sprayed over their slick bodies, he ordered her to tell him.

"Say it, Anna. Tell me."

"I love you, Kaleb. Oh, I love you more than you could possibly understand!" As she flew over the edge into madness, he exploded inside of her.

* * * * *

An hour later, Anna and Kaleb lay on his bed, wet and dripping and drained from their shower. Kaleb lifted his head just enough to look at her.

"That might be the cleanest I've ever gotten."

He allowed his head to fall back to the mattress as she smiled toward the ceiling. "You and me both. I've now had two showers today, and it's not even noon."

"Want to go for three?"

"No." She sat to reach for the towel and began to dry off. "I have to get back to finding those hands."

"I know the closest pair you could have right now." He tried to use them on her, but she shoved him away. "Spoilsport."

"Not those kinds of hands, McMurran. The hands in my grandfather's ring."

"Want me to help?" He reached for his own towel.

"I would love your help."

They dressed in companionable silence, Anna for the second time that day. When they were finally seated at the kitchen table over two mugs of coffee, Anna brought him up to date with the books she had found and the painting she and her grandmother had discussed.

"Apparently, I'm not the one who was supposed to find this picture now, but Grandma thinks I may have found this copy for a reason. The original is still out there somewhere."

"You have it with you?"

"It's in the book in the car."

"Why don't you go get it?"

Anna retrieved the book, and Kaleb studied the picture intently. "Your grandmother was quite a hottie."

"She'd be thrilled to know you felt that way about her."

"It just gives me something to look forward to when you're her age."

For a moment, neither of them said anything as they let the awkwardness of the moment pass. Anna continued about the picture.

"I think Grammy feels that one of my brothers will find the original. I wish you could have been there to hear the story of how my grandfather convinced her to let him paint her portrait. Her father would not allow them to be together, and it took another two years for them to find each other before they could finally be a couple."

"Sounds familiar."

Anna realized the sudden intensity behind the truth of that statement. "But to listen to her tell the story and watch her face as she did...you could just see how much she misses him. I know not all relationships and marriages are easy, but they really made it look like theirs was."

"So what do you want to do about this today?" He gestured to her stack of books and notes.

"You'll really help me?"

"Anna, when are you going to believe me?" He reached for her hand across the table; she took it gingerly. "I love you. I cannot say that enough to you. Yes, I'll help you. I haven't enjoyed being with anyone as much as I have enjoyed being with you. Ever."

Anna knew that was the moment her decision had been made. She gripped Kaleb's hand tightly. "Then there's something I need to show you." She bounded from the table to get her shoes.

"What?"

"It's something I've been him-hawing about, and now I know it's the right thing for me to do. But I need to find Maddy. And your dad."

"My dad?" He scratched his head, worried that Anna was losing her mind. "Don't tell me you've decided that older men are better for you?"

"No, silly. But I cannot get into this right now. What time is it?" She glanced at his kitchen clock. "When will be Maddy get out of school?"

"She has just about three more weeks, but I don't think I can wait—"

"No, I mean today. How much time?" She brushed through her hair.

"Couple more hours. Look, Anna, what is going on? You've got me worried."

"No need. It's just one more step in the process of finding my part of the ring. I need you to call Maddy at the school. Tell her you'll pick her up at the end of the day. And then I need the two of you to meet me at this address." She scribbled it down on scrap paper she found near his phone and handed it to him.

He gave it a cursory glance. "It's at the other end of the island. Kind of near your brother Ian, isn't it?"

"Yes. Huh, I hadn't thought of that. Anyway, that doesn't matter. I need you to do this for me." She went to him and took his face in her hands. "Please, Kaleb, trust me."

How could he do anything but? Once those pale eyes were on him, he was lost to her. "I do trust you, but—"

"Good." She gave him a loud, smacking kiss. "I'll see you at the end of her school day. I have to call your father. I hope my cell phone is in my purse. I'll see you later!" She was a blur of color and out the door.

Chapter XI

Kaleb could barely concentrate as he finished up for the day at the lighthouse. He could barely concentrate as he pulled in front of Madelaine's school. Anna's behavior was odd, to say the least. And it was slowly eating at the inner lining of his stomach.

He spotted Maddy come flying out of the building, the afternoon sun hitting the red in her hair at just the right angles. Her long flowered skirt fluttered against her shapely legs in the breeze, and her expression was grim as she yanked his car door open.

"Kaleb, what is going on? Is Anna hurt?" She sat and strapped herself in after tossing her book bag onto his backseat.

"No, she's not hurt. But something weird is happening. We have to go meet her somewhere right now." He pulled out into the heavy after-school traffic.

"Did you two make up from last night?"

"How did you know about that?"

"She spent the evening with me. Oh, God."

"What?"

"I just hope that she's not upset over what I told her about you and me."

"You and me? What about you and—" He stopped mid-sentence and aimed a cool look in her direction. "Maddy, please tell me you didn't tell her about my ridiculous attempts to—woo you by the fire."

"You call that 'wooing'?"

"Maddy..."

"I'm sorry. Yes, I told her." At his exasperated sigh, she hurried to explain. "I was trying to let her know that I thought she was wrong for not telling you about New York. And I was trying to explain what you were like when she left. Somehow it all sounded like a good idea at the time."

"I cannot imagine why telling Anna about our little—episode would be a good idea. Did you tell her that you rejected me? And that I was grateful?" he asked as he rounded a corner a bit too sharply.

"No, Kaleb, I told her that you and I stayed in bed for a week because you simply couldn't stay away from me." When he swore, she punched him lightly on the arm. "Yes, I told her." He continued to search the streets for their destination. "You have no idea what this is regarding?"

"No, I do not. Believe me, I wish I did. It has something to do with my father."

"Your father?"

"Yeah. Apparently, she had to call him into this. I have no idea why." He intercepted her question before she could even form the words.

They finished their ride together and pulled into a parking lot where they saw Anna first and Kaleb's father second. Anna was grinning like an idiot, and Marcus looked sheepish.

Kaleb was out of the car like a shot and hurried to them. "Anna, what is going on?"

"Let Maddy get here, too."

Madelaine skipped across the gravel to their sides. "Hello, Mr. McMurran. Okay, Anna, this had better be good. You know, I like how you assumed that I would have nothing to do after school today, and I could just go wherever you needed me to go."

"Did you have anything planned?" Anna asked behind a small smile.

"No."

"Okay then—"

"Anna, Dad, if someone doesn't explain soon, I think I'll blow."

"Anna, this is your doing, so I think you should get the honors." Marcus winked at his son and stepped aside for her.

"Well...I'm renting this place." She angled her head toward the deserted building while Kaleb and Maddy stood with mouths open.

Madelaine spoke first. "Why?" All she could see was dust and broken glass.

"I'm starting my business here."

"You're opening a bakery?" Maddy asked incredulously as she indicated the old sign that now lay against the back of the building near the alley.

"No! I'm changing it into a dance studio!" She hugged herself from the excitement. "Well, it's not mine yet, but your dad says that once he puts the paperwork through, I should have no problem getting approved." No one spoke. "Well, what do you think?"

Maddy burst into screams and headed straight for an embrace. "Anna, I think it's incredible! You're going to own a studio! You'll be living here! On the island! I can hardly stand it!" She rocked her friend back and forth.

Kaleb remained quiet as he approached her and took her hands. "Are you sure this is what you want?" His eyes were stormy and inquisitive and unsettled. Anna found the combination to be alluring, arousing, and disturbing all at once.

"Yes. I've made my decision. I will be happy teaching here."

He hugged her so hard and so fast that it knocked the air from her lungs.

Marcus McMurran stepped forward. "Would you like to take them on the tour, Anna?" He dangled the keys in front of her face.

Anna twisted the knob and knocked cobwebs out of her face to let the group through to her new plan. Each of them walked around the building slowly, examining the workmanship and checking for things that would need to be renovated up to code. Kaleb had questions for his father while Maddy was spewing out numerous ideas for decoration and usefulness. Eventually, some of the initial excitement died down, and Madelaine inquired about Anna's living arrangements.

"Apparently, the former tenant had added a suite above with the owner's permission and lived there on occasion. Once I fix it up, I'll stay there. Until then, I'll just stay with my mother and father." She could feel Kaleb's eyes boring holes into her, but she dared not look at him for fear of revealing what her heart truly wanted from him, of him. From them.

Kaleb cleared his throat and asked, "Do your parents know?"

Anna turned to look at him for the first time in several minutes. "No. I'll tell them in my own time. Until then, I just want to celebrate!"

"That's my cue to leave. You should take your girl out for a nice dinner, Kaleb. And her friend, too, so that the three of you can plan together." Marcus began to leave.

"Mr. McMurran," Anna began, not at all sure of her footing in this area, "I don't think it would be fair to leave you and your wife out of the celebration. After all, it was you two who helped me to find this place."

"Mom's in on this, too?"

"'Fraid so, son. We were sworn to secrecy."

"Kaleb, if it's all right with you, I think we should include your folks. This celebration just won't be the same without them."

Kaleb looked down at the woman who had turned his life upside all those years ago and began to understand that she would do so for as long as he knew her. He touched her cheek, and neither of them noticed the curious look his father sent them nor the sigh Maddy released. He nodded, and the group was on their way to Kaleb's childhood home.

Several minutes later, Anna was apologizing to Rita McMurran for imposing on her hospitality. "When I suggested that you and your husband be included, Mrs. McMurran, I never though they would just barge into your home and take over like this." Anna looked around her at the chaos that was only just beginning.

"First, you call me Rita—like I told you before—and my husband Marcus. You're certainly old enough to do so. Second, I live for chaos. Raising two boys in this house settled my nerves over noise a long time ago." She reached for a large plastic bowl.

"My mother raised three children, and she could never have people over spur-of-the-moment like this. She'd be frazzled."

"It takes all kinds of people to raise children. Your mother is the kind of woman who likes order. That's all." She began to peel potatoes.

"You obviously know her kind very well." Anna fidgeted, not knowing what to do next. "Would you like some help, Mrs.—Rita?"

Rita smiled and handed Anna the peeler. "You go right ahead and peel these for me. I'll make mashed potatoes in a bit. For now, I'd better go see that my husband fired up the grill." She left through the back door.

Kaleb snuck up behind her as she hummed a tune and wrapped his arms around her waist. "Have I told you how happy you make me?"

Anna stopped her work long enough to hug him. "No. But I wouldn't mind hearing it now and again."

"I'd like to be able to tell you every day, Anna. Every day I'd like to be able to wake up next to you and tell you how lovely you are, how your smile starts my day on the best foot. To know that you are going to start your own studio right here within arm's reach…I don't know how to describe what that does to me. In fact, I'd like to talk to you about those living arrangements you told Maddy about. I was thinking—"

He had turned her around during the last moments of his speech, and she was looking up at him as he began to caress her shoulders. He was cut off by Evan slamming through the front door, baby in tow.

"Kaleb, stop pestering Anna and help me with all this stuff." He set Marissa down on the floor in her carrier while he held the door open for his wife with his hip. Michelle brought in a bag of groceries.

"Your timing could not be worse," Kaleb grumbled at him and took the other bag from his brother.

Anna quickly went back to peeling the potatoes as Michelle walked into the kitchen. She knew that look in Kaleb's eyes; she understood what it had meant.

She realized what he had been implying when he spoke of her living arrangements. And she silently scolded herself for almost saying "yes." Imagine what her mother would say if she were to live with a man! Anna, herself, had always said that she would not do such a thing without being married to him, but she was sure the farthest thing from Kaleb McMurran's mind was marriage.

She jumped at Michelle's voice. "Take it easy there, darlin', you might cut your hand at the rate you're peeling those." Michelle snapped a carrot in two and began to nibble.

"What? Oh, yes. Thank you." Anna ran the potatoes under the faucet.

"Are you all right?" Michelle asked.

"Yes, I'm fine. Just nervous. I'm sure Rita told you what I'm doing. It all seems very unreal still."

"I'm sure it does. I hope it's okay that they invited us for dinner, too. Mom said she wanted us to celebrate with you, but truthfully, they'll use any excuse to see little Marissa." Michelle's face appeared luminescent as she mentioned her daughter. "They're really marvelous grandparents."

"They seem cut out for it." Anna placed the stack of potatoes into the large pot on the stove.

"I imagine they'll want more grandchildren, but I don't think I'll be up to it any time soon. Guess they'll have to start bugging Kaleb."

Michelle watched Anna's expression cloud and wondered if her intentions were to stay with Kaleb. By the looks of things, Anna appeared either unsure of Kaleb or unsure of herself. She made a mental note to keep an ear open for the remainder of the day with regard to both of them to see if they were truly that blind to the other's needs.

Anna had never been a part of such a noisy and messy event. Rita and Marcus certainly kept a clean home, but they did not mind when something spilled or if someone spoke too loud to make him or herself heard over the rest of the din. She answered their questions as best as she could but mostly just watched and listened. Their family dynamic was very fascinating.

Kaleb kept an easy conversation going with his parents, Maddy, and his brother, but he watched Anna out of the corner of his eye. He saw that she seemed overwhelmed by all of it—the noise, the clamor, the four conversations going at once. He had a quick image in his mind of dinner at her home—candles, quite music playing in the background, "please" and "thank you" being tossed around every four seconds. Rose would likely fold the napkin across her lap, quite prim and proper, before she delicately sliced into the meal on her China that had probably been prepared by someone else. This image was interrupted by Marissa spitting up hugely all over her grandmother as she made fussy noises and told Michelle not to worry. She would clean both the baby and herself in the kitchen.

Dessert was eaten outside on lawn chairs in the early evening shade. Madelaine and Michelle discussed the school and what Michelle and Evan were going to do with Marissa once she went back to work in the fall. Kaleb and his father argued over something they had seen in the news while Rita and Evan played with the baby, who had recently begun to stay awake for longer periods of time. Anna was quietly content with her cup of coffee until her cell phone rang. She went to her purse to answer it.

Rose's voice pierced her solitude. "Anna, dear, where are you?"

"Hi, Mother." Kaleb shot her a glance before she turned away. "I'm at the McMurrans' home for dinner. They invited me."

"Oh. Well, are you having fun?"

Fumbled by the question, Anna answered quietly. "Yes. It's been lovely."

"Darling, Richard called again and needs an answer soon. I told him not to be surprised if you bought a plane ticket as early as next week. Now you know you are welcome to stay with your father and me for as long as you want, but why wait when you have opportunity practically banging your door down? Also, I have invited your brothers for dinner this coming weekend as a sort of going away party for you. They are both available, so I thought I should book them as soon as possible. I will not bother you anymore this evening. You enjoy your visit. I will be spending the day with your grandmother tomorrow. You are welcome to join me. Call me later if you plan on being out all night again." Rose disconnected before Anna could respond to anything she had said.

As she folded her phone back into her bag, her head began to throb lightly at her temples and at the base of her neck. She was rubbing them absently as Kaleb came up behind her to place his hand on her shoulder. She jolted at his touch.

"Everything okay?"

Her eyes were lost again, as he had seen so many times before, especially more recently. He cursed her mother silently for dimming their light and taking away from the enjoyment of her evening.

"It's going to be much harder to tell her than I had imagined."

Kaleb put his arms around her. He pressed his lips to her head, which caused his mother to place her hand over her heart, link her other hand with her husband's, and sigh.

"Would you like me to be with you when you tell her?"

Anna almost broke down at that small and simple offer. Her heart rolled slowly in her chest. "No. This is something I need to do on my own. It has to come from me." She picked her head up from his shoulder to look up at him. "But I thank you. Not only do you love me, but you are becoming such a good friend to me."

The family had been quietly watching their exchange while they tried to continue talking. Marcus broke into everyone's thoughts. "I see my little granddaughter is asleep. Why don't we put her down in our bed and play cards? Who's in a betting mood tonight?"

The murmurs soon became shouts as each person tried to claim his or her champion status. As soon as Marissa was tucked safely and surrounded by pillows on her grandparents' king size bed, the adults gathered around the table for a raucous game of "Bullshit." Anna had never played cards, nor had she ever heard of such a game, so she was somewhat appalled that she would have to yell the word "bullshit" at any one of them at the table if she thought he or she was bluffing. She realized to her horror that she would need to say this to even Kaleb's parents. After Kaleb caught her bluffing a couple of times, she loosened up, and by the end of the evening, got the hang of it. When the winnings were claimed by Evan, he rubbed it in his wife's face. No one had beaten Michelle in quite some time.

"So, Anna," Maddy began as she cleaned up the cards and dishes, "when will you be able to start renovating your new studio?"

Madelaine asked the question with such enthusiasm that she tried to settle her stomach subconsciously as it caused her to think about her mother and what she would say when she told her. She deserved this evening of happiness and was not going to allow anyone to spoil it.

"Mr. McMurran—Marcus said that I should have my answer from the landlord by tomorrow, so I guess I could start in a month after I sign the lease and close." She smiled brightly.

"I, for one, cannot wait to help you!" Madelaine bubbled over with excitement. "You've been gone for so long, and now I get you back in my life— just like that! It's a gift, Anna, a real gift." Maddy discreetly wiped at her eyes.

"Don't make me cry, Madelaine Murphy. I don't need that right now." Anna wiped at her eyes, too.

"I think we should take our little one and go home. It's late, and I have work in the morning." Evan took the car seat with him into his parents' room to gather his daughter.

Once Evan, Michelle, and Marissa were pulling away in their car, Maddy said "goodbye" to Rita and Marcus and Anna and Kaleb. Then Kaleb walked Anna out to his truck.

He pressed her body up against it. "Anna, stay the night with me. Let me take you back to my apartment."

She ran her hands over his firm butt. "I thought you'd never ask."

As soon as Kaleb bolted the front door to his home, Anna pounced. She grabbed him and pushed him back against the wall. Fusing her mouth to his, she took possession of him. The assault to his senses was devastating. He was suddenly craving her skin in a way that meant he had been starving all this time and was finally being fed. He tried to undo her shirt, but she pushed his hands away as she ripped his from his shoulders, sending buttons flying. She undid his buckle and threw it aside, not sure if she heard it crash into a lamp or if the crash came from somewhere deep inside of her. She forced him down to the ground, but he went willingly.

Her hands were everywhere at once, and he thought he would go blind from the insanity of it all. There was such heat, such untapped passion, that he wondered why no one was coming to their rescue. And he would have gladly turned anyone away. For he could allow her to claim him like this each time, every time, and still it would not be enough.

When her head dipped below his waist, he gripped the carpet for support, arched his hips, and almost gave in to the swirling needs that were sure to erupt from him. She was a witch; she was an angel. Her hair caught the light from the kitchen, and he saw it evolve into warmth around her face, the wicked gleam in her eyes adding to the danger and the arousal. He wanted to cry out, to beg for something, but did not know what to beg for. He had allowed other women to initiate intimacy with him before, but this was something entirely different. This was life-giving and destructive, and if he died from the sheer pleasure of it, he could think of no other or better way to leave this world.

Anna ripped her clothes away, exposing slick flesh, and grabbed his hands to take possession of her. He remained on the floor, writhing beneath her, but now he could finally roam over her form freely as she arched her back and took him deep inside her.

The first orgasm slammed into her and sent her flying, calling out his name, rearing her head back and forth. But she was still not finished with him. She kept him beneath her, slowly riding him up, up, up to the edge of madness and back down again. He brought her mouth down to his and devoured her. She felt the liquid pull stirring again as she began to mount him faster and faster until neither could see the end nor the beginning.

She arched back one last time as she crested. He emptied himself into her on a cry of only her name.

* * * * *

Kaleb stared into the dark from his place on the floor. Anna breathed steadily by his side. He wanted to move her to the comfort of his bed, but she was already sleeping, so he decided to wait a bit longer.

What had happened between them only moments ago? He sure was not complaining, but this side to Anna was so different, even from the Anna who had seduced him just a couple of weeks ago.

Had it only been that long? How was it that he was losing track of time? She had done this to him. When he thought back to earlier in the year, he had begun to work on the island's landmarks and had gotten settled into this apartment, but he had known deep down—even then—that he was not considering this a permanent solution. Nothing had felt permanent back then.

Not until Anna Keller had walked back into his life.

He pulled her closer, and she stirred. Sensing she was partially awake, he lifted her to him and carried her to his bed. She shivered, so he closed his windows a bit and pulled the covers over them. She pressed her body to his, which awakened his. Anna had needed to burn out the fire earlier that night. She had a rage inside of her that she had needed to quench, to satiate. And he had let her. Now Kaleb needed something from her.

He rose above her and made love to her in a way that would settle his heart, commit her to him in his mind.

He did so all throughout the night.

Chapter XII

The next day Anna split her time between a meeting with Marcus at his real estate office and reading through the books that related to her search for the ring. Her mother was gone to her grandmother's house, which created both tension and comfort in her. The tension was a result of Anna knowing that eventually she would need to tell her and her father about her latest endeavors. The comfort was a result of cowardice—Anna did not have to face the music yet. She could hide behind her mother's absence for the day and put off the inevitable until later.

Her meeting went well, her application for the lease approved quickly as Marcus had predicted. She sat in his office signing a multitude of forms and hugged him before she even realized that she had. He seemed pleased about it, though, and laughed off her unease. He promised to put in a call to the landlord to see if he could get her the keys sooner so that she could begin renovations earlier than she had anticipated.

Without anything more to do that afternoon, Anna decided to visit her grandfather's grave.

She rode her bike to the north end of the island where the cemetery was nestled between an old farm and the small airport, which only allowed residents of Grosse Ile to fly their own single engine planes for recreational purposes. As she glided through the wrought-iron gated entrance, she felt guilty for not bringing flowers along with her. Then she chuckled because her grandfather would call her foolish for thinking that she had to do so in the first place.

Finding his marker was easy since the plot had been chosen all those years ago when he had moved her grandmother and himself to this corner of the world. The tombstone was not yet placed since his death was so recent, but the color-coded ribbon allowed onlookers to know who had been buried here. Anna breathed in the fresh late spring air and wished fleetingly for a jacket. She leaned her bike against a nearby tree and knelt down at the foot of his burial place.

She remained quiet for a time, allowing the air to stir the senses and the memories she had of this man. All at once she could feel the stubble of his cheek pressed against her face as she laughed up at him while she threw her arms out to be taken into his as a child; his laugh exploded out of his chest as she told him about one of the few pranks she had played on her brothers; his eyes, so very much like hers, dimmed when she boarded the plane for New York.

Anna suddenly missed Patrick O'Connor with an intensity she had never before experienced.

She felt her heart speak out to him and decided that if anyone saw her talking to an unmarked grave, she did not care if she appeared silly. The words were already forming on her lips.

"Pappy, it's nice to be home." She brushed at some grass that had stuck itself to her leg. "Grammy misses you terribly, but I think you've been visiting her in her sleep, and that gives her comfort. I'm sorry I wasn't here when you were so ill in your final days. I'd always thought the dance was more important than anything. And I know, you wanted me to keep at it. So it's unwise to waste energy on any regrets. But you're not here to tell me otherwise, so if I decide to regret a little, I'm entitled." She swallowed the tension in her throat. "The dance is no longer what it used to be, Pappy. For the first time in as long as I can remember, I feel whole. This place feels like home. Kaleb feels like home. You remember him, don't you? He was usually getting into some kind of trouble—but not too much. Just enough to cause my mother to worry about my hanging around with him. My mother is another issue. I'm finally content with the decisions I'm making in my life, and I cannot even share them with her. Not yet. And you've left the three of us a—project, I'd guess you'd call it. She's very unhappy with you about it. And for the first time that I can ever recall, I don't care. I want to find this ring. My part of the ring. And you know what? I think the search has helped me to put areas of my life into perspective. It's certainly helped me to bond with people instead of music. I feel like I am the kind of friend Madelaine deserves. Kaleb, too. Maybe that was your intention. To help your poor lost granddaughter to gain some perspective. Well, if it was, then I thank you." She stood and brushed off her shorts. "I'm sorry it took me so long to stop by and see you. I'll try not to keep too much time between visits from now on." She went to her bike and climbed onto the seat. "I love you, Pappy. I hope you knew how much before you left."

As Anna rode off down the bike path, a circle encased in white gold began to pulse, reinforcing the new bonds of friendship.

138

* * * * *

Kaleb decided that working side-by-side with Evan was very therapeutic. Throughout their childhood, the two of them had sweated out many a summer working outdoors. Although Kaleb had always been the one who felt more successful with the hands-on approach, Evan had still been able to hold his own. He did so now as they installed dry wall in the upper most section of the lighthouse.

Evan caught his arm on a nail and swore. "I gotta wash this off," he said as he climbed down toward the sink.

"Wimp. I've had bleeders before. You just need to run with it."

"I am. Right to the sink."

"Fatherhood is making you weak."

"Ah, but it actually makes me stronger. See, I figure if I take care of this now, I won't get an infection that will lead to an illness that could lead to my untimely death. In this way, I'll actually be around to ward off the boys that will surely be knocking at my daughter's door." He wrapped a towel around his arm and applied pressure.

Kaleb hammered in the last of the nails on the corner piece and stepped down from the ladder. "Pour me some of that iced tea Michelle sent with you."

As Evan obliged while trying to keep balance with only one arm in use, he turned the conversation to Anna. "You plan on helping her with the studio?"

"If she wants my help, yeah." He chugged the cold beverage greedily.

"So she hasn't asked you for help." Evan drank from his own glass thoughtfully.

"No, not directly. I mean, she has sort of implied it in the way she talks about her plans." Kaleb fidgeted.

"So what exactly are her plans then?"

Kaleb shrugged. "She's going to open the studio and teach little kids. I'm sure she's working on some designs right now."

"Oh, so that's where she is today?"

Kaleb huffed out a breath. "What is with all the questions? I don't know where she is today." And that was really what was bugging him in the first place.

"Interesting." Evan refilled his glass.

"Why is it interesting? Because we're a couple, you think we need to know where the other is all the time?"

"So you are a couple."

"I never said that."

"Yes, you just did." Evan removed the towel from his arm and ran it under the cool water from the faucet.

"Look. We are seeing each other. No, Anna has not told me what all of her plans are. Yet. I don't even think she's told her folks, and when she does, she's going to need a friend." The thought of that discussion caused his stomach to rile a bit.

"Kaleb, I'm worried about you. I saw what her leaving did to you the last time, and—"

"She's not leaving, Evan. She's already signed the lease. You were there last night for the celebration."

"I know. And we are all very happy for her. But, Kaleb, what if this thing the two of you have is something to give her the encouragement she needs along the way? When I see you look at her, I see things I never thought I'd see floating around in that head of yours. But when she looks at you, I see something altogether different."

He thought about this all throughout the remainder of the day as he and Evan finished the dry wall in the upstairs. Never wanting to admit his brother might be right, Kaleb did his best to ignore the raw feeling he carried with him into his gut as he cleaned up from the job later that evening. He had not heard from Anna all day, and that more than bothered him. His brother's words plagued his mind as he drove first to Anna's house, then to the would-be studio. No one had been at her home, and he thought she might have gotten the keys to the building. Upon seeing her car in the empty lot, he gripped the steering wheel harder. He slammed his door shut and walked up to the screen in the back of the building. He stood in the doorway, gazing in at her in awe.

She must have been working like a fiend for the past several hours because most of the cobwebs were gone, and she had obviously pushed aside some of the lighter pieces of equipment and furniture. That left just enough space for her to begin to envision the middle of the dance floor, and it seemed that she was doing exactly that.

She was wearing skin-tight hot pants in black with an off-the-shoulder black leotard, leg warmers, and ballet shoes. Her small portable stereo was plugged in at the corner, and she crouched down in the center of the floor, her face shielded by her knees as she bent her head down into them. She had pulled her hair into a loose ponytail, and small pieces were beginning to escape and stick to her already perspiring shoulders. As the music began to float from the CD, Kaleb could see by the lost look of intensity in her eyes that she was not really there in that told dusty bakery, waiting to transform it into a newly renovated studio. She was somewhere where only the music could reach her, and he could not.

He watched, studied, observed. He had never seen her perform before this moment. Yes, he had bundles of newspaper clippings, but those were moments frozen in time because some clever photographer had the keen sense to capture the strain of her muscles and the anticipation of the next move in the dance. But to witness a live performance, where he could hear her labored breathing, see the sweat begin to pool on her back, and feel the music as it crested and washed over her, was an entirely different experience.

Kaleb's heart fell just a bit farther into the abyss.

When she stopped moving, he realized the music was over and that she was staring at him. His vision had blurred for just a second until he, too, had been transported to whatever place she had been taken during the dance. She turned the stereo to "off," grabbed her hand towel to wipe her face, and shot a smile in his direction.

"Hi, sexy."

His heart was in his throat, and he was almost ready to tell her to go back—that New York should not have to sacrifice such talent and passion—that she belonged on that stage. Then he saw her tuck the necklace—his necklace—back into the top part of her leotard, and all of those thoughts drained from his head.

"Hi, yourself. I've always wanted a private performance." He walked to her and gathered her close against her small protest.

"Kaleb, I really need a shower."

"You smell just fine to me. In fact, I kind of like the slick look. Imagine how slippery you are with all that sweat." He began to nibble on her right ear as she squirmed against him, which only added to the excitement.

"Kaleb, please. I've been running around doing something all day." She pulled away as she laughed.

"So you managed to get the keys ahead of schedule." He surveyed the room.

"Yes. I've been quite busy."

"I can see that." He began to pace the room slowly.

She could sense the tension and wished she had not been the cause of it. "I'm sorry I didn't call you today, Kaleb. I had a lot going on."

"I can tell."

"Kaleb—" She went to him and pressed her fingers to his arm, lightly. "I can see that you're frustrated with me, and I suppose I don't blame you. But after your father gave me the keys, I needed to be here on my own for a while. I needed to begin to get a vision of things to come. I've never done anything like this for myself, and I needed to see if I could really do it. I hope you'll forgive me."

He looked down into her pale eyes. Seeing his future in them did not ease the panic he still felt lingering at the edges of his stomach. But he took her hand in his and quieted her by pressing his lips to the center of her palm.

"There's nothing to forgive."

"Thank you. Look at everything I've done today. Maddy's called me five times with different ideas, and she swore she was going to stop by to see me, but I quietly pleaded with her to give me some space, and she gave in. Which is really a big deal for her. I don't think I'll be able to prevent her from coming out here tomorrow, but I figure by then I'll have had enough time here to start accepting other people's ideas on this place." She ran a hand lovingly over the trim around the window.

"Sounds like you've got it all planned out."

Anna could hear the worry, and although she did not like it, she could not help but feel partially pleased that she caused it, considering how Kaleb had turned her world upside down in such a short amount of time. She smiled but remained where she was, across the room from him.

"Not all. I was hoping you could help me."

"Me?"

"Yes. I know you have so many projects going right now, but I could really use your assistance. If you can squeeze in some time for me."

Kaleb remained where he was across the room from her as he considered all that his brother had said earlier in the day. He had known that in the most intimate recesses of his mind this was all that he had been waiting for.

To be needed by Anna.

He crossed to her, took her hands in his, and said, quite simply, "I can squeeze you in."

Smiling like fools, they locked in to each other for a staggering kiss.

A sound at the doorway caught their attention, and they turned to see her mother, gaping at them.

"Mother." Anna's shocked voice reverberated around the room as she could feel Kaleb's arms tighten around her waist as she would have surely tried to escape them.

Rose took a gingerly step forward. There was ice in her eyes. "I heard about your new little venture."

"Who—who told you?" Still Kaleb held her.

"Not the person who should have, Anna Keller." She said her name with such disgust that Anna was almost ashamed it was she her mother spoke of. "There I was with your grandmother having a delightful lunch at the club when one of the wait staff drops by our table to send her congratulations to you on your new—purchase." Rose looked around at the room, scorn emanating from her entire being.

"I did not purchase it, Mother. I'm leasing. And I was going to tell you and Dad—"

"Really? When would that have been, Anna? At the wedding? Because I am quite certain that Mr. McMurran is going to make an honest woman of you. Isn't that right, sir?" She angled her head toward him ever so slightly.

Kaleb released Anna and took a step forward. "Now you listen—"

"No." Anna reached for his arm before he could finish his sentence. "I will handle this, Kaleb."

Rose watched in quiet surprise as her daughter blocked the man to face the woman.

"Our relationship is not any of your concern, Mother. Not right now. And it has never been."

Anna saw her mother arch her brow for a brief second before quickly regaining her composure. "I tend to disagree, Anna, particularly when other people have made observations about the two of you—observations that I do not care for in the least."

"I don't care about their thoughts, Mother, any more than you really do."

"Now you wait a minute, young lady—"

"No, you wait." Anna took another step toward her mother, causing Rose to flush subtly at the tone of her daughter's voice. "You only care because Kaleb is not what you thought I should have. Well, I'm sorry that you feel that way, but you have had no right to interfere. It is not as though Kaleb is dangerous to me, Mother. How did you manage to keep his letters from getting to me?" As Rose paled, Anna felt the slight victory and went with it. "Of course I caught on to that. How could you keep that from me? Those letters were mine to read. And the letters I sent back to him? Who did you pay off at the post office, Mother? You know, that's a federal offense, messing with someone else's mail. You're lucky Kaleb doesn't want to press charges."

Rose closed her mouth on the silent protest. Anna continued, the rage inside of her simmering nicely.

"And now I'm following a dream. *My* dream, Mother. I'm sorry if you don't like it, and if you would like for me to repay you and Father all of the money you've invested in me over time, I gladly will. Because I really believe that I can make this work. And there isn't anything you can do to stop me. I'm staying. I'm home for good. And this is where my heart is now. It's never been in New York, Mother. Like yours was."

Silence can be heavy when it is imposed by an unwilling speaker, and this was no exception. Rose swept her hand over the material of her summer suit, allowing her gaze to do the same over the room. Finally, she rested it on Anna's determined face. "So my opinion means nothing, then?"

Anna sighed. "If it's not a good one, then, no, it does not. I'm sorry if I'm hurting you, but I need to do something for myself. Something that makes me feel like getting up in the morning."

"And this will?" She gestured at the empty space, the dirt, the sallowness of the color in the walls.

"I think so. Yes."

Rose continued to stand another minute in silence. She made no move toward Anna nor toward Kaleb and eventually walked out of the building without saying a word.

Anna let out the breath she had been unaware she had been holding. "Well. That was—much worse than I could have ever anticipated."

Kaleb stayed near the edge of the room, sensing Anna needed her space right now and did not need to feel crowded. "Are you ready to throw in the towel?"

Of all the things Kaleb could have said at that moment, this question was the least expected. "What?"

"Maybe she's right. I'm sure you could sense the feeling that she thinks you're going to fail. I'm sure you could pull out of the lease. You've only recently signed, and you may only lose your deposit."

Anna stared at Kaleb in disbelief. "Why would you say these things to me? Of course I'm not going to pull out of the lease! I've made a decision to build a studio, and by golly, that is what I intend to do."

"Good." He went to her now and placed his hands on her shoulders. "At least you've stopped shaking."

Anna stepped back as she understood what game he was playing. "Nicely done, McMurran."

"I could say the same about you, Keller. You handled her—and yourself—very well. Maybe you should do battle for me some time."

She hugged him and pressed her face into his shoulder, breathing him in as she spoke. "I think I'm done with battles for the day, McMurran. I'm suddenly very tired."

"Then why don't I take you back to my place and let you relax there for the night?" He brushed his hands over her hair, a gesture he was getting quite accustomed to doing on a regular basis.

"I really don't think you want me to rest. I have a feeling you have other things on your mind. You might take advantage of me in my vulnerable state."

When he chuckled, she eased back to see him as he spoke. "I love it that you can see right through me."

Chapter XIII

Anna considered this new venture a true labor of love, and as she saw Madelaine scurry away in fear of a large black spider, she knew she would need to do a lot of convincing in order for her friend to stay and help.

"You know, I have final exams to prepare. I could be spending my Saturday doing that. But oh no, I'm here with who knows what kinds of creatures lurking around every corner all because you implored me with those big eyes of yours."

"I also mentioned that Adam might stop by." Anna continued to sand the window frame.

"Well, if he does not show up soon, you are going to need to find yourself a new friend. Why isn't Kaleb here taking care of all of this macho stuff? I'm sure he's dying to prove his love for you." She eyed a large box suspiciously before mustering the courage to move it.

Anna stifled a laugh at her friend's fear. "He said he'd be by later. Had something to take care of." Which concerned her because she had thought he would jump at the chance to work with her on her project.

"So things are pretty hot and heavy with you two, huh?" Madelaine sneezed as dust engulfed her.

"Not that heavy. I'll admit I've been eating better than ever since being home, but still…" She spared Maddy a glance as her friend rolled her eyes. "Sorry, bad joke. Yes. I think we're pretty serious."

"So, why not move in together?"

"Madelaine, I am not going to ask him to move in with me. It's probably enough that we've become a couple. There's no need to rush anything. I like the pace we're taking." Anna began to sweep the sanding into the dust pan.

"So are you really going to stay here? I'd offer you my place, but somehow I think you want your own room. And after what you told me about your discussion with your mother, I don't think that will be terribly comfortable for long."

Anna made a sound of agreement as she heard a car pull up. She went to the window and saw Adam get out of his vehicle, followed by Ian. "My brothers are here."

At Maddy's excited shriek, she ran into the bathroom to freshen up. Anna greeted them at the door, bandana around her hair, dust on her face, and the sander in her hand.

"Well, what do you think?"

They stepped inside to view their sister's latest idea, neither understanding nor accepting just yet. Adam was the first to speak.

"I can't believe you're turning this into a dance studio." He kept his hands in his pockets as he slowly took in his surroundings, afraid that any speck of dirt might ruin his expensive slacks.

"That's okay. Sometimes I can't either." Anna was grinning foolishly from ear to ear.

"Have you started thinking about a clientele base?" he asked as he toed loose boards out of his way.

"Yes. Leave it to you to worry over such things. But I cannot promise an opening date until I get things lined up. I plan on doing some work myself. And Kaleb said he'll help. Plus, he has connections with contractors, etc. I just have to keep banging away."

Adam and Ian exchanged glances at the mention of Kaleb's name but said nothing to indicate their concern over their sister's sudden change in direction.

"This really could turn into something big, Anna, if you market it right." Adam brushed off part of the counter and leaned on it.

Anna turned to Ian. "I know you've got something to say, but you're certainly taking your time about it."

"He always does," Adam commented as he turned to the opening of the bathroom door.

"Well, well, look who the cat dragged in. Adam and Ian Keller, it is so nice to see you both!" Maddy beamed as she clasped her hands together and walked in Adam's direction.

Anna waited expectantly for Ian to comment. "I think you know what you're doing. And that's precisely what I told Adam. So, I'm happy for you." He walked to her and hugged her, fast and awkward as tears stung the backs of her eyes.

"You weren't supposed to give in that easily, Ian." Adam smirked at his brother.

"I think she's been given a hard enough time over this. She deserves some well wishes."

"So, you've spoken to Mother." Anna now stood in the middle of the group.

"Yes, we've spoken to her."

"Or rather," Adam interrupted, "she has spoken to us. She wanted us to come here to talk some sense into you."

"I don't think she needs you to do that for her." Kaleb stood in the doorway, hands in fists at his sides. No one spoke, mostly because of the intensity behind his eyes.

Adam stepped toward him. "I guess we'll decide that, seeing as we are her brothers."

Anna put up her hands. "Fellas, please. I have had enough heartache over this place to last me a while. Let's just everybody shut up, or someone wish me good luck."

For several full seconds, no one spoke. Madelaine was rather enjoying the raw chemistry that was somehow knocking itself around the room. Adam and Kaleb continued to look at each other until Ian spoke.

"Good luck. Now, Adam, why don't we offer what we came here to do?"

Adam shook himself free of Kaleb's penetrating stare. He glanced at Anna. "We came to offer our services."

Anna's jaw dropped open. "You came to help?"

"Well, we figured that you were probably strapped for cash, and we have some time on our hands, so yeah, we're here."

Anna let her head fall forward into her hands as she collapsed to her knees in a sobbing heap on the floor. Kaleb was at her side in two strides.

"What is it, Anna? What's wrong?"

She lifted her face away from her hands. "I don't know what I've done to deserve all of this, but I am going to be eternally grateful to all of you." She laughed, and it was a watery sound as Adam went back out to his car to fetch a change of clothes, and Ian began hauling garbage away.

They worked with the easy rhythm of a common goal. Rock music blared out from Anna's portable stereo while Madelaine flirted none-too-shyly with Adam, and when he was not giving her advances the attention they deserved, she turned the charm on to Ian, who would blush and try to move her out of the way. Anna and Kaleb fought over how much work she should be allowed to do. After all, she was just recently putting on some weight and could not lift a lot, but she felt that this should not get in the way of hard labor. Eventually, she was shoved out the door, along with Maddy, to buy a bucket of chicken, biscuits, and stuffing for lunch. She opted for the restaurant's lemonade instead of homemade, considering the environment.

As they stuffed their faces and their bellies as much as possible, Kaleb began to question Anna about her progress with her search for the ring.

"Admittedly, I have not been as diligent as I could be," she answered over a mouthful of mashed potatoes. "But I've had other things on my mind. And I think my grandfather is okay with it. Somehow, I think all of this was a part of his plan." She gestured to the room from her crouched position on the floor.

Adam dug into the bucket. "What makes you think our grandfather knows what you're doing?"

"I went to see him and got the feeling." At everyone's blank stare, she elaborated. "His grave. I went to visit his grave, and I was overcome with a rather—peaceful feeling. I think I'm supposed to be on this journey. Maybe there isn't even a ring to find, but it was part of the reason why I came home. Maybe that was all he wanted." She broke a biscuit in half to split with Kaleb.

He gave her words some serious thought. "I think there's a ring to be found."

The group looked at him in quiet wonder until Madelaine encouraged him to continue.

"Your grandfather had a different kind of soul, true. But, he loved each of you for entirely separate reasons, none of you more than the next, but separately. I could see it in the way he would play with you as children or in the way he would speak of you in town as you grew older. I think his intentions with his letter were to prove that to you one last time. And for you to have some fun with it. If your family's legacy is true, then your great-grandfather set forth something that can only be solved by the three of you. I know I've helped some, but anything of value to the cause that has been found, has been found by you, Anna. So far, you're the key to the friendship piece."

She collected her thoughts as she began to clean up their mess. "Adam, Ian, I haven't shown you the painting of grandma, have I?"

They each nodded negatively. Kaleb cut in, sensing how tired she was but still trying to maintain the energy to work. "Why don't you show them another day? We've done quite a bit here today, Anna. Maybe we could all reconvene tomorrow early in the morning and work like dogs then."

Adam took a good study of his sister and wondered why he had not noticed the fatigue in her face or the dark circles under her eyes before Kaleb mentioned it so subtly. He motioned for Ian to pack up their belongings.

Madelaine jumped to her feet excitedly. "No one can leave until we take a picture!" She dashed out to her car to retrieve her camera.

Anna groaned. Turning to the group, she said, "Maddy took a picture of this place before I could start anything this morning. She said I'll want it for posterior's sake. But I just know that I look a mess. Why I would want to be reminded of that, I'll never know."

Kaleb came to her side, brushed at the film of dirt on her cheeks. "You've never looked lovelier."

She blushed because her brothers were watching intently as Maddy bounded back into the room. "Okay. I just have to set this thing up to go off in ten seconds. Line up over there by that window. It seems to be giving off the best light right now."

As the group assembled, Madelaine set the camera and ran into the photo in the nick of time. The five of them looked exhausted but content when the flash went off.

* * * * *

As Kaleb slept by her side that night in his bed, Anna watched the rise and fall of his chest, the way the early summer breeze of the night ruffled his bangs. She brushed her fingers over his hair to wipe it away from his face, and he stirred. She remained still so as not to awaken him. His breathing was deep and steady, and she knew he would wake early to help her as much as possible before he returned to his own job at the beginning of the week. She wanted him to get as much rest as possible.

Madelaine's words played back in her mind, as did her brother, Adam's, before he had gone home. He was willing to allow her to stay in his spare room until she found her own place, which she thought was so sweet of him, but she knew that would be very uncomfortable. She also realized that staying with Kaleb was becoming more and more of a habit. This, too, made her uncomfortable. Not because she did not enjoy sleeping by his side, but because they were each contributing to a situation that neither had set boundaries for.

She knew she did not need those boundaries, but she theorized Kaleb probably did.

Moving as quietly as possible, she slipped from his hold and walked out to his living room area. She looked out at the quiet street and noticed the moon was full and very bright. Sitting on his sofa, she reflected on their recent romantic developments. She knew that he loved her, and she felt comfort knowing she had shown her love to him so easily. But is that where it ended? Were they destined to be lovers only, spending the night in each other's bed only on occasion? This uncertainty created tension in her shoulders, and she rolled her neck from side to side to ease it.

Yes, she loved Kaleb McMurran, but was that enough?

She would need to face her mother again, and she had yet to speak to her father. Although he had been out of town, she was sure her mother had phoned to tell him everything Anna had done recently. What would his reaction be? If he was disappointed in her…funny, it had not occurred to her to be so worried about her mother's disappointment.

She turned to see Kaleb standing in the dim moonlight of the hallway. He walked to her and pulled her off the couch and into his waiting arms. "Couldn't sleep?"

She smiled. "No. I thought I would come out here for a while so as not to disturb you."

"It disturbs me when you're not sleeping by my side. That's what woke me."

She shifted, uneasy at his choice of words, as though he had been reading her mind. He noticed the movement but stayed quiet.

"I didn't mean to wake you. Why don't we go back to bed?"

He knew there was more here to explore but decided he could badger at her later to get to the bottom of whatever might be troubling her. "I've got just the remedy that will knock you out."

She was laughing as he fulfilled his promise.

* * * * *

Early the next morning, Anna brought the gang breakfast courtesy of Frannie and her diner. She figured fuel for the day was in order since the temperature would begin to soar before noon; it would be the first hot day of the season. They each gobbled down eggs, bacon, toast, pancakes, hot coffee, and juice. When Michelle and Evan arrived, Anna bobbled her glass.

"Kaleb told us you could use more hands." Evan moved in to snatch toast from his brother's plate.

"But Michelle shouldn't be working here. She just had a baby."

Michelle smiled. "I already went for my six week check-up two weeks ago, and I'm fine. Besides, I needed to get out of the house and hang with some adults, do something adult. This feels great." She drank coffee deeply.

"Something adult, you say?" Evan wiggled his eyebrows at his wife. "I could have thought of something a bit more fun than helping out here."

"You already did—last night." Michelle sashayed her way over to the pancakes that were stacked on the counter.

Kaleb choked on his bacon. "Thank you for sharing. Too much information—way too much." But he walked sheepishly toward his brother and slapped him on the back.

"Well, if all of the hormones are under control around here, I think we should ask Anna what she would like to accomplish today." Madelaine threw her plates in the garbage can and stood facing the group.

Anna explained that she would like the main floor cleared out entirely if possible. She was hoping to begin to look at paint samples, but she knew they needed to focus on making the place look clean first. She had already booked the floor sander for later in the week when she thought she would need it but realized that they should paint first. She pulled out her cell phone to call the hardware store to reschedule.

As the men hauled old appliances, equipment, and rotting shelves out to the street, the women sanded door frames, swept out corners, and removed old lighting. By the time the afternoon arrived, they had cleared out the main floor space and could begin to see progress.

Anna was sweating as she stood by Madelaine's side to ask her friend for help. "Listen, I don't want to bother anyone else with this because this is my place. And I really should have a hand in what goes on here. Plus, I didn't ask all of you to help with this while I'm off designing—"

"You didn't ask all of us. But we came anyway." She smiled.

"The point is, I don't feel right taking time away from the main floor to worry about my own concerns, but—"

"Anna! Would you please get to the point?"

"It's hard for me to ask for help."

"I know." Maddy smiled, understanding.

"I need to work on the upstairs office."

"Well, no one around here is going to feel like you are abandoning us. That's all a part of it." Maddy brushed her hands on her shorts.

"No, not just that. I also need to transform part of the upstairs into—into my place. To live," she expanded at Maddy's confused look.

"Oh. Does Kaleb know?"

"Why does he need to know? Maddy, I cannot assume that I can stay at his place every night. Besides, I'm sure he would appreciate being able to stay at mine from time to time."

"Personally, Anna, I don't think he'd care if you stayed with him all the time. But if you're so set on having your own space—"

"I am."

"Then I will help you."

"Thank you, Maddy. It means a lot." Anna picked up the hand sander again.

"I'll go get the broom, and you and I can get started right now."

"I want to release everyone early so that they can all go home to rest, and then I can really dive in to what I want to do up there."

"Just go sneak upstairs, and I'll follow shortly."

Anna began rummaging through what the previous tenant had left behind. Nothing seemed to be of value, so she began hauling boxes down the outside steps and out to the curb. Each time she made the trek, she appreciated having her own entry into what would soon be considered her own flat. As she worked, she thought about the fact that she had never really lived on her own. When she had been in New York, she had lived by herself, but because she had been so young when she first arrived, she was made to live in a dorm-like setting with the other dancers, and a "den mother" was assigned to check in on her and others like her. Once she was of age, she became the den mother until she had fallen apart and returned back home.

Now, no one would be there to check on her. It would all be completely up to Anna. No one would see if she needed anything before toddling off to bed.

Not even her mother.

She was sad for that, but she was beginning to see that Rose could not really help who she was. She had certainly had a fine upbringing, but for Rose, her parents had not been enough. What had been her father's efforts to make the child come more alive had been viewed as foolishness in the mind of a premature adult trapped in the body of a girl. Anna considered this. Had her mother ever really been young? Or had she always been Rose O'Connor Keller? The fact that she seemed cut out for dinner parties and the high life had never been questioned. Although Anna's father was far more relaxed, he still seemed to just accept Rose for who she was and allow her to be in charge of the family.

Even though Anna understood it was time for her to take charge of herself, she thought perhaps she should begin to accept Rose for who she was and stop looking for the kind of mother she knew Rose would never be to her.

At this, she paused and leaned against the wall as Madelaine came back up the steps.

"You've been quiet for a while."

"Hmm? Sorry. I was just lost in thought, I suppose." Anna went to one of the wide windows and breathed in the summer air. "I can't believe I'm doing this, Maddy. It's funny how everything comes around full circle."

"My parents always said it would, and as a kid, you never believe them, but I can see now that they were right." Madelaine removed the rubber band from her hair to redo the ponytail knot.

Anna turned slowly to face her. Realization was dawning heavily, and she needed a minute to allow it to sink in. "Full circle. Maddy, what if that is the key to finding my part of the ring?"

"What are you talking about, Anna?"

"Think about it. My great-grandfather left behind an old family legend—some call it a curse—on my grandparents because he did not like who my grandmother had chosen for her mate, for her lifestyle. He swore that his legacy would be that future generations would pay for this error in judgment."

"Yeah. So?"

"So, my mother should have been of a generation of three, but because my grandmother was too weak to have more children, she could not be of such a generation. But we can. Adam and Ian and I. We are the generation of three that my grandfather spoke of. And my mother is the one who is displeased this time with my choices. My error in judgment, according to her."

Anna paced the small room slowly, her index finger resting lightly on her lips as she kept her gaze to the ground, giving herself time to think. Madelaine watched while she allowed Anna's thoughts to roll around inside her own head.

"Full circle, Maddy. That's what this all comes down to. The ring is a complete circle. Our situation is a circle. If I can figure out what I am supposed to return to, maybe I can find my part of the ring. The hands that represent friendship."

Madelaine thought her friend might have figured out a missing piece to the puzzle and was happy to be a part of it, especially since this was putting a lovely, healthy glow into Anna's cheeks and a smile about her lips. Even with the dirt smudges across her face, Anna looked soft and dreamy and somehow more complete than she had. Ever.

Kaleb bounded up the stairs from inside the building. "What are you two ladies up to here?" He was holding two cold beers out to them. Maddy reached for hers right away and popped the top.

"Anna here thinks she may have found another piece to the puzzle. The ring she's supposed to find," she explained at Kaleb's quizzical expression.

"Really? Want to tell me about it?" He swallowed his bottle in a few quick gulps.

"Yes. I do. But not yet. Not until I can clear my head of all these cobwebs. The room, too. Look at this place! So far, all I've managed is to move the garbage out to the street. It's still terribly dusty up here, not clean enough for anything other than us." She looked down at her grubby clothes.

Kaleb laughed. "Well, the gang is hungry, so I thought we could order some burgers and fries from Frannie. She'll be astonished to see how much we've already accomplished so far."

Anna twisted her bottom lip in her top teeth. Madelaine could sense that whatever she was about to say was not going to be received by gentle ears, so she volunteered to go back down to the main room and see how the rest of them had been progressing.

Kaleb sensed something, too, so he asked, "What's up, Anna?"

She twisted her hands in front of her. "I'll be happy to pay for everyone's meal; they certainly have earned it. But then I want everyone to go home and spend the remainder of their Sunday night in the comforts of their own homes. I want to work up here for as long as I can."

"Oh, like a little private party. Sounds like a beautiful idea. I'll go get the food, and we'll shoo them out as fast as we can. You know, there's no working shower facilities yet, but I think a little dirt—" He had begun to saddle up to her when she put up her hands to block his advances.

"Kaleb, I was thinking of working here tonight. Alone."

That stopped him. For a moment, he said nothing. Then he let the small "oh" escape his lips. The two of them stood there studying each other until finally he proceeded with their dinner order.

"Well, can't blame a guy for trying. I'll get you a cheeseburger—extra pickles, no dressing. I know how you like it. I'll be back shortly." He brushed past Michelle as she came up the stairs.

"What's wrong with Kaleb?" Michelle looked to his retreating figure and then to Anna.

"I think I just blew it with your brother-in-law. Big time." Anna dropped her face into her hands and let out a frustrated sigh.

Michelle felt a bit awkward, considering the situation. She did not know this girl that well, but if her instincts were close, she could see how much the two of them meant to the other. Maybe they just weren't sure what to do about it. She decided to take a chance.

"Anna, why don't you open that beer and take a break for a few? Tell me what happened before Kaleb and Evan get back with dinner."

Chapter XIV

Later that night, as Anna soaked in the tub of her childhood, she reflected on the day. Allowing the bubbles to froth around her, she tried to empty her mind. Her muscles were taut; her skin had been filthy. Now she listened to the quiet ping of the classical music as it drifted in through the hidden speaker while the deep conditioner worked its magic on her hair. She had always loved indulging now and again in bubble baths, but tonight had to be out of necessity. Her muscles had screamed at her to stop work shortly after one in the morning, and her eyes had closed themselves off into slits as she had driven home minutes later. Grateful her mother had already gone to bed, and that her father had returned safely from his trip and had joined her mother, she had crept up the stairs to lose herself in this very female ritual, but instead of preparing for a date, she was preparing for sleep.

Her mind would not shut off now, though, especially since it kept replaying her conversation with Michelle and her very awkward goodbye with Kaleb. She knew he was upset, and she supposed she could not blame him entirely. But he had not really given her much chance to explain, had only grunted at her the few times she had spoken to him. The rest of them had felt the change, too, and were uncomfortable because of it. She thought she had seen Michelle give Evan a bland look that told him she would explain all later, but the rest had dutifully eaten their burgers, drank their beers and sodas, and tried to make small talk with jokes. Anna felt okay with her decision for the evening, so she did not spend too much time rehashing it and was not all that uncomfortable.

Until Kaleb had practically brushed aside her kiss goodbye. Then she had been hurt and embarrassed.

But she would not allow that to ruin her plans. The building was cleared out, and she could allow some of the contractors that Kaleb had helped her find to work on bringing the building up to code. That would open her focus to the business end of things, the legalities of owning her own studio.

This thought caused her to jerk awake, splashing water and bubbles onto the tiled floor.

Realizing she had almost drowned herself in her parents' bathtub, she drained the water and dried off, padding her way to the bed. Crawling under the covers, she drifted off immediately, her wet hair soaking the pillow.

* * * * *

Kaleb spent the next several days in meetings with his boss and other contractors. The lighthouse was progressing quicker than any of them had thought possible, and they began to talk of other jobs on the island, of hiring more hands to help. Kaleb's interest in taking over as a foreman on the upcoming transformations was noted by his subtle show of interest. He knew it had taken him a long time to reach this point in his life, and he finally felt that people around here were taking him seriously.

Everyone but the one person who actually mattered.

Anna had not left his thoughts this entire week, and as he drove past a group of teens who were obviously feeling the pleasures from their newly released status from school, he regretted that they had not seen each other since that Sunday when they had all worked so hard to help her get the studio started. Flashes of her dancing, unaware that she was being watched by him, faded in and out of his mind as he turned into his brother's driveway. He could still feel the passion of her movements, smell the dust mixed with the sweat as she leaped through the air. The music from that day had left him unsettled.

He leapt from his truck and ran up to the back door, swinging the six pack as he did. He caught Evan in the kitchen preparing their evening meal of steaks and baked potatoes.

"Brought your favorite beer." Kaleb set it on the counter and then held the door open for Evan as he carried the platter out to the grill in the back yard.

"I figured we'd eat out in the yard tonight," he commented as he tossed the potatoes onto the grill and loosened his tie.

"You just get home from work?"

"Yeah, we had a meeting run over. You?"

"I stayed late for meetings, too. Who'd a' figured?"

They laughed and sat on the deck.

"Where's Michelle?"

"She's trying to get Marissa to sleep. It's been a rough day for her. Baby's got a cold."

Instantly concerned, Kaleb sat up in his chair. "Shouldn't you take her to the doctor's?"

"Relax. And yes, Michelle did. She's fine. Just one of those things."

As he finished his sentence, Michelle came out to join them on the deck. She bent to kiss her husband's cheek and then flopped down into a patio chair.

"You look beat." This came from her husband.

"I am. Had no idea something so little could scream for so long." She brushed the hair out of her eyes. "How've you been, Kaleb? Seen Anna lately?"

"Well, you sure don't take long, do you?" He swallowed more beer, a bitter taste moving around in his throat. "No. Not since Sunday."

"I kind of figured."

"Why?"

"Because of what she told me that day."

"What did she tell you?"

Michelle looked at her brother-in-law incredulously. "Please tell me, Kaleb dear, that you have given her the chance to explain things to you." At his blank and guilty stare, she huffed out a breath. "I should have known. You are ridiculous!" She began to rise, but he stopped her with a hand on her arm.

"Be a pal. Fill me in."

"I don't know why I should." When her husband turned his pleading eyes in her direction, she laughed ruefully and gave in. "Fine. But this is the only help you get from me regarding Anna anymore."

* * * * *

She knew it had been foolish to hope for a phone call, much less a visit. But Anna still hoped, and it was almost a week later. Throughout the week, Madelaine had been kind to her and had helped with some items at the studio, one of those being providing her studio with a name. She still was not sure. In the meantime, she had running and clean water, working electricity, and a beautiful floor plan.

Anna could not ask for more.

When she had brought her father there a few days before, her stomach had been in knots. Her mother had, of course, told him of her ridiculousness, but he had reserved judgment for himself. And his praise had settled something inside of her. The way he had looked when she had shown him all that she had done without anyone else's help had almost healed her heart. Almost. He had beamed with pride when she had spoken of the questions she had asked of Marcus McMurran and how professional she had sounded. Now she felt she could move forward with her plans on more solid footing.

They had not broached the subject of her mother.

Now as she sat at a makeshift desk by her lamp in her upstairs office, she pondered several items: Kaleb, the ring, the studio, Madelaine, her parents...Her head was swimming until her eyes went blurry, and she tossed the paperwork aside. Licensing and other such nonsense would have to wait until the morning. She called her first early night in a week and stood to gather her things and go home.

Kaleb was in her doorway, watching her. She let out a quiet startled gasp and held her hands to her chest. He remained in the doorway.

"Michelle and Evan say 'hi.' They wanted to know why you didn't accompany me to their house for dinner tonight."

Anna set the folder down on the desk. "I don't recall being invited."

"You weren't. Which is another thing they wondered. Why I didn't invite you. When I told them you and I had not really spoken this week, Michelle knocked me upside the head. She always figures it's the guy's fault. Being married to my brother would give her reason to think that." He shrugged his shoulders and kept his hands in his pockets.

Anna laughed subtly at his remark but also remained where she was. "I would have enjoyed dinner with them." *With you.*

"You've made quite a bit of progress around here." He edged his way in and walked the length of the room slowly, admiring the craftsmanship he saw. "It's certainly a lot cleaner."

"Yes." She folded her hands in front of her.

Kaleb sighed and turned. "I'm sorry I jumped to conclusions. Michelle told me about your conversation. Now don't be mad at her," he said and held up his hand to quiet her before she could respond. "I pried it out of her. And she gave me a lot to think about. I had never considered that you would have a need to build this for yourself. I'm sorry."

The simplicity of his words softened the edges around her heart. When she had first turned and had seen him in the doorway, she had wanted to stay angry. He had hurt her feelings. But now, she could see that he, too, was hurt and unsure of how to handle the next move. So she went to him and wrapped her arms around him, pressed her cheek to his.

"I've missed you, Kaleb McMurran."

He brought his arms around her as well, held her tight. "Want to spend the evening with a fool?"

"Only if you'll spend the evening with one, too."

He looked down into her eyes, laid his hand on her cheek. Her pulse quickened as needs that had lain dormant for almost seven days now began to stir. He saw the change come into her eyes and raised a brow at them. She looked away shyly, but he brought her gaze back to him with the simple touch of his finger to her chin. Pressing his lips to hers, she felt her knees turn to liquid.

They kissed like that for a time, allowing the week's frustrations and insecurities to be washed away. Bodies brushed, hands roamed, whispers breathed, skin heated. Soundless sounds emanated from the brushing of their clothing as they moved to music no one else would have heard. Kaleb walked to the lamp to shut it off and saw the mattress in the corner. Raising his brow once again, Anna began to explain, but he stopped her with his finger pressed simply against her lips.

She turned her head and took his fingers into her mouth. The moan escaped before he could stop it.

They locked around each other again, but he held on to the slippery and fiery reins of control. The sun was just beginning to set, and traffic outside was light. There was no breeze on this early summer evening to settle the heat as it built layer by layer between the two of them. She bent her head back to accept the light assault he played over her neck. Gripping her hips, he pressed his body against hers like a dancer might during an opening performance—skilled, taut with nerves and energy, and craving more than it should be allowed. He wanted her more than he ever had and wondered how the two of them did not die from the intensity of it.

She ran her hands down the length of his torso, grabbing the material of his white t-shirt as she did, eventually pulling it out of his jeans and up over his head. He brought his mouth back to hers and devoured. Blood had pooled itself in the center of her gut, and it now shot out in every direction, making her limbs feel heavy and heated all at once. She arched back to press his face against her still-clothed torso.

Kaleb laid her down on the mattress and removed each article of clothing with the care and precision of unwrapping glass. The lightest touch of his fingers on her skin sent shock waves spiraling out of control until she was no longer sure where to grab on or if she even wanted to do so. He breathed over her—on her neck, down her torso, over her breasts until her nipples were sharp and pointed. Flicking his tongue over them, she cried out, feeling the first shock waves course through her, electrifying her and weakening her all at once. She grabbed hold of his hair to bring his mouth back to hers, but he held her wrists in his hands and removed them, holding them down on the cool sheet beside her head. He traveled lower and lower until his tongue dipped inside of her, and she went blind from the torment. She knew she would beg if he did not hurry. Trying to gain purchase, she flew over the edge once again as he treated her to the delights she knew he would show only to her—just her.

Thinking he would let her be, she began to relax as Kaleb pulled himself above her, met her mouth demand for hot demand, using his hands to pleasure her more and bring her deliriously close to the edge again. She wrapped her legs around his waist as he slipped into her at a maddeningly slow pace. Cupping her bottom with one hand and her face with the other, he kept his eyes on hers as he slid in and out of her, allowing the pace to set itself, until he could stand it no longer. He thrust himself in and out at an alarming rate, sweating, raising himself up on his hands to get a better view of her.

When she cried out for the last time, he poured himself into her.

* * * * *

They lay quietly in the dusky light, wrapped gloriously around each other, their thoughts dim and nonsensical. Anna began to giggle at nothing in particular until Kaleb turned to her and asked her what was so very funny.

"I don't know. I'm just happy, I guess."

He flipped her so that she would lie on top of him, and he could still feel the swell of her breast against his damp skin, the rate of her heart beating strongly against his rib cage.

"Anna, pretty Anna—He brushed the hair from her eyes as the laughter in them died down. He knew she could sense his mood. "Do you think we'll ever tire of each other?"

"Why don't I answer that in about twenty years?" She saw his eyes darken and instantly regretted her choice of words. She moved away from him and sat up, pulling the sheet around her as a protective shield. "Are you thirsty?" She hated hearing her voice crack. "Why don't I get us some water?"

"Anna." He forced her to look at him. "Why would you think hearing that would upset me?" When all she did was move her shoulders in a noncommittal gesture, he took hold of her face in his hands and asked again, "Why would you think hearing that would upset me?"

She let out a breath; it ruffled her bangs. "Because I don't know if you see us together for the long haul." Oh, it was humiliating to hear the panicked edge to her voice, to know that he had such a hold on not only her heart, but her entire being.

"Do you see us together for the 'long haul'?" He smiled.

She bit her bottom lip. "I'm not sure that I do. But I'd like it." She got up from the bed, leaving him naked while the sheet pooled around her feet as she paced, holding most of it close to her chest to keep covered. To feel protected. "Kaleb, I know we've never really spoken about any kind of commitment, and I certainly had not anticipated discussing it with you under these circumstances. But, yes, I'd like to see us together for a while. There. I said it." She faced him as she finished and braced herself for his response.

Nothing could have prepared her. "Then I don't see any other choice. You'll have to marry me."

The silence that hung in the air was only pierced by a seagull in the distance and by a lone car driving past, the driver on his way home from work. Anna and Kaleb look at each other for several moments as he lay propped up on his elbow, grinning like a maniac.

"I'm sorry. What—what did you—what?" she finally managed.

"The way I see it, you're back—for good. There's been no one else since you—and I do mean since you. We obviously don't do well when we're apart, so it's logical that we should be together all the time."

"Are you giving me a logical proposal?"

Because he caught the hint of irritation, he knew he should switch tactics quickly. He had not planned any of this for tonight, and if he did not settle this matter quickly, he would throw himself at her mercy and do whatever it took to make her a permanent part of his life.

"Anna, I'm giving you what I've wanted. Now I just need you to agree. Will you marry me, Anna Keller? Have children with me. Be my family."

She stared at him. He was offering her so much—and yet..."I won't give up my studio. I won't give up the dance. I need those things for myself. If you listened—really listened to Michelle the other night—"

"When did you hear me say that I wanted you to give up any of those things?" He sat, pulled on his jeans, continued to look at her from his position so close to the floor. "Anna, I fell in love with the woman who wants those things, with the woman who has struggled to get those things. They are a part of who you are, as much as you are a part of me." When her eyes filled, he crossed to her. He kissed her gingerly. "Marry me, Anna. Take my heart, take my name, and take my life."

"Okay, Kaleb McMurran. I will marry you."

He picked her up and swung her around.

Chapter XV

They did not know whom they wanted to tell first, but they certainly knew whom they wanted to avoid. As they dressed the following morning, Kaleb discussed Rose with Anna as calmly as he could.

"She's going to need to know, Anna. We can't send her photos of the wedding after the fact."

"Why not?" she asked, only half-kidding as she brushed her hair.

"I think I should do this properly anyway. I'll need to ask your father's blessing. I think he would like that."

"Yes, I think he would, too." She smiled at him.

"Then it's settled. I'll phone your father today at his office and tell him you and I want to meet with him and your mother tonight over dinner to discuss some things with the studio. Then I'll ask for his blessing. It should be fine." He tried to wet his throat but found it was dry as sandpaper.

Anna came up behind him and put her arms around his waist. "You're nervous, aren't you?"

"I think a guy has a right to be nervous when he's about to ask for his woman's parents to say it's okay to marry their daughter." He turned to face her, and she laughed at him. "Yeah, I'm nervous."

Later that day, she found that notion to be unbearably sweet while he found it to be unbearably uncomfortable. Anna worked in the quiet solitude of her office as she made plans for her building, oblivious to the chaos of what was going on below her. The work crew was stripping, polishing, and installing, and she was humming under her breath and smiling as she wrote checks and tried to figure out her new computer system. This was how Madelaine found her.

"Summer vacation is God's gift to teachers!" she exclaimed from the outer doorway. Anna turned her beaming smile toward her friend. "Well, someone sure is in a good mood."

"Yes, I am." Anna got up to pull something out of her printer.

"I slept in today until the sun had already been up for over two hours!" Maddy clapped her hands together and giggled.

"That's wonderful." Anna tried reading what was on the page in front of her but could only see blurry letters; nothing was making any sense.

"Anna, what's going on with you? You look giddy."

She set the paper down and faced Maddy head on. "Kaleb proposed to me last night."

Stunned silence filled the same room once again until Maddy let out a loud yelp and engulfed Anna in a fierce hug.

"But, Maddy, you cannot say anything to anyone yet! I just had to tell someone. We're telling my parents tonight, so no one else can know until they do. Promise me."

"I promise, I promise. How? When? Oh, please give me the details!"

Anna sat Madelaine down and told her the entire story. She appeared clam and excited, giddy and nervous, up until she began to talk about her mother. Then her insides began to chew on themselves, and Madelaine had some advice.

"Do you love him, Anna? I mean, really love him?" When her friend nodded, she continued. "Then nothing she says or does can really make a difference. Right?"

Anna sighed. "I know, but it would be so nice to have a mother who simply said 'congratulations' and left it at that."

"My goodness, you're greedy." At Anna's look of confusion, Madelaine continued. "You have a new business that will soon begin to bloom, a hunk of a man who wants to spend his life with you, and me for your best friend. Now you want your mother to be happy for you, too?" When Anna laughed, Madelaine took her hands in her own. "You and Kaleb will be fine. He won't let a thing happen to you, I just know it. Trust him, and the two of you will be all right."

As Anna was replaying Maddy's advice later that evening and dressing for dinner, Kaleb went to his mother's florist to purchase flowers and tell her the good news. After she finished crying a bout of delightfully shocked tears, she hugged her son fiercely and told him to take as good of care of Anna as his father had taken of her. She then insisted on having both families over for a barbeque for the following weekend to celebrate. Of course, Kaleb had to make her promise on three Bibles that she would not do anything yet since he still had to get through the evening's dinner.

The phone call to Anna's father had been relatively easy, and he had a small suspicion that Gregory Keller knew what was up Kaleb's sleeve. But he had said nothing more than agreeing to bring his wife to the restaurant that night. The rest would be up to Kaleb.

When he picked her up with a bouquet of wild flowers in his arms, she was glowing. They had arranged for some time alone before dinner so that Rose would not be home when he came to get Anna, and he was very grateful that he had been clever enough to think ahead like that. His tongue fell out of his mouth when she walked down the path to his truck ahead of him.

She had chosen a filmy and floaty turquoise dress with strappy sandals. She had strategically placed small white and raspberry-colored flower petals throughout her hair, and her scent lingered just ahead of him. When she turned to look back at him and sent him her most dazzling smile, he was lost to her again.

They went for a quiet walk down by the water and held hands and gazes for long periods of time. Now and again they would speak of future plans, but mostly they allowed the breeze and the boats to make noise while they simply reveled in the company of the other. When it was time for dinner, Kaleb held her door open to make sure she was settled comfortably and then drove off.

They arrived first, and Anna explained that a late arrival by her parents would be a strategic move on her mother's part. This still did not bother him. He went ahead and ordered champagne. When the cork popped, and the frothy liquid spilled over onto the carpet, Anna squealed as she tried to capture the golden beverage with her flute. He caught her in a kiss as Rose and Greg approached the table.

The first moments were a bit strained since Anna had not really spoken to her mother ever since Rose had shown up at the studio so unexpectantly. The four of them exchanged pleasantries, and Greg kissed his daughter's cheek.

"You look lovely, Anna. Now, what are we celebrating? It looks like we got here in time for a champagne toast." He pulled out a chair for his wife to sit, and she did so stiffly.

"We are celebrating. I'm glad you could both make it." Kaleb poured champagne for them as well and held up his flute. "Before we order dinner, I'd like to share some news with you. Please join me in a toast. Your daughter has agreed to marry me, and I would greatly appreciate your blessing."

They all tried to ignore the loud gasp Rose sent out as she spilled champagne onto the table. Anna's eyes never left Kaleb's face.

When at last someone did speak, Greg turned his attention to Anna. "Is this what you want?" When she looked at him, her eyes filled with love and tears, a lethal combination in any young woman, and nodded, he had his answer. "Then I will propose a toast. Welcome to our family, Kaleb."

As they bumped their glasses together, not one of them missed Rose's reaction. She was sitting very still, her champagne flute on the table, a stoic outer shell dominating her fine features. She continued to stare at the table cloth until Anna pleaded with her to say something.

"You want me to react to this?" She picked her head up and gazed at her with ice in her eyes. "You want me to bless this union? If you want me to fake happiness for you, Anna, I will not. This man is well beneath you, and I cannot simply stand by and tell you that this is a good idea. And I will not apologize for that either." She stood and turned to her husband. "Our daughter belongs where even the stars would dim next to her. After all of the time and money we have invested, how can you not see it?" With that, she made a grand exit, causing some from nearby tables to stare in wonder.

Anna began to cry, silent, molten tears that slid gracefully like the dancer she was down her cheek. Kaleb and her father turned to see her state of mind in time to watch as she dabbed gently at them with her napkin. No one knew what to say to ease the pain of the moment.

"Well, I certainly had not expected her to ask me what colors I've chosen, but I don't think I expected that." She sipped champagne, and its grip was like shards of delicate ice sliding down her throat to settle sharply in her hollow belly. "Honestly, I wasn't sure what to expect."

Gregory took his daughter's hand in his on the table, forcing her to look into his eyes. "Anna, I don't expect you to be kind right now, but this has all been so much for her. Your grandfather's death, this search for the ring, your return from New York, your purchase of the studio...I am not excusing her actions, but perhaps if we gave her a little time."

She sniffed and laughed the laugh of one who knows she has been defeated. "Dad, you know as well as I do that however much time we give her, she will never come around. If that means my own mother will not be at my wedding, then so be it. I know I'll have my two favorite men." She took Kaleb's hand in hers, making the three of them a joined circle. "If it's all right with you, I would like to celebrate still. You have given a beautiful blessing to us, and I really think we should revel in that. So..." She picked up her delicate glass once again. "I propose another toast. To us," she said and smiled at Kaleb, the candlelight reflecting worlds in her shining eyes. "We have my father's blessing, and we will be married. Soon." They each sipped and tried to get through the meal with as much joy and dignity as possible.

Later, when Kaleb held her in his arms in his bed at the apartment, he tried to protect her against the shutters that racked her body. She was dreaming, and it was obvious to him that her dreams were as unsettled as their dinner had been. Her father had ridden home alone; obviously, Rose had taken a cab, or perhaps some other unlucky soul from the restaurant had agreed to take her home, someone she knew to be of good blood and good money. He had watched Anna battle the heavy gloom that had settled over her as she had sat next to him in the truck on the drive back to his place after stopping of at her home to pick up a few of her things. She had tried so hard to be cheerful about their engagement, especially when he had made love to her softly and gently only an hour before. He thought lighting the candles and throwing open the windows to the late evening breeze would console her as he reminded her why he loved her so very much. But now, in the quiet of the aftermath of their loving, her spirit would not rest, and he was silently willing her to settle, to relax, to be.

Just to be.

In the morning, when he awoke, she was gone. All that had been left behind was her scent. Worried about her emotional stability, he dressed, drank less than a half a cup of coffee, and drove out to find her.

* * * * *

Anna felt as though a piece of her had been removed, not quickly and sharply, but with precision, like that of a surgeon's scalpel. Her mother had been working on her for a time, and she realized now that she would never be what her mother had wanted from her for so long. So she went to the one other person who might understand Rose even better than she did.

As her grandmother listened to Anna's story through tears, smiles, and sobs, she made tea, nodded her head, stroked Anna's neck, and made mental notes to have a discussion with her only child. She knew Rose had grown into a cold woman, but she had never anticipated the chill that would try its best to intercept others' happiness.

Olivia allowed her only granddaughter to finish the story by wiping down her face with a dishcloth. Anna's eyes were red and swollen and desperate. She had not seen Anna look so desperate in all the years of her life.

Except when she had been sent away to New York.

Now she needed to get to the bottom of this situation in order to ease the pain Anna most definitely did not deserve.

She finally spoke after having been silent for so long a time. "Anna, you are one of my most precious jewels. Your grandfather and I were so blessedly happy that you did not take on your mother's traits." At Anna's shocked look, Olivia laughed and sipped the rest of her tea. "Don't be so surprised. We have always known the kind of woman Rose has become. We tried to instill in her the same fantasies your grandfather had, but it was not to be. And that was when I had to cut her loose. I will always love her, Anna; she is my daughter. Someday, when you have a child of your own, you will understand what it is I speak of."

"But I would not do this to my child."

Olivia smiled tenderly and brushed Anna's cheek with her hand. "I know. And I don't believe your mother is doing anything intentionally to cause you harm. She simply cannot see past her own desires to see that what she is actually doing is causing you great suffering. For that, I am sorry. But, your grandfather warned me this would be part of the curse. It's just hard to accept when it's your own child who fulfills the legacy." She absently placed her hand over her womb, feeling almost like she did all those years ago when she had carried Rose there.

Anna's head snapped to attention. "What do you mean she's part of the curse?"

Olivia looked back into her granddaughter's face and realized she had spoken that last part aloud. There was only one way to handle it now. She had always believed that children deserved the truth. Even when her grandchildren had been young, she had not believed in disguising anything from them. And now was her chance to prove that.

She went to the sink to rinse out her cup. "Your great-grandfather left that ring in three pieces because of me."

Anna watched Olivia's back for a moment as the older woman looked out through the kitchen window and onto her lawn. She gave her time to compose herself until she turned back, sat down, and finished the tale.

"He had—connections with all things spiritual. He was a wise man; he was nobody's fool. But I'm afraid I may have made him out to be before he past into the next world."

"I don't understand."

"Your great-grandfather cursed this family because I did not follow in the path he had chosen for me. And because of it, I was not allowed to see my family again. Not even my mother."

The tragedy struck Anna at that moment, and she understood all that her grandmother had given up to be with her grandfather. She reached across the table to take the arthritic fingers in her hand as she silently willed Olivia to continue on with the story.

"My father had a very proper Englishmen selected for me, not some ill-bred Irish vagabond, who did not have a pot to pee in, nor a window to throw it out. When I told him about the painting, he was seething, humiliated, crushed. I did not understand because all I could see was love. Your grandfather had this marvelous ability to block out all other sights whenever he was around me. But my father did not appreciate this in the least, so I was, of course, forbidden to see him anymore, and I would be married to the Englishmen at once. When Paddy came to speak with my father about my hand in marriage, my father threw him out—literally onto the street. He could only hear the Irish brogue—the cheapness of it rather than the beautiful music that carried it to your ears. I locked myself into my room for days when I was rescued by nightfall by your grandfather. He had heard that I was to marry that stranger, and he could not stand it. So we rode away on horseback into the dusk and never returned to see any of my family again. Quite a romantic story, some would say." She chuckled softly and looked down at their joined hands. "We shipped off to America immediately because we knew my father would never look for us there. And we built a life, the life you've known about. And here we are." Now she looked back at Anna directly and squeezed her hand as much as she could.

Anna's face was damp yet again, but this time she shed tears for a young English girl who surely must have been terrified of the life she was leaving behind and the one she was about to embark upon. She had so many questions rolling around in her head, but she asked her heart to guide her as she spoke.

"And if you had to make the choice again?"

Olivia released her hand, not before giving Anna a solid squeeze, and touched her face. "If you have to ask, then I have not done as good of a job as I thought telling the story."

Anna had known the answer before she had asked it, but somehow having her grandmother verify it for her relaxed her even more in her decisions. "But what about the ring? This still does not explain how the ring came to mean so much to our family, particularly to Adam and Ian and myself. How does it hold such importance?"

Seeing her granddaughter's quizzical face revived something in Olivia. She wanted the feel of adventure again, and she thanked her husband—quietly—for giving her such a marvelous gift before he had left her. She tried to explain.

"Anna, your great-grandfather said that a type of disquiet would settle inside of my family for having betrayed him and his wishes, and that the only way to be rid of it would be to have a generation of three locate the pieces that tied so closely to them. At the time, I did not understand that this disquiet would actually root itself inside of my daughter—the quickest way to get to a mother's heart, seeing her child so full of discomfort and unhappiness. He could not have known that she would go on to have three children, who would then be given the chance to find the pieces. But know this—if any of you should fail, you will lose all. There is no chance for one of you without a victory for all."

* * * * *

As Anna finished relaying the story to the group spread out before her, she looked quietly around the room. Madelaine's eye were wet, discreetly so. Adam looked grim while Ian appeared concerned. Kaleb was seated on the floor in front of her, holding her hand in her lap. They had gathered together in the upper flat of Anna's studio, where she had been working like a fiend to get it ready for company. Convincing Adam to give up an evening at the club had been difficult, but the others had come willingly and without much effort. They were each now finishing up slices of pizza and bottles of wine. Anna and Kaleb had begun the evening with the announcement of their engagement, and although Anna could sense that Adam was holding out on his true opinion, he still had congratulated them and hugged her fiercely. Now he looked distrustful as he allowed the words his sister had spoken to replay themselves inside of his head.

"So your grandmother gave up everything for your grandfather? I—I don't know what to say." Maddy choked back a silent sob.

"Why have we never been privy to this story before now, Anna?" This came from Adam as he refilled his wine glass. "If this was such a turbulent time for her—for them, why wait until our grandfather is dead to tell us? It's a fine story; I would think he would have enjoyed telling it."

"If you could have been there to see her face as she told it…" One single tear glided down her cheek, and Kaleb reached up to take it onto his finger. He pressed it to his lip as she looked down at him. "Don't you see? I cannot be the only one to find my part of the ring. All three of us need to look. If any one of us fail, we will lose all. All of us will lose all. I don't know what that means, but it scares me to consider the possibilities." Adam shrugged and looked away. "Please, Adam. Open your logical mind and consider the possibilities for just a moment."

"I have." All eyes turned to Ian. "I know it will surprise you, but I have been doing some research of my own in my spare time. My piece of the ring is love, according to our grandfather, and I have discovered that he is probably right. That should be my piece."

"You're going to encourage this nonsense?" Adam asked incredulously. "I cannot believe the pair of you! An old man leaves a ridiculous letter in his dead hands, and you two run off on a wild chase!" He stood to pace the room.

"Why is it so hard for you to imagine, Adam?" Anna was now on her feet, the intensity behind her stance surprising everyone in the room. "How much has our grandmother asked of us in our lifetime? How much have I? If we entertain the thoughts of a foolish old man for the sake of the love he has left behind, what harm can there be? Is it really that bothersome to you that people at the club will whisper about you behind your back? I would have thought you would make such decisions for yourself, not because of others who don't matter. That's the brother I grew up with and have grown to love. I don't understand you now. Excuse me." Anna walked from the room to the stairs and went to the main floor. Madelaine, stealing one last look from Adam, joined her.

The three men remained in the silence for a time, Kaleb and Ian seated on chairs across from each other, Adam standing near the lone window, looking out onto the empty street. The tension was there in his shoulders; the humor of the situation was lost on him. For a man who had always had a plan, this fork in the road was disconcerting.

"I've know Anna for a long time," Kaleb began as Adam turned to face him. "I realize I haven't known her as long as the two of you have, and I also realize that you are not entirely sure I am right for your sister. Agreed?"

Adam cocked his head. "On both counts."

Kaleb nodded and continued. "What I am sure of is that your sister does not fly by the seat of her pants. She has been a follower for a long time. Someone else carves out the plan, she goes with it because she figures they only have her best interests at heart. And now, for the first time in her life, she comes to you and asks you to take a leap of faith. Anna—level-headed Anna, who has always made wise decisions. Decisions that would certainly never rock anyone's boat. I'm not a faith man, myself." Now he addressed both brothers. "I need good, solid proof. But when I fell in love with your sister, hard, I had no idea if she would believe me. But I had to believe that she would. I put my faith in her, and she has done the same. I won't let her down this time either." Kaleb stood to go to the stairs.

"Anna is different." Adam stopped Kaleb with just his words. "She's level-headed, yes, but that's something that we've all come to depend on. It's something about her that we appreciate. So to hear her ask us to go on a treasure hunt…" He stuffed his hands in his pockets. "I'll go down the other stairs. Tell her that I'll try." With that, he left Kaleb and Ian alone.

"He will try, Kaleb," Ian stated in his matter-of-fact tone. "If there's ever anyone from whom you can trust a promise, it's Adam. He's just more solid than the rest of us. He's more set in his ways."

"Sounds like someone else I know from your family."

The dryness of the remark was not lost on Ian. "You probably won't get my mother's blessing for your marriage." Ian stood and prepared to leave. "That may be another thing my grandmother was preparing you for. Think about that."

As Ian drifted down the same stairs his brother had taken, Kaleb was left to do nothing but think.

Chapter XVI

Anna worked with more determination on her studio than she thought she could muster. The workers were running things at a fast and smooth pace, which gave her the confidence she needed to run advertisements for a fall opening.

And would allow her to plan for a late summer wedding.

Excitement bubbled out of her as she approved some lighting fixtures. She was skipping across the room when a woman, whom she did not recognize, was found standing in the doorway, watching her.

Anna approached her with a friendly smile in place. "Can I help you?"

The woman looked shakily around her as she tried to surmise the situation. "I'm not sure. I was told this is going to be a dance studio, but I can see that you're busy. Maybe I should come back later."

Anna could see that under the in-your-face-confidence was a thin layer of nerves. She wondered idly if the woman was jumpy because of all of the machinery or if there was another reason.

"No, you can stay. Just watch out that they don't cut off any of your toes." When the woman looked at her somewhat horrified, Anna tried a smile. "I was only kidding. Why don't we go upstairs to my office where we might be able to think above all this racket?" She watched the woman consider this as she looked back behind her shoulder. Then, as though she had received some sort of approval, she came forward to follow Anna up the back stairs.

When they were finally closed off into a more silent space, Anna invited her to sit. As she did, she noticed the woman's quick scan of her surroundings. Feeling as though she needed to defend her territory, Anna began to explain.

"I only leased the building a few weeks ago. You should have seen it then." When her laugh was not well received, Anna extended her hand, trying a different tactic. "I'm Anna Keller—well, soon to be McMurran. Oh, I suppose I'll have to ask him if he wants me to take his name," she said, almost to herself. "In any case, it's nice to meet you, Miss…"

"You're engaged? I didn't see a ring." The woman shook Anna's hand quickly.

"No, I suppose there hasn't been time for one. He only proposed two days ago." Why was she defending herself to this stranger? She supposed it could be because of this woman's dark eyes. They were probing and protected all at once. And Anna had never seen eyes so black in all her life.

"I didn't catch your name."

"I didn't give it." At Anna's arched brow, the woman relaxed. Obviously, this waif of a woman would not be intimidated easily. Looks were often very deceiving. "I'm Nina Connors. And I'm interested in knowing your opening date for my daughter. She really wants to take tap lessons."

The excitement Anna felt at the prospect of her first real student stuttered only momentarily at the idea that this woman had a child. Such attitude was not usually associated with motherhood—or at least that was Anna's opinion.

"Well, I was just discussing that with the contractor downstairs. It looks like I'll be able to hold my first lessons in the fall, probably around the time your daughter starts school. How old is she?"

"She's seven. And full of spit and vinegar. In fact, I should be getting back to her. I told her to wait in the car. You looked like you had a lot going on, and I didn't want her getting in the way." Nina rose to leave.

"I'll have to meet her. Why don't I walk you out to your car?"

As Anna led her to the steps, Nina hesitated for only a minute. Then she agreed, and the two of them found her little girl standing outside the car kicking at rocks and flirting with Kaleb. Nina shot across the lot like a bullet.

"Jacqueline! I told you not to speak with strangers!" She went to her daughter protectively and scooped her up, all the while glaring at Kaleb.

"Not too many of us are strangers around here. You'll learn that soon enough. I'm Kaleb McMurran." He nodded at them in what Nina would have sworn resembled the movement of a cowboy tilting his hat at a young Philly.

"McMurran…oh, you're her fiancé." She still held her daughter as the two of them studied the couple, who now had their arms around each other.

"You've a strong memory," Anna commented, as she stared at the uncanny similarities between mother and daughter.

"I'm a quick study," Nina returned, as she saw kindness and trust emanating from them as only a newly engaged couple could understand. Fortunately for her, Nina understood that was not always the case.

"You must be Jacqueline," Anna stated as she stepped forward to get a better look at the girl.

The energetic seven-year-old bounced out of her mother's arms and down to the ground. "I'm Jack. I'm seven. And we were just kicking around at the rocks, Ma."

"Sorry?"

"Mom," she corrected and earned a raised brow, oddly resembling Anna only moments ago.

"I suppose it's my fault. I invited her inside to see the studio, and we got to kicking." Kaleb actually managed to look sheepish.

Anna shoved at him playfully while Jack bounced up and down. "Please can I see the inside, Mom? Please?"

Nina looked from her daughter to the mess of workers and shook her head no. "Miss Keller is too busy right now. We'll come back another time when we sign you up for lessons."

"Really? I get the lessons?" Jack's mouth hung open in sheer delight.

Nina had seen enough to know the dance instructor could be trusted. "Yeah. You can have the lessons." Jacqueline whooped her way to the car and continued her seat-dancing inside of it. "You sure you want to deal with the likes of her several days a week?" Nina hooked a thumb in her daughter's direction as she added a touch of humor to the question.

"I think I can manage. Why don't you stop by in a few weeks? By then, I should have a schedule printed out."

"That sounds fine. Nice meeting both of you." She began to walk away.

"Are you new here? I don't recall seeing you around before."

She faced them and gave them both a dazzling smile. Anna saw Kaleb's eyes sway. "Yes. We've just recently moved." With that, she hopped behind the wheel and drove off.

"You can put your tongue back in your mouth now, McMurran," Anna said as she turned toward the building.

He came out of the fog long enough to hear the sarcasm in her voice, if not the exact words. "I'm sorry. Am I not allowed to look now that we're engaged?" He smiled, trying to pull off embarrassment. It did not work.

"You do any more than look, and I'll have one of the boys around here hide the body after I'm done with you." She trotted up the stairs.

Kaleb was not far behind. "Deal." Then he was pulling her into his arms for a searing kiss. When she surfaced, Anna tried to speak without a quiver in her voice. She knew it was there and cursed him for enjoying it so much.

"That might make up for that little fiasco in the parking lot."

"Maybe this will, too. While I was at work today, I made some phone calls. I thought I'd make you dinner tonight, and we could go over some ideas for our wedding." He had caught her off guard and was enjoying himself immensely.

She was almost stunned and pressed a hand to her belly where the butterflies were engaged in a vicious war. "Are you serious?"

"Yes, Anna. I don't want to put off marrying you any longer than I need to. I'd marry you tonight if I could, but they won't approve the license so fast. I know—I checked."

She felt so warm, so much so that when she wrapped her arms around him and asked him a question, she was not ready for his reply. "So that puts the end to that little affair you had only minutes ago with the sexy new stranger?"

"She wouldn't have lasted past the night for me anyway. Well, maybe one night."

He dodged her swats and fell laughing with her on the mattress.

* * * * *

The community was abuzz with the news that Kaleb McMurran had proposed to Anna Keller—and that Anna's mother was not happy about it at all. Everyone seemed to be in on the gossip, including Melanie Wilson, and when she ran into Kaleb at the corner market, she learned sadly that her old tricks would no longer work. It seemed that even though Mrs. Keller was going to give them grief, Kaleb could not be happier or more devoted.

There was a spring to his step as he prepared chicken Florentine, a Greek salad, and cherry cobbler for dessert. He popped the cork from Anna's favorite bottle of wine to allow it room to breathe. He centered the flowers in the middle of the table and lit every candle that was available. When Anna walked in minutes later, she would have sworn she had entered a dream.

He played soft music and danced with her in the middle of his living area while the chicken finished on the stove top. Brushing his hands over her shoulders, he could feel the tension and knots in her shoulders. Assuming this was due to how hard she had been working, he began to knead her shoulders and heard her give a moan. This stirred his blood, but he wanted to wait until later to have her again. For now, he would feed her well and talk about the ideas his mother had found for their wedding, keeping everything simple and elegant.

That was how he saw her.

She ate the salad nimbly and pushed the chicken around on her plate, barely taking any bites. When he joked with her about it, she tried to brush it off and managed two more nibbles before she pushed her plate away. By the time he had dessert on a plate in front of her, she had finished two glasses of wine and was working on a third.

"So, Mr. McMurran, where did you learn to cook so incredibly well?"

He eyed her; the sentence had come out almost slurred. "When you live on a ranch in Colorado, you get tired of steak every day. I taught myself." He laughed. "Actually, their cook taught me. Her name was Phyllis, and she could make a mean roasted turkey. I'll have to try that out on you sometime."

"So, once again, you were a hit with the ladies." She focused on him through blurry vision.

"Phyllis was three hundred pounds if she was an ounce, and she had been widowed for the better part of the previous thirty years. Not too many paid her much attention until I came around. She told me I was her favorite ranch hand and cried when I left to come home."

"My mistake." Anna got up to wander the room for no particular reason.

Kaleb waited a beat and then asked, "Anna, what's bothering you?"

She whirled on him. "I think my mother is going to cut me out of her life!" She fell to the sofa in a heap, and he instantly went to her. Placing his arms around her, he listened as she relayed the events of earlier that afternoon after she had returned from working at the studio. She was getting ready to come over to his home, spent a lot of time on her make-up and hair, which she now realized would be ruined from the mess she was making. Her mother had come into her room, and without her father's knowledge, made it clear that she was not sure what their relationship would be like if Anna were to marry Kaleb.

"Of course, she didn't say your first name. She's always careful not to, like it's a disease or something." Anna sniffed and wiped her face with the back of her light sweater. "Oh, Kaleb, it was awful! How will I stand losing my own mother?"

He said nothing, watching the plans he had of the evening drain slowly away into nothing. She was right; how would she stand it? Kaleb knew no one could ever take the place of his mother, but he had certainly had visions of Anna and he raising a family of their own so that he would pass his family's traditions and morals on to their own. But what could he offer Anna when it came to her mother?

He knew the answer and swore viciously inside his head at the single word that kept popping into view.

Nothing.

So he would formulate a new plan, one that would somehow fix this great mess and make it all better for Anna. Because in the end, her fulfillment was all that would matter to him.

He tucked her under the sheets in his bed, held her close as she slept from too much wine and exhaustion from her crying jag. He knew what he had to do. As much as he did not want to do it, it would be necessary.

* * * * *

Kaleb pulled into the narrow drive and just sat for a moment, looking at the house. In all the years he had been a part of their lives, and they a part of his—however unwillingly—he had never been invited into this house unless it was by Anna. And even then, they had been quick little jaunts inside, just long enough to pick her up for a date, never long enough to stay for conversation.

Rose O'Connor Keller had not been interested in having a conversation with someone she felt was beneath her.

He marched up to the door, a determined set to his jaw, his gray eyes putting the storm on hold. He knocked soundly and waited to be greeted by ice.

She did not disappoint.

The minute she saw who it was that was knocking, she tried to slam the door in his face but to no avail. He lodged his foot in quicker than she anticipated, and he smiled. With an edge.

"Hello, Rose. Lovely to see you. Can I come in?" Without waiting for reply, he pushed past her and into the living room.

She closed the door at his back but remained standing firm in the foyer. "I suppose it will not do me any good to say I could call the police for breaking and entering, now would it, Mr. McMurran?"

He caught the fury in her words, but there was something else. Something else just under that top layer, and he could have sworn it was nerves. It struck him as funny that he could activate Rose O'Connor Keller's unease.

"We need to talk."

"I have nothing to say to you." She opened the door for him and indicated that he should leave.

He remained where he was. "I have plenty to say to you. If you wish to stay there in the foyer while you listen to me, I have no problem with that. But I thought we could make ourselves more comfortable than that."

She waited, understanding that he was playing a game, and she desperately needed the upper hand. She stepped forward into the room but moved no closer to him. Folding her hands in front of her waist, she stayed silent, curiosity getting her as to why he would brave her for a visit.

"I want to marry your daughter. I love Anna very much." When she rolled her eyes, he simply paused and waited for her to settle again. Once she did, he continued. "There is nothing I won't do for her. She offers me more than I ever thought any woman would. And I know that I do the same for her."

"Do you now?" Now she did speak, and this time, he could actually feel his blood turn cold as she turned that feral gaze on to him. "You think you offer everything possible to Anna? Mr. McMurran, my daughter has dined with diplomats. She has performed in front of audiences of thousands. She has a ballet that is actually going to be written for her specifically." Rose did not bother to feel guilty about the lie. When she had last spoken with Anna's director, it was she who had dropped the idea into the man's lap, only to have it dismissed. But she figured all that would soon change. "My daughter needs nothing from you, Mr. McMurran. You are surely a nice change of pace from the—cultured men she generally entertains, but I see this as nothing more than a phase. Once she realizes her mistake, she will kick you to the curb like no more than yesterday's news."

"Anna said you weren't sure about your relationship with her if she marries me."

"That is correct." And that is when she saw it. The panic, just the hint of it, that Anna would be without her mother. Sensing he really did care about her daughter did nothing to curve her next action. "You say you care about my daughter? You say that you would do anything to keep her happy? What of it, Mr. McMurran?" She tapped a slim finger to her lips. "I wonder just how much you are willing to prove that."

* * * * *

The two girls giggled helplessly over the pictures they saw in the magazine. Madelaine flipped to a new page and showed it to Anna. "How about this one? You could go down in history as the puffiest bride of them all!" Laughter bubbled out of her.

Anna sat back and ran her hand through her hair. "Oh, Maddy! I'm getting married! Can you believe it?" She sighed and reached for another bridal magazine.

"I say it's about time. Of course, all it does is remind me of how sincerely far away I am from my own nuptials. I can't even get a second date from your brother!" Exasperated, she threw herself back against the couch.

"Believe me, Adam is no prize."

"He is from where I'm sitting."

They laughed again, and then Anna became quiet until she said, "I hope I didn't scare Kaleb last night."

"How?"

"He made me a really fantastic dinner and had all these brochures available for me to browse so that I could pick the perfect wedding setting. Then I went and got all sloppy about my mother. Made for a bummer of an evening."

"I imagine it did. But I'm sure he understood. Anna, he's going to be your husband, so I think it's okay if the two of you have serious conversations." Madelaine tossed the magazine onto the floor and faced her friend.

"Yes, I know. But still...I never thought my mother would tell me that she would not be there for me if I married Kaleb."

Maddy's face registered pure shock. "Did she actually say that to you?"

"Not in so many words. But her intent was there. One of the things I said to Kaleb was how would I survive without my mother."

"Oh, Anna..."

"I know, it's pathetic, isn't it? Here I am, an adult, having lived on my own, and my mother still has that kind of hold over me." She got up to pace.

Madelaine considered. "I don't think it's pathetic at all. If my mother were to let go of me because of some guy, I don't know what I'd do."

"But it's not just some guy, is it, Madelaine? It's Kaleb. I want to have children with him."

"Oh, Anna." Madelaine went to hug her friend. "I know this is different. And don't worry. Everything will work out just fine. It's you and Kaleb. The fates have been waiting for the two of you for quite a while."

"Maddy, will you be my maid of honor?"

When Madelaine pulled back to look Anna in the eye, she gasped with delight. Then she hugged her again, tighter and with more fervor. "Anna, nothing would please me more! I thought you'd never ask!"

* * * * *

Anna was still laughing over Maddy's reaction hours later while she waited for Kaleb at the lighthouse. Only Madelaine Murphy could reply to such a request the way she did. And it warmed Anna's heart to know that Madelaine was hers.

She was finally belonging.

But now she was worried. Kaleb had told her earlier to meet him at the lighthouse because he had some things he had wanted to finish up before they spent their evening together, and he had yet to show. She tried tidying to keep her hands busy, but since the place was still under construction, there really was not much she could do. She sat to flip through the bridal magazines, and after another hour passed, she gave up and went to the window. She figured he must have gotten tied up talking to someone in town.

She went outside at dusk to skim along the water's edge. Several fishermen were tying their ends for the day, and she waved to them out of habit like she had when she was a little girl. All at once she felt so content. This was where she had been raised; Kaleb had always called this place "home" as well. Now they would create their own family, and they, too, would feel the way she and Kaleb did about it. Nothing pleased her more at the moment.

She imagined her little girl waving to fishermen on the water's edge and went giddy with it. She skipped over to a pile of rocks and tossed them just to see the ripples.

She simply could not wait for the ripples Kaleb and she would cause together. But where was he?

Going back inside the lighthouse, she sat down on the couch to wait for him and fell asleep.

* * * * *

The next several days felt like Anna had been trapped inside a dome in which she was captive, but anyone looking in had not the faintest idea of the hell in which she was barely surviving. She knew Kaleb was safe; she had heard from several people that they had seen him around the island. But every time she tried to reach him, he was unavailable. She had been to several of his work sites, his brother's house, his parents' house—but none of them were talking. She knew they had ideas about where he was, and not one of them would tell her no matter how she pleaded. So she began to slowly turn inside out.

Madelaine tried to help by working with her on the studio, but when Anna would ask if any of this made sense, all she could do was nod her head and hold Anna while she fell apart.

Anna knew that this was the end. Deep down, she understood that Kaleb had left her, and she could not see why.

As she lay awake in her bed at night at her parents' home, she would replay their last moments together. She wondered idly if he had been bothered by all of her crying over her mother, and she thought that if he was, then he was not the man she had thought him to be.

At this point, this was quickly turning out to be the case.

She began to lose weight again, not enough to sound off any alarm bells, but enough that her family and friends noticed. Adam vowed that if he could get his hands on McMurran, he would enjoy hearing him plead for his life. Anna just brushed this off, like she might a bothersome fly, and went back to the routine of her life.

None of it made sense. How could Kaleb just disappear for almost a week and not tell her? If she did not get answers soon, she would go quietly mad, and they would find her in a puddle of what had once been she, useless and transparent.

When Rose came into her room one afternoon to soothe her with tea, she sat on the side of the bed and pulled back the covers to look at her daughter. When she saw the heavy and dark circles under her eyes, a twinge of guilt found its way to the surface, but she held it at bay, knowing she had done everything for Anna's sake.

"Why don't you have some tea?" She offered her the delicate white cup.

Anna looked out of hollow eyes. "No. Thank you. I'm fine. I just need to sleep."

"Anna, you will turn to a bag of bones if you keep this up."

"I said I'm fine, Mother. Just let me be."

They sat there for another few minutes, Anna staring into nothing, and Rose holding the cup as the tea inside of it grew cold. Then Anna spoke, quietly at first.

"I know you're happy about this. You got what you wanted."

"How can you say such a thing? Seeing my daughter in this kind of pain is never what I would want." Rose took hold of the tray and stood to leave. "I'll leave you alone."

As her mother tried to leave, Anna let out a choked gasp. When Rose turned to face her, Anna's cheeks were already soaked. "Please, Mother. Stay. I don't know what to do."

Rose set the tray on the dresser and went to her daughter once again, taking her in her arms while Anna sobbed. She knew her child needed to purge herself of all that had happened in recent weeks in order to get back on track. To get back to the way her life should be. She gave her the time she needed and then set her against the pillow to study her tear-ravaged face.

"Anna, you will survive this."

"How?"

"Do you not remember when that young man—what was his name?—I believe it was Darren Carter—rejected you? You were barely fifteen, and you wanted so badly to go to the dance with him. He turned you down. I seem to recall having a conversation with you right here on this very bed about him. And you moved on just fine."

"Mother, that was a young girl's foolishness. This is different. I was to marry this man and make a family with him. Kaleb made me such promises..." She sobbed on a fresh wave of tears.

"Darling, this too shall pass. Not all men are good at keeping their promises." But she hoped desperately that Kaleb was a man of his word as she recalled the promise he had made to her during their last conversation.

"Kaleb was. What if something terrible has happened to him? His family doesn't seem to know where he is. They are concerned. Maybe if I go to his brother, Evan, he'll help me to find him—"

"Anna, there's no need to fuss like that. I'm sure Kaleb is fine; he has just decided that now is not the time to take a wife, especially one of your calibers. He must have realized his mistake."

Anna studied her mother's face. Suddenly, everything was falling into place. "Unless someone realized it for him."

"What are you talking about, Anna?"

"Was he here? Did you speak to him?" And because she knew her mother so well, she caught it—the faint shift before she could cover with a lie. Anna leaned back once again and felt terribly weak. "You told him to leave. You must have. It's the only reason why he would be away from me."

Rose began to fuss, but Anna grabbed her wrist. She could see the intensity behind those eyes, eyes she had created, and knew when the battle was lost.

"Obviously he felt that going away was easier than sticking around and fighting for you. I would not want to marry a man like that."

She thought about it, and Rose saw it, too—the image of slapping her mother across the face—and feeling that kind of heat on her hand was so potent, she almost transferred the idea into reality. But not even that would heal this wound.

"The letters." Anna had spoken so softly that neither of them really knew if she had said it aloud. She repeated herself for the both of them. "The letters. Mother, what do you know about the letters?"

"I do not know what you are referring to."

"Yes, you do. When I went away to New York, I wrote to Kaleb, and he to me. Yet, neither one of us ever received any correspondence. What about the letters?"

Rose sat perfectly still for a full minute. *Damn Kaleb McMurran for coming back into her life and ruining all!* When she finally spoke, her voice was hoarse, showing some fear for the first time that Anna could recall.

"I had an arrangement with Gloria in our post office here and one with your den mother in New York. It seemed to work well at the time."

Like a shot, Anna was out of bed and tossing items from her dresser. She whipped off her nightshirt and pulled on thin cotton pants and a loose-fitting blouse. Rose watched out of defeated eyes.

"What are you doing, Anna?"

"I'm going to find him. And after I do, I will not be able to stay here anymore. I'm not sure if my decision will allow you to have a relationship with me, but I know for certain that your decisions will not allow me to have one with you." She found a hair tie and pulled her hair into a loose knot.

"Be careful, Anna. Make sure this is what you want."

She met her mother's eyes with all the scorn she could muster and found that in reality she felt immensely sorry for her. "I've known what I've wanted for quite some time. And here I've been feeling guilty over what I've been doing to you. I suppose you haven't lost much sleep lately." She slammed her way out of the room and out of the house.

Rose was left to her own tears inside her child's bedroom.

* * * * *

She drove as though she were on fire. She had no idea where to find him, but she knew she could get help.

Pulling in front of Evan and Michelle's house, she came to a screeching halt and tore out of the car, running wildly up the walk. Banging on the door, she was frantic by the time Michelle answered in a robe.

"Anna? What's wrong? Come in. You look a mess."

She made room for Anna to enter as Evan came down the hall looking disheveled and somewhat sleep-deprived.

"Anna, what's going on? Why are you here so late?"

"Please, I beg of you. Tell me where he is. I don't know where else to go." Her hands wrung themselves around her purse, turning her knuckles stone white. Evan and Michelle looked at each other, obviously distressed over what they saw on Anna's face.

"Anna, we would love to help, but—"

She cut Evan off, cleanly and abruptly. "My mother. My mother did this. She told him to go away, and he did, but I don't want him to. He has to know that. I still want to marry him. Look." She tossed her purse down on the floor to free up her hands to retrieve the necklace from under her shirt. "I still wear this. Because he gave it to me. I never needed a ring. I just needed him." Desperate for answers, she fumbled with the clasp, her hands shaking violently.

Michelle stepped forward to remove the chain for her. Anna pressed it into her hands.

"You give this to him and tell him that I will be waiting for him at the lighthouse. If he wishes to keep the necklace and not me, then I won't expect him. But even if he just wants to return it to me and let me explain, I'll be waiting. Michelle, please don't keep this from him."

As Anna left, the couple felt a pain neither had felt in a long time. They turned to see Kaleb standing in the doorway, his feet bare and a bottle of beer in his hand. Taking the necklace from his sister-in-law and saying nothing, he disappeared back into their basement.

* * * * *

She slept in fits and starts on the couch with only the blanket Kaleb had once covered her with to keep away the chill. Every time she heard a car, she sat up and ran to the door, only to discover that it was no one.

She tried to keep a positive thought; after all, Michelle had looked sincere when she had promised to tell him that she would be waiting for him here.

So why hadn't he shown?

As she drifted off yet again, she thought she heard a noise. Opening one eye, then the other, she saw him. She bolted up from her position on the couch and found him watching her from the open door. He stepped through it and closed it.

For a while, they simply stared at each other. Kaleb cursed himself for the heaviness he saw under her eyes; he had often thought they were her best feature, and once again, he was responsible for putting the weary and hurt look in them.

He felt his heart split. If she could sense this, she gave no hint.

Finally, he broke the silence. "You should not have come here to sleep. Someone could have seen that you were alone in an unlocked building, and then what? This was not a good idea."

"I'm already mostly gone. Whatever some stranger may have chosen to do to me could not possibly be much worse."

It was not just the words; it was the utter despair that she put into them without even trying. He knew he was responsible for that, too.

"I tend to disagree." He came toward her and held out the necklace. When she made no move, he set it on the center table. "You'll need to be out of here soon. I'll be finishing up, and then I'll be packing my things."

He would not look at her, and she thought that might be a good start. "Where are you going?"

"What business is it of yours?"

The minute the words were out, he regretted them. He could feel the heat drain right out of her. Only able to bear a quick glance, he tried the same cold and distant tactic.

"You need to go, Anna. I've got things to do."

"Do you realize that's the first time you've said my name since you've walked in here, Kaleb?"

"Well, it's not as though I've forgotten who you are."

"You could have fooled me."

"Don't do this, Anna. Please."

"Don't do what, Kaleb?" She threw the blanket off and stood to meet him

185

toe-to-toe. "Don't tell you that I love you? Don't tell you that I still want to marry you? Should I also not tell you that I want to have your children, Kaleb, or would it make it that much easier to follow my mother's orders if you just didn't know?"

Now he did look at her, full on, and the heat from that searing blast almost knocked her flat. She sucked in a breath and pressed a hand to her stomach in defense of the storm brewing there.

"Your mother's orders? You think I did what *she* wanted? Let me make something very clear. I do nothing to make Rose happy. But I knew that it would be that and so much more for you. In the end, that's what I knew would make you happy."

"Not being with you would make me happy? How does that even make any sense, Kaleb?"

"Because I will not be responsible for taking you away from your mother!"

The words were spoken; there was no taking them back. And now it was all quite clear to her. She understood. So she eased back and seared him with a look of her own.

"And you didn't think this was something I should decide for myself?"

She held her ground as she spoke the words. They were delivered quietly, which allowed their punch to pack a bit harder, a bit deeper. Her hands were fisted at her sides while he raked his through his untamed hair. She had him in knots, and he had no idea how to proceed.

She made it easier for him. "I see that I had more faith in us than you did. I suppose I'll take my necklace and go."

She made it as far as the table when he spun her around. "What right have you to say that to me? I have faith in us! I'm the one who pushed your brother just over the edge to help find his part of the ring! Of course I believe in us! Without you, there is barely me, Anna." The last part ended on a choked and somewhat desperate whisper.

"You have no faith, Kaleb. You stand here and remind me of all that you've done; yet, you made the decision for me. You never bothered to ask what I might decide, what I might feel is best. Instead, you took it upon yourself to guide my future. Well, I've had enough of that, thank you. From now on, I decide for me. I won't have you or my mother or anyone else doing so."

He held her gaze and realized he held her arm just as firmly. When he released her, she rubbed at where the bruise was surely already forming. He tried to find the words.

"I only went to your mother because—"

Anna held up her hand to stop him. "What do you mean you went to my mother?"

He sighed. "I went to her house—your house to try and settle this. By the time I left, I had promised her that I would leave you alone. For your own good." He laughed pitifully. "She actually had me believing it for a while. I was doing it for you. You were so sad when you told me that you might lose her over this—over me. I couldn't bear the thought of you ever regretting that decision, Anna. I loved you too much."

Anna breathed deeply and slowly. She rocked back on her heels. "Kaleb, you did all of this because I had been sad?" When he nodded, she shook her head and sat down on the couch. "If I lose my mother because I marry you, that is her decision, not mine, and I would hope, not yours. I asked you once to be my friend, to trust me. How does any of this show that you respect me?"

He knelt in front of her, finally coming close enough to touch but still holding back. "I am your friend, Anna. I was willing to sacrifice you for you." When she met his gaze, she was lost once again.

"Kaleb McMurran, do you still love me?"

"Anna—"

"Answer my question, please."

"Yes."

"Do you still want to marry me?"

"Anna—"

"Answer." She arched her brow.

"Yes. Desperately."

"Will you still be my friend?"

He took her hands in his and pressed them to his face. "As long as you'll be mine."

And when he kissed her, they both felt the pulse of it, the energy. He pulled away from her only to watch her eyes go dark with curiosity, then wonder, then discovery.

He asked her, "What is it, Anna?"

She simply pointed, and he turned.

Above the entryway to the lighthouse glowed a circle of light. They stood and walked over to it. Anna reached up to touch, and suddenly in her hand she held it.

"My part of the ring."

The two hands of friendship circled in the light for another few seconds, warm and reassuring as they stared at it in disbelief. He wrapped his hand around hers as she continued to hold this part of the ring until he said, "I guess this is what I'm supposed to give to you as a promise."

As he placed it on her finger, and the light subsided, Anna replied, "It's what we're supposed to give to each other."

Printed in the United States
37746LVS00005B/184-201

9 781413 767858